Misconception

Christy Hayes

Copyright © 2012 Christy Hayes

All rights reserved.

ISBN: 1477628983
ISBN-13: 978-1477628980

DEDICATION

To my parents and in-laws for setting such good examples.

OTHER BOOKS BY CHRISTY HAYES

Angle of Incidence

Dodge the Bullet

Heart of Glass

Shoe Strings

The Accidental Encore

The Sweetheart Hoax

Golden Rule Outfitters Series:
Mending the Line, Book 1
Guiding the Fall, Book 2
Taming the Moguls, Book 3

Kiss & Tell Series
A Kiss by Design, Book 1
A Kiss by the Book, Book 2
Kiss & Makeup, A Kiss & Tell Novella

ACKNOWLEDGMENTS

To Cassie Cox for her help with this book. To my family for their love and support, always.

CHAPTER 1

"I'm sorry," Pace said into the receiver. "I didn't hear you." The boys ran through the house, chasing their chocolate lab puppy, Cooper, screaming at the top of their lungs with a dog toy chirping in each of their hands. They passed through the kitchen and up the stairs, where, coincidentally, Cooper wasn't allowed to go. "It's mass chaos here. For a second I thought you said I was pregnant."

A pause on the other end of the line, just a slight hesitation, told Pace she'd heard right. "I did say you're pregnant, Mrs. Kelly. Just got the labs back this morning."

The noise disappeared, as if it had been swallowed into a vacuum and the only sound was the buzzing in her head. "Wait…" she struggled to get the power of speech back. "That can't be right. My husband's had a vasectomy."

"I've seen it happen before. You two didn't follow the doctor's orders and use condoms until they could test and make sure it worked."

"My husband had a vasectomy three years ago."

The silence on the other end of the line wasn't just a hesitation. No, it seemed more like a cavern of deep contemplation. "Oh…"

"Listen, there has to be some kind of mistake. I know I haven't been feeling quite right, but I'm not pregnant." Pace didn't know who she was trying to convince. She'd been tired, listless, occasionally nauseous, and her periods were all over the board, but pregnant? "Those tests aren't a hundred percent accurate, right?"

"I'm sorry, Mrs. Kelly. I'm looking at the blood test results. Your file indicates you aren't taking any medications. Is that correct?"

"Yes, I mean, no...I mean, I'm not on any medication other than multivitamins."

"Then there's no doubt about it," she said. "You're pregnant."

When the phone call ended, Pace still had the phone dangling from her frozen fingers as Jason rushed into the kitchen, talking a mile a minute into the ear piece that since his latest "big deal" had started, seemed permanently attached to his head.

"Jason?" He swallowed the dregs from one of the kid's orange juice glasses still on the table and shoved an uneaten bagel half into his mouth. He raised his eyes to heaven and with his free hand pointed to the earpiece, as if she didn't know he wasn't talking to her about the glazing ratio of the atrium glass. "I need to talk to you." He kissed her cheek and headed for the garage.

"I'll call you from the car," he whispered.

She'd come to think of his out-of-town meetings as his weekly escape. This deal, some skyscraper in Chicago that caused him to pop Tums like candy, had him out of town at least three days a week for the last two months and the boys pushing the limits of her patience.

As if she'd summoned them, Dillon and Mitchell rushed back through the kitchen, puppy in hot pursuit, in their habitual loop around the main floor—kitchen, dining room, den; kitchen, dining room, den—just as she sank into a kitchen chair. Mitchell dragged his disgusting old blanket and Dillon still wore his pajama pants. She eyed the clock. Eight-eleven and the bus arrived at the corner at eight-twenty.

"Did you guys brush your teeth?"

Her perpetual question always received the same answer. "I forgot."

They both headed back upstairs with orders to finish getting dressed as Pace lassoed the puppy and shoved his getting-bigger-by-the-day body out the back door. He needed to run off some energy chasing the remaining squirrels that hadn't come to grips with the fact that he was there to stay.

Pregnant? Pace felt as if she'd been knocked over the head with a two-by-four. She leaned against the counter and laid a hand on her stomach as the boys conducted what sounded like an aerobics class above her head. Her body didn't feel any different than it did ten minutes ago. How in the world could she be pregnant? She and Jason hadn't even had sex that much lately.

"Let's go guys," she shouted up the stairs. "I'm not driving you to school today." But when she turned and saw the bus pass in front of the house, she knew she would, in fact, be driving them to school. Not that missing the bus never happened; she knew they loved her driving them in as much as she loved their few minutes alone in the car, but the mayhem she embraced everyday with a heartfelt smile seemed like the straw that would break her back on the heels of the nurse's bombshell.

It took twenty minutes to find Mitchell's missing shoe and to re-make Dillon's sandwich. "Tommy Butler is allergic to peanut butter," he explained as she searched the junk drawer for her keys. "Mrs. Finegold keeps throwing my sandwich away."

Pace quit rummaging around and slammed the drawer shut. No more peanut butter and jelly? Why didn't they just stick a knife in her back? What in the world would her picky son eat for lunch? "Dillon, why didn't you tell me about the no-peanut-butter policy? And how can your teacher just throw your sandwich away when she hasn't notified the parents about the new rule?"

As Pace grumbled under her breath and considered calling the principal to complain about the teacher, Dillon began frantically fishing through his backpack. If his teacher could see her now, the lightweight everyone considered a pushover—throwing bread on the counter, drumming her fingers on the open refrigerator door as she surveyed its contents, trying to figure out what Dillon would possibly deem worthy of his discriminating palate, slamming mayonnaise and cheese on the counter—she wouldn't be so quick to label her a nice, easygoing parent, someone whose son everybody wanted in their class.

Pace knew everyone thought she was too nice, too proper to make waves. Little did they know her life had just been turned upside down. Dillon interrupted her frantic attempt to make an acceptable sandwich, a sandwich he'd probably throw away because he wouldn't eat it, and handed her a crumbled note. "Mrs. Finegold told us to have you sign this. I forgot."

No wonder he'd been ravenous when he came home. She'd stupidly attributed his hunger to a growth spurt. Dillon brooded the whole way to school about the turkey and cheese sandwich she made even after Pace had filled it with potato chips like they sometimes did at home. Mitchell kept tugging off the sock cap she insisted he wear in the rare Atlanta cold snap. "But it itches," he whined as they idled in the carpool line.

An hour later, the boys safely delivered to Parkside elementary school and the dog asleep in his bed in the corner of the den, Pace checked the phone. No calls, no messages. *Darn it, Jason. Call.* The whole ride to school and back she'd thought of nothing but the nurse's announcement. Hadn't everyone heard the story about the woman who, after her husband got a vasectomy, had a tummy tuck and then found out she was pregnant? She'd thought that was an urban legend, like being able to tell the sex of a baby by peeing into Drano.

She and Jason had agonized over whether to have more children years ago after watching two parents juggle more kids than adults at sporting events and school activities. They'd made their decision official three years ago with a thirty-minute outpatient procedure and a recovery weekend of March Madness and rotating bags of frozen peas. And now—when the kids were both finally in school and Jason was stressed to the breaking point with this deal and his boss—now she got pregnant? They'd sold every scrap of baby stuff they had lurking in the basement at the neighborhood garage sale last summer and she'd just started laying the groundwork for a home-based business. Despite the appealing chance to experience it all again—the first smile, the first steps, the first word—she couldn't help but feel a little disappointed that all of her plans had gone 'poof' with one thirty-second phone call.

After trying Jason and getting his voicemail, Pace headed upstairs to make the bed and had to stop at the top to catch her breath. Her lack of endurance and shortness of breath, two of the symptoms that had led her to the doctor in the first place, now made sense knowing she was pregnant. So much about how she'd been feeling became clear even as her future went dim and out of focus.

She eyed the phone on the bedside table and knew Jason wouldn't answer the phone if he was still talking to his boss, Tarks, or one of his clients. He longed to start his own firm and a big part of her wished he would go ahead and do it so he'd stop complaining about his job all the time. Whenever he started one of his diatribes about Tarks, Pace had to bite her tongue to keep from telling him to go ahead and quit after they'd practically broken their backs for the last ten years paying off his student loans because he was too stubborn to borrow money from her parents. They'd finally managed to stash a little money into savings and start a college fund for the boys and she'd hoped to have a better buffer in place before he risked his steady income. She glanced at the phone on her nightstand and willed it to ring as she piled throw pillows on top of the comforter.

After picking up the boys' dirty clothes from the floor and turning off every light blazing away in their rooms, she went back downstairs, looked at the mantle clock in the den, and realized Jason had probably already taken off. She was about to go crazy keeping the news to herself, but felt a little relieved at the delay. Pace knew her husband would freak when she told him the news because, as much as they both wanted him to, he'd never be able to leave the security of his job with another baby on the way.

* * *

The whole way to the airport, Tarks wouldn't quit nagging Jason about the atrium design. Yes, the man was a world-renowned architect, yes, his reputation was beyond reproach, and yes, he'd taken Jason under his wing. But working so closely with him, as much of an honor as it should have been, had become Jason's number one reason to get out on his own.

As he did during most of his quiet moments, he thought of the future on the flight to Chicago. In just a few weeks, his back and forth travel would slow down and he could relax, enjoy the holidays, and start making concrete plans for his own firm. He dreaded announcing his departure and the hit to his bank account wouldn't be easy to stomach, but the call he planned to make when he got home would help ease the sting.

After mulling it over for weeks, he'd decided to accept the offer on his grandfather's land. The farm had been sitting empty for years, a sentimental investment that could finally be put to good use. The bid hadn't even come close to their asking price, but he had to be realistic about what a hundred and twenty-five acres of South Georgia farmland would fetch in a down economy. If the buyer accepted his counter, the deal could close in sixty days and he could have his new firm up and running by spring. Just the thought of starting his own firm and proving everyone wrong who thought he'd married Pace for her money had him smiling as he returned his seatback to the upright position in preparation for landing.

Pace. Damn, he'd told her he'd call from the car. She seemed weird when he left, staring at him as if she couldn't believe he had to run out the door to catch his flight. He knew she hated the travel as much as he did, but she couldn't understand the pressure he was under. And the boys. They'd barely even stopped chasing the dog long enough to kiss him goodbye. He even caught them high-fiving in the hallway when they saw his suitcase and knew mom would order pizza for dinner. Nice to know they'd throw him under the bus for a slice of pepperoni. His hectic schedule wouldn't get any easier when he started his own firm, but at least he'd be able to pick and choose his clients and try to keep the travel to a minimum.

As soon as the wheels touched the ground, Jason dug his phone out of his briefcase and called home. The answering machine picked up after four rings. "Pace, honey, I'm sorry I didn't call sooner. I just landed and I'll be free to talk for the next half-hour if you get a chance to call. Love you, babe."

His phone rang just as he got into the cab for the ride to the hotel. "The Hilton on Michigan," he told the driver before saying hello to Pace. She sounded funny, although he could hardly hear through the jumble of talk radio the driver blared at top volume.

"I'm in the cab," he explained when she asked where he was. "Sorry about this morning. I'm hoping to wrap this up as soon as possible and get back home by Wednesday."

"Jason," she cut him off. "The nurse from Dr. Hidel's office called this morning. You're not going to believe this. She said I'm pregnant."

He knocked on the plastic partition between the front and back seat and asked the driver to turn the radio down. The cabbie lifted his hand in acknowledgment, but Jason didn't register a change in the volume. Perhaps it was because his ears were ringing. "What?"

"The nurse from Dr. Hidel's office said I'm pregnant."

Cars swooped around the cab, their exhaust like small puffs of smoke from an old man's cigar. The sky, gunmetal gray, promised showers later in the day. The driver nodded his head to whatever the commentator had just said. Everything seemed so normal, everything but what his wife had just told him.

"Pace...are you kidding?"

"No, Jason, I'm not kidding." His perpetually happy wife, his little Tinker Bell, sounded annoyed. He couldn't wrap his mind around the idea of another baby, but her attitude came across loud and clear. "What do you think I do all day? Sit around and think of ways to throw you off stride?"

"Okay, okay, I'm just..." he swiped a clammy hand over his face, "...thrown off stride. I don't understand."

"Neither do I, but she said there's no mistake. I'm sorry to spring this on you when you're out of town, but I tried to talk to you this morning."

"Jesus." Of all the things he thought she'd be upset about, his leaving in such a rush, his falling asleep on the couch last night—again-, a problem with the boys, he never thought he'd hear those words come out of her mouth. No wonder she'd acted weird. "Well..." *Shit, shit, shit.* "What do we do?"

"The nurse said they don't want to see me back until two weeks from now, but she suggested getting you checked out. Something obviously failed in terms of the vasectomy."

"Ya think?" The cold from the cracked window seemed to have made its way to his bones and he pushed the button to close it. He blew out a big breath and tried to think as all his plans went up in smoke. Another responsibility was the absolute last thing he needed right now. "Okay, so I guess we're having another baby." He rubbed the pinpoint headache from his temple. "How do you feel?"

"I don't know." Her voice sounded tiny and very far away. He imagined her tapping away on something, the counter, her coffee mug, the wall. She tapped her fingers when she was nervous or upset. "Anxious and more than a little confused. How do you feel?"

About six feet under and wishing she'd gotten her tubes tied like he'd asked her to, but admitting his annoyance wouldn't do any good right now. He wondered, for a fleeting second, if his father had felt this way when he'd heard the news of his unexpected arrival. "The same, I guess." The cabbie hit the brakes with such force that the phone nearly slipped from his grasp. He fumbled for the seat belt he hadn't bothered to put on. "Pace, I can't deal with this right now." He couldn't fit the belt into the latch practically buried in the crevice of the seat despite repeated attempts. It could have been that his hands were shaking. "I've got to go before the cab driver kills me. Let me get through this meeting and I'll call you as soon as I can."

On the other end he heard her sigh with frustration. She didn't answer when he told her goodbye.

Jason looked out the window as the taxi exited the interstate and darted through the streets of Chicago. People passed on the sidewalks, bundled from head to toe with their heads ducked against the strong wind, going about their lives as if nothing had changed from the day before. For a moment he forgot where he was or why he was there. Pregnant? What the hell? The cab came to an abrupt halt in front of the Hilton. The valet opened his door and ushered him out into the chilly morning air. He could see the valet's breath as he spoke, but didn't hear a damn word he said. He paid the cab driver and watched him pull away with his briefcase and presentation tucked into the backseat where he'd left them.

CHAPTER 2

Tori Whitfield pulled a scarf from the retractable rack in her closet and had just tied it around her neck when she heard her husband come in from his workout. Colin had left early with a gym bag and a spring in his step he'd usually exude on a morning round of golf. When she peeked around the corner at him, he tossed the bag on the bed and sat down on the chaise by the bay window to unlace his shoes. Despite the color in his cheeks, every hair on his salt and pepper head was in place and he didn't look as though he'd broken a sweat.

"How was your workout?" She gave herself major points for asking without sarcasm. After all these years, she hated her habit of analyzing everything he did or said, but his good mood made her more than a little suspicious.

"Great." He stretched his stocking feet in front of him and folded his hands behind his head. "I should have listened to you and Pace years ago. There's nothing like getting your heart pumping first thing in the morning."

If only she and her daughter had more in common than their addiction to exercise. Tori watched Colin's eyes drift closed as the sun streamed in from the window, casting him in golden light. From the smile on his face, she'd bet his heart hadn't been the only thing pumping this morning. "I take it you're happy with Matthew?"

He dropped his arms and sat up. "Didn't I tell you? Matthew and I couldn't sync our schedules, so he passed me on to Tricia. She's a real ball buster."

She tried to recall the trainer he'd referred to, but, other than the very effeminate Matthew, she couldn't differentiate the girl he mentioned from the throngs of blonde beauties at the club who motivated their clients through sheer jealousy. She should have known Colin would find a way to get out of the birthday sessions she'd carefully arranged with the club's only male trainer.

He moved into the adjoining bathroom and turned on the shower. The room quickly filled with steam. He poked his head out as Tori picked up her brush from the vanity. "I'm heading to Washington tomorrow for a meeting Trey's arranged with Senator Billings. His endorsement, on the heels of his coup with the labor board, should put an end to any talk I'm anti-union." He rubbed the shampoo onto his head and winked. "Wish me luck."

He had real competition for his senate seat for the first time in years and he seemed more energized by it than discouraged. Her cynical mind couldn't help but chalk his attitude up to residual cheer from his morning of "exercise."

She stole a glance at him as he stepped out of the shower and wiped off the mirror. Still thin and impossibly handsome, a stranger would think that he was the one, not her, who ran three times a week for the past thirty years. Would anyone ever guess her friends had teased her for dating the shy boy with big dreams? Tori straightened her shoulders, sucked in her stomach, and tightened the tie on her belted cardigan. Father Time, it seemed, had caught up with only one of them.

In the bedroom, moments later, dressed in a suit and tie, Colin swooped behind her and kissed the back of her neck. She couldn't help but notice his scent, soap and the sandalwood cologne he'd always worn. Desire, so unexpected and foolish, sprang to life.

"Will you be home for dinner?" She felt as though she had to beg for a sliver of his time.

"I'll check my schedule and let you know." With a grin and a pat to her bottom, he disappeared.

She took a deep breath and tried to be grateful that her busy schedule left little time to mope. She'd spearheaded the capital campaign for the children's hospital and had committed to take an active role in the Junior League's toy drive. With Colin's campaign about to gear up, she wondered if she had it in her to play the part of the doting wife, especially after he'd stoked the flames of her insecurity with the trainer. Would she ever be able to relax without looking over her shoulder for trouble?

* * *

Pace took a brisk walk around the block with Cooper to calm down after Jason's phone call. He couldn't deal with this right now? Did he think she could deal with it alone? She hadn't exactly gotten pregnant by herself. Maybe she should have waited until he'd gotten home, but she just couldn't hold it in any longer. She had to tell someone and he'd have been angry if she'd told Sherry or…her mother before telling him.

Her mother. Pace couldn't imagine what Tori would say when she found out. Her mother could barely tolerate the mess and noise of Pace's life with two rambunctious boys. God only knew how she'd react when she heard they were having another baby. Maybe it would be a girl. Was it too much to hope the unplanned and highly unlikely pregnancy would give Pace the daughter she'd only imagined?

Pace spent the morning scouring the internet and discovered the rarity of a vasectomy's spontaneous reversal. She had to wonder if not having sex very often made a woman more fertile. God knew if she and Jason were to have a surprise pregnancy, it should have been when they were in college and couldn't go a day—heck an hour—without it and they weren't necessarily all that careful about birth control. She pushed away from the screen when she realized the absurdity of thinking an unexpected pregnancy in college would have been better than now.

She nearly jumped out of her skin when she heard a knock at the side door. She looked around the kitchen as she made her way to the door. The morning's breakfast dishes still sat in the sink and the laundry she'd pulled out of the dryer to fold sat atop the table. The puppy happily tore the newspaper to shreds in the den. She would've liked to blame the shock of the nurse's call for causing her to let things slide around the house, but, truth be told, she'd been trudging through daily life for weeks. The pregnancy certainly explained her absentmindedness and lack of energy.

She spied her neighbor Sherry through the glass door, holding her toddler Katie on her hip. Great. The supermom whose house always looked Martha Stewart perfect got to see Pace at her worst.

"Hey." Pace stepped aside to let her in.

Sherry entered the kitchen and glanced around at the mess. "What's wrong?"

"Nothing." Pace wanted to drag her to the table and tell her about the pregnancy, tell her about Jason's unbelievable reaction, and let Sherry's enthusiasm for babies ease the sting of the news. But she knew she couldn't do that, at least not yet. "I wasn't expecting anyone."

"Sorry to interrupt, but I'm in a bit of a bind." She set Katie down on the hardwood floor with a distinct look of distress at the state of the house. "I know you're not interested in being room mom for Dillon's class, but I just talked to Juliet and she said you're helping out with Mitchell's, so...I thought maybe you'd reconsider because I'm desperate?"

"Sherry..." She felt cornered. How could she say no to the woman who volunteered for everything, had less time than anybody else she knew, and still managed to make it all look easy? Pace didn't have a crafty bone in her body and didn't like having to beg overworked and cash-strapped parents for countless donations or favors.

"I know you don't want to, Pace, but when I say desperate, I mean desperate. My sister's moving to Charlotte with her boyfriend and, without my babysitter, I can't get in the class too often. And you know how I've had to beg for parents just to answer my emails."

If only room mom duties were all Pace had to worry about. She wouldn't have any free time until their new little bundle of joy was in preschool—four years from now. "You know the only reason I said yes to Juliet is because she won't take no for an answer. Isn't there anyone else who can do it?"

Sherry followed Katie as she wobbled toward the sharp corners of Pace's desk. "I came to you first. Will you just think about it?" She maneuvered Katie in another direction and then turned abruptly to face Pace. "What's this?"

Oh, God. The corners of Sherry's mouth tilted upward as she pointed at the computer screen and the pregnancy website Pace had stupidly left on display. Pace lunged for the desk and stepped between Sherry and the evidence of her predicament. "Ah...nothing."

"Nothing?" The knowing glimmer in her eye told Pace she'd already placed bets on the due date. "Is there something you want to tell me?"

"Don't be silly." Pace lifted the pad of paper she'd jotted a few dates on and pressed it to her chest. *For God's sake, Pace, act natural.* "I'm just doing some research for a potential client." So much for her freelance career. She certainly wouldn't have time to edit corporate communications projects while feeding an infant every two hours and chasing after a toddler.

Pace raised her brows, daring her friend to call her a liar. Sherry knew she'd been planning to do some work from home, which made her asking Pace to be room mom even more annoying. "Listen." Pace clasped Sherry's arm and turned her away from the computer. "I'll think about it, but I really don't have time. Please pester the other moms."

"I'm not pestering you, Pace."

"I know, I know. I'm sorry. I'm a little out of sorts today. The kids missed the bus and I've got a mountain of stuff to do." At least the state of her house confirmed the obvious. "You know I'll do it if you can't find someone else, but please try."

"Okay, okay." Sherry slung Katie onto her hip. "Are you sure you're all right?"

"I'm fine." She plastered on a fake smile and gave Sherry a jaunty wave, all but confirming her status as the world's worst liar. She watched Sherry walk back to her car and strap Katie into her seat. She knew as soon as they drove away Sherry would reach for her phone and start the rumor mill flowing. Great.

The puppy streaked by with little strips of newspaper hanging from his mouth. Pace gave a passing thought to wrestling the paper from his mouth and putting him outside, but decided she didn't have the energy. As bad as Cooper behaved when the kids were in school and unable to wear him out, a baby would be a thousand times more work than the dog. She'd never planned to have a baby at thirty-five. Oh God, she thought, she'd probably have to have an amniocentesis. Pace *hated* needles.

She went back to the computer and after another internet search, felt thoroughly depressed. Her chances for miscarriage, birth defects, placenta previa, ectopic pregnancy, low birth weight, and a premature delivery were significantly higher now than five years ago when Mitchell was born a healthy eight pounds. She ordered herself to stop reading the internet and just think for a minute. Most of the kids' friends had moms older than her. That meant most of them had had kids when they were over thirty-five. She thought about Mary Blisston, her neighbor with six kids, the youngest of whom was in preschool. Mary had to be well over forty. She was also overweight and exhausted all the time. Pace's body had bounced back pretty well the last two times, but now that she was older... She sat back in the chair and stared up at the ceiling.

Just the thought of carrying a baby in the heat of the summer made her head spin despite the crisp November day. She dragged herself away from the computer and vowed not to look up any more pregnancy sites. If Jason could tuck this little grenade in a closet and deal with it later, so could she.

After dealing with the dishes and folding the laundry, she knelt down to begin picking up the newspaper bits and spotted an article about advancements in ultrasounds. Resigned, she plopped down in Jason's favorite chair to read. Who was she kidding? Pace couldn't believe she was pregnant, much less forget. As the parents in the article raved about the three dimensional images that allowed them to bond with their unborn baby, she realized she had to stop thinking so negatively. How could she even consider a pregnancy a ticking time bomb? She and Jason had created a life and she should feel thrilled to have another child with the man she loved. Just because he worked all the time and didn't exactly sound overjoyed to hear she carried his darn-close-to-a-miracle love child didn't mean they wouldn't get past the shock. She crawled on her hands and knees searching the scraps for the end of the article, determined to keep a positive attitude, only to discover that Cooper had ransacked the magazine bin in the spare bath.

* * *

It took Jason two hours to track down the taxi that had his briefcase and another hour to wait while it was delivered. He didn't know what he would have done if they hadn't recovered his laptop and he practically kissed the driver who handed it back. After he'd downed two rolls of antacids, the taxi pulled up to the client's building with just enough time for them to say the partners had another meeting and he'd have to reschedule.

When he finally made it back to the hotel, he guzzled a twelve-dollar mini bottle of Jack Daniels and tried to find a silver lining. The only thing he could come up with was that the delay had probably saved him from stumbling through his presentation. Between the stress of recovering his laptop and Pace's announcement, he couldn't sell beer to an underage college student, much less a multi-million dollar project he'd spent months of his life creating.

Fuck. He'd planned for the bonus check from securing this, his biggest deal to date, to help set him free from Tarks, but all the missteps put him firmly back under his thumb. His boss had even threatened to fly up for Wednesday's meeting to smooth things over with the client. The thought of him swooping in and taking control of the deal Jason had orchestrated meant he'd spend half the night tightening his presentation to ensure Tarks wouldn't hop on a plane and take over. And then it hit him. With another baby on the way, he couldn't possibly leave the security of his job to start his own firm. He was barely present to raise the kids they had now and the long hours and financial constraints inherent to a risky venture wasn't an option when they'd have medical bills, diapers, and another mouth to feed.

He just didn't understand how Pace could be pregnant. Even the painful, anxiety-inducing procedure he'd endured years ago couldn't derail his potent little swimmers. As much as he wanted to joke about his virility, he couldn't feel proud of his sperm when a new baby changed everything.

After a hot shower where he thought long and hard about his options, he called the real estate agent handling the farm. "Don," Jason said with a throat clearing cough. The bourbon had done just enough to make his stomach queasy. "It's Jason Kelly."

"Jason. I was fixin' to call you in the mornin'. I tracked down Billy Miller this afternoon. I think he's gonna accept your offer without a counter. I expect to hear from him by tomorrow at the latest. He's pretty eager to get this thing wrapped up by the end of the year."

Just when Jason thought he couldn't feel any worse. "Listen, Don, things have changed. I'm going to have to back out of the deal."

For a moment he couldn't hear anything but Don's exhalation of breath and the squeak of his office chair. Jason pictured him, leaning back with his feet up on the scarred metal desk, some retired bird dog snoring away under the window. "Why? You know how long we've had this thing listed and with the economy the way it is..." With a final squeak of his chair he closed the deal. "Son, I don't reckon you'd get this good a deal for at least as long as it takes for the market to improve—whenever that may be, God willing and the creek don't rise."

Jason smiled at Don's expression. Pace had once said everyone from South Georgia spoke in parables. He'd take stories any day over the snob speak of her childhood friends. "I was hoping to use the money for something specific and the opportunity, well, it's not available anymore. It won't be for awhile. I'm afraid if I sell now, I'll end up pissing the money away."

"Jason, if you don't sell now, there's a chance you never will. Truth be told, son, Belton's a dying town. A few years from now you might not be able to give it away."

So Jason reluctantly agreed to move forward with the contract, if Billy Miller contacted Don like he expected, and let another part of his dream slip away. Jason took several calming breaths before reclining on the bed to call Pace. Hearing the commotion on the other end did little to soothe his nerves. The puppy had ransacked the house and done a number on Dillon's favorite stuffed animal, so things weren't going so well there either. He and Pace could barely talk with the kids interrupting every five minutes with fights and "emergencies" that couldn't wait until she was off the phone. He could tell by her terse, one-word answers she was still pissed—as pissed as his wife could get. Then she told him to hang on, shut herself in some confined space, the pantry or the hall bath he imagined, and told him that she'd decided to look at the pregnancy as a little gift from God.

"Sometimes the best things in life happen when you're not looking," she whispered in the Sunday school voice he teased her for when she got on her moral high horse. "You and I are classic examples of that being true." When he didn't answer, she said, "I know you're upset about this, Jason, but I can't be disappointed that our love made a baby."

And just like that, she reminded him of everything he loved about her and everything he hated about himself. He knew he should feel excited, but he couldn't seem to feel anything but pissed that he was stuck in a job that sucked the life out of him. "You're right, honey. Just give me a few days for it to sink in." He needed to buck up and deal with reality, because he wouldn't be able to live with himself if he let his kid think he didn't want it. Going through life like that, like a big fat mistake your parents made, was no way to live. He could certainly attest to that.

He spent all day Wednesday in meetings. First the CFO, then the CEO, then the Board of Directors. He felt so tired by the time he dragged himself back to the hotel after dinner and drinks with a few of the guys that he fell directly into bed and didn't see the flashing message light on the room's phone. He forgot to take his phone off vibrate and it kept going off through the night. Or at least until midnight, he realized the next morning when he scrolled through the calls he'd missed from Pace. Three. Guess she'd given up and gone to bed.

He caught her first thing Thursday morning. He could hear the boys fighting over who got the biggest bowl of Choco Crunchies as she clipped her answers off in the exasperated tone she usually reserved for her mother.

"I told you I forgot to check my messages, Pace. I don't know what else you want me to say."

She sighed and in it he heard all the ways he'd let her down. "I guess hearing I'm pregnant hasn't thrown you for a loop the way it has me."

"Why do you think I left my briefcase in the cab? You'd just dropped the little bomb and I couldn't even think straight." He rubbed the now throbbing pulse in his temple. He needed to calm down. This wasn't her fault. It was nobody's fault and getting mad at her wouldn't do anything but make him feel guilty. "Look, I know a baby is not a little bomb and it's not a disaster. You're right—it's a blessing. Hell, it's a damn miracle, but I need to concentrate on business right now so I can get home and we can deal with this, okay? I'm not saying it hasn't hit me, but I'm trying to keep it at bay so I can do my job and get back."

After a long pause where he knew she reined in her rare show of temper, she said, "I don't want to fight about this, Jason. I just want you to come home."

"I do too. I already changed my flight to Friday. I'll be home by dinner.

CHAPTER 3

Tori pulled her car into Caroline Prenzy's drive and marveled at the beauty of their estate as the sun fought its way through the soaring trees that surrounded the old Tudor mansion. The Prenzys lived directly behind the Whitfields, hidden from sight by towering hedges and the creek that ran between their properties. Those barriers had never stopped Pace from wading across and roughhousing with the Prenzys' two Airedale terriers. Caroline's girls were older and much prissier than Pace. They never gave her much attention, but the dogs eagerly played when Caroline's youngest, Graham, wasn't around. Tori couldn't count the number of times Pace had come home covered in mud with a mile-wide grin after hours playing fetch. Tori would scold her, of course, because she would have invariably ruined another school uniform or designer outfit, but Pace loved those dogs too much to let the threat of punishment stop her. Tori would never forget the way Pace carried on when the old dogs died within weeks of each other.

Mary Beth, Caroline's long-time housekeeper, greeted Tori at the door and ushered her to the kitchen where Caroline set a tray of sandwiches on the table next to a tureen of soup and a pitcher of her famous peach iced tea. "I thought we were going out?"

Caroline wiped her hands together and raised her palms in the air. "I didn't feel like dealing with a crowd and you know you love Mary Beth's chicken salad."

Tori plopped her purse on the counter and took a seat at the large farmhouse table. She slipped her shoes off and burrowed her feet into the almost threadbare rug beneath. There was nowhere she felt more at home than Caroline's kitchen. She looked around the cozy space, with its white cabinets and robin's egg blue counter and shades lighter walls. Caroline had set the perfect table, with cloth napkins and her sunflower plates. They always made her food seem so happy. "There are only two places set. Isn't Ginny joining us?"

Caroline sat at the end of the table, flopped her elbows down, and steepled her hands. "I asked her not to come."

Ginny and Caroline had been friends for years, good friends. Her asking Ginny not to come couldn't be good. "Why would you do that?"

"I wanted to talk to you alone. Just the two of us."

Tori's stomach clenched and her hand froze in mid-air where she'd reached for her glass. Play it light, she told herself. This didn't have to mean what she thought it did. "Well, I guess I should be relieved there won't be an audience for whatever you've got up your sleeve." She glanced at Caroline and saw the deep furrow between her brows. "But somehow I'm not." She folded her hands in her lap so Caroline couldn't see them shake. "What's this about, Caro?"

The feel of Caroline's hand on her arm caused her to jerk.

"I think you already know."

Tori dropped her head and let out the breath she'd held. "I suspected." She looked up into her friend's pitying eyes. "Who told you?"

"Edward saw them a few nights ago. He said it could have been innocent, but after I talked to you the other day I had a feeling things weren't going so well."

"Am I that transparent?"

"To those who love you..." Caroline squeezed her arm before letting go, "...yes, I guess you are."

Tori twisted the napkin in her lap. It was the same color as the walls. "It's my fault. I arranged a trainer at the club, a male, and an effeminate one at that. I should have known Colin wouldn't stand to be bossed around by a girlie-man. He switched to one of those blonde mannequins that pose as motivators." She hated to ask and, really, what difference did it make? But the words were out before she could snatch them back. "Do you know which one it is?"

Caroline reached for her arm again. "First of all, I don't ever want to hear you say it's your fault. It's his fault and no one else's." She pulled away and sat up in her seat. Tori watched the steam rise from the soup bowl between them. "Secondly, she's not blonde and she's not a trainer."

And Tori thought it couldn't get any worse. From the look on Caro's face she could tell that it would. "Who?"

"Paulina Hathaway's daughter."

Tori's mind raced. Paulina Hathaway's daughter worked as an intern for Colin. Paulina had called Tori herself just a few months ago and asked if she could pull a few strings and get Heather's resume in front of Colin. She'd asked him to consider taking her on while Heather took some time off from school. "But she's...twenty? Twenty-one?" She snorted at the absurdity of it. Their own daughter was thirty-five. "That can't be right."

"They were having dinner at The Palm last Wednesday. Ed saw them leave the restaurant and get on the elevator. It was going up." Caroline averted her eyes. "He saw them embrace before the elevator doors closed."

"So much for innocent."

"Tori..." Caro had her arm again, this time in both her hands. "I hate telling you this."

"Then I guess we're even because I hate hearing it." She pushed back from the table and stood up. The walls, the pretty blue against the white cabinets that had always reminded her of the sky with puffy clouds, closed in on her now.

"I didn't want you hearing from someone else, from someone who didn't know you, who wouldn't have your best interest at heart."

Tori spun around to face her. "Who else knows?"

Caroline dropped her head and shrugged. "Ed wasn't alone. He was with Dick Hensley and a few other guys from the club."

Tori thought of the group she'd mentioned, a pack of alpha males, most of whom probably had mistresses of their own. She doubted they'd run off at the mouth about Colin, but Ed did come home and tell Caro…

"What are you going to do?" Caroline asked.

Tori surprised herself by laughing. Somehow, some way, in the face of all the madness, she laughed. "Do? What does one do when she discovers her husband is bedding a twenty-year-old?" She circled the island. "Get a face lift?"

Caroline stood, her beautiful butcher-block island between them. "I'm serious, Tori. I can't watch you go through this again."

"Then you'd better shut your eyes, Caro, because it looks like I've got very little choice."

Mary Beth walked into the kitchen as Caroline and Tori faced off over the island. She coughed, hung her head, and backed out of the door.

"You have a choice," Caro said. "You've always had a choice."

Her comment ignited Tori's temper. It was irrational, the anger she felt toward her best friend and her seemingly flippant advice. Easy for her to say, Tori thought, when Ed had never once looked at another woman. "That may be what it looks like from the outside, Caro, but from where I'm standing, things aren't so black and white."

"I'm not suggesting you up and leave him. At least not right away." Caroline gripped the edges of the island. "But damn it, Tori, you've got to deal with this. He can't get away with treating you like this."

Judgment, even from a best friend, still stung. "Why not? It's not the first time."

"It could be the last." Caroline slumped her shoulders and leaned heavily on the island. "What's the worst thing that could happen?"

Tori said the only thing that came to mind. "He could leave me."

Caroline pushed the bowl of tomatoes out of the way and reached for Tori's hand. "Not if you leave him first."

* * *

By Friday night when Jason walked through the door, Pace was in a complete frenzy. She'd had all week to obsess about the baby and tried not to be upset that Jason hadn't. She immediately noticed his signs of stress, the finger tracks through his hair and the way his shoulders slumped from exhaustion. The boys jumped on him like a piece of gym equipment. Once he had a chance to disentangle himself from them and the puppy, who'd left a happy-pee puddle by the front door, he walked into Pace's arms and kissed her in a way that told her he'd been thinking about the pregnancy as much as she had. In a split second, all of her anger evaporated.

Jason always had the ability to calm her with a look or a touch. Pace often wondered what she gave him in return, other than anxiety and stress. It never ceased to amaze her that he chose to spend his life with her, someone so full of neuroses, thanks in large part to her upbringing. He'd said he didn't know who she was when they met and was glad for it. If he knew then what he knew now, Pace wondered if he'd have turned and walked away that first night. God knew her mother would have been happy if he had, but Pace wouldn't ever have found the peace his love brought her and the family they'd made together. Tori called it suburban hell, their simple life of domestic bliss. This from a woman who'd rather plan and host a party for two hundred strangers than babysit her grandsons.

"Hi." She could smell the hint of aftershave he'd used hours ago and the scent he often carried when he came in from traveling. Airport smells.

"Hi." They stared at one another with a look of wonder. What had they done, his look said to Pace. His eyes, the kelly green of his name, could say more than words at times. His eyes had drawn her to him the night they'd met, as he stood in a corner of the fraternity house nursing a drink and using those eyes to track her movements. She'd had too much to drink, not the keg beer he sipped that she later tasted on his tongue, but some vodka concoction her roommate had made up before the night began. Pace had seen him staring at her and didn't know if he was interested in her or if the alcohol had given her the singular sensation it still did when she drank. When it became clear that he wasn't going to stop staring, Pace, emboldened by liquor, sauntered up to face him.

"You're staring at me." She'd hoped her words didn't slur.

He shrugged and took another sip, eyed her coolly over the lip of the cup. They faced each other silently before she began to feel stupid for trying to engage him in conversation. Now that she'd stepped closer, she could see he wasn't just cute, with his long hair and dare-me-to-care clothes, so out of place at the frat house. He was gorgeous.

"Why?" She finally asked, unable to help herself.

His eyes dropped to her chest. She'd never forget the feel of the blush that crept, or more aptly ran, up her face. She'd been called pretty before, in a Sally Field-as-Gidget sort of way, but it certainly hadn't been because of her less than stellar chest. He'd laughed and the dimple she had to kiss while they made love appeared out of nowhere. He reached out to finger the cashmere collar of her red sweater.

"In a room full of black, she wears red." Pace had been too drunk to be impressed with his third person reference and she felt her brow furrow in question. Later, he'd confess he'd almost walked away, almost written her off as another dumb sorority girl.

"What's wrong with red?" Pace thought she'd missed some joke. She never gave much thought to clothes other than to cover her appropriately for the weather. The fact that she'd had on a black sweater earlier and tossed it aside right before leaving ran through her mind.

He dropped his hand. "Nothing."

"Then why are you staring at me?"

"I'm taking an art appreciation class." That was all he'd said, as if that explained anything.

"I've had too much to drink to assimilate any meaning from that vague answer." Her use of the word assimilate, he'd later admit, had kept him interested.

"The eye is drawn to certain elements in...paintings, pictures, sculptures. Colors have meaning beyond just the clothing or item they represent. Red's the color of passion, emotion, anger. A woman who wears it wants to be noticed."

Years later, when they'd scraped enough money together to buy a fixer-upper townhome, they painted the kitchen red. He'd said it made him hungry to see the color, but not as hungry as seeing it on Pace that night. It was the first room they made love in besides the bedroom.

Pace sighed into his chest and snuggled closer. "I've missed you." She wished the boys and the dog wouldn't complain if they slipped off to the bedroom for an hour. She physically ached for his touch.

"You have no idea, Pace." His mouth found hers and on his tongue she tasted his desire. If she had to choose right that second whether to be pregnant and make love to him that night or not be pregnant, but not have him, she'd choose pregnancy every time.

The boys thundered back and peeled them apart. Mitchell dragged his blanket that, since Jason started traveling so much, had become a permanent appendage to his body. Pace would have thrown the tattered blanket away if she didn't think it would crush him. Dillon tried not to act too excited to see him, but his smile gave him away.

As Jason's fingers untangled from her hair, Pace felt the spell burst from around them and resumed cooking dinner in the kitchen. The kids squealed in the den as Jason pulled gifts he'd bought at the airport from his bag. The puppy danced in a circle and barked. The noise that only yesterday would have set her teeth on edge made her laugh. Everything she'd worried about in the last week floated off her shoulders. Now that Jason was home, she knew they'd be okay.

* * *

Pace came in the bedroom after checking on the boys as Jason tossed his shirt and suit pants into the dry cleaning hamper.

"They're out like a light." She kicked his dirty socks from the bed to the floor and smiled at him in a way that stirred his blood. He was exhausted, but since they hadn't had sex in weeks, he couldn't beg off as being too tired. He ran his hands over her hair, the same tawny color it had been since childhood, and pulled her to him. Her baby pictures had only hinted at the beauty she'd grow to become. Mitchell, the baby, well…for now, he had her hair.

After they made love, Jason lifted the silk of her gown—she never slept naked since the boys came along. "What if they come in the room and I'm naked?" she always said when he'd beg her to leave it off. He missed sleeping skin to skin like they used to. He kissed her smooth belly, still as flat as the first time he ever touched it, and kissed the spot where he assumed their third child now grew. Maybe this time it would be a girl. "Hi in there." When her muscles tensed, Jason realized she was crying.

"Pace? Baby, what's wrong?" God, she was pregnant. She'd gone through the roller coaster of emotion the first two times; she'd go from laughing to crying in less than a second and he never knew what to do. Pace wiped away the tears and shook her head, snuggling against him.

"Nothing."

Since she'd told him about the baby, all he'd done was think about how it would affect *his* job, *his* plans to quit, how much longer *he'd* have to work to get this kid through college. He hadn't considered how a baby would change her life and her plans to work from home. God knew they could use the money.

"I've been an asshole about this."

"I know." She leaned up to face him and they laughed. She always managed to pull him out of even the worst funk. Her smile faded and she studied him for a long time, her clear brown eyes on his face. "Can you believe this?"

"Honestly, no. I can't believe we're having another baby."

"I messed up your meeting, didn't I?"

Jason kissed her nose. "It threw me, but we'll either get or lose the account on the merits of the proposal." He'd thought this repeatedly on the plane ride home. "I know you weren't trying to sabotage my career."

"Aw, Jas. A baby." She shook her head. "I'm too old to have another baby."

"Apparently not." He shifted to move the pillows behind his head and hoped she didn't hear the disappointment in his voice. He could barely keep his eyes open. "I'll call the urologist on Monday." He yawned and turned on his side. "I hope I don't have to have the whole thing done over again." Actually, he wouldn't put himself through that again and even as tired as he felt, he knew bringing it up for discussion now wouldn't be the wisest move.

"If it failed once, it may fail again," she said, turned out the light, and wrapped herself around him.

In this position, their arms and legs intertwined as if each one were a part of the other, he felt an inkling of her optimism. He'd get through the shock and get excited. Pace would turn the whole thing around to where he'd have to try to remember they didn't plan to have a third child in the first place. Having another baby wasn't the end of the world.

"If it comes to that, I can have my tubes tied after..." she rubbed her face against his shoulder, "...well, after the baby's born."

Monday, on his way to work, Jason called Dr. German's office. When he explained to the nurse what had happened, she managed to squeeze him in that afternoon. He didn't really have time to go over to the doctor's office, especially considering he had another eight months to worry about it, but scheduled the appointment anyway. It seemed like the only constructive thing he could do.

As he sat in the waiting room, he looked around. The place had been recently updated, with contemporary furniture and carpet that still carried the new smell. Business must have been good. He decided he wasn't paying for the visit since the vasectomy didn't work the first time. He wanted to say something to the men sitting around him. They weren't all at the office for vasectomies, but he felt like issuing a warning anyway. "Hey guys," he imagined saying. "Don't count on this working one hundred percent of the time."

When he realized he would probably have to jerk off into a cup with a magazine like a fifteen-year-old, he found himself squirming in his seat. Last time he took the cup home and he and Pace had some fun with it. Definitely no fun this time. After thirty minutes, a nurse called his name and led him down a brightly lit hallway. As he'd suspected, he had to whack off so they could determine the extent of the reversal. *It's reversed enough to get my wife pregnant!* He wanted to shout at her. She led him to a room lined with magazines and DVDs, a mounted plasma television, and a leather couch. He could have sworn the nurse smirked at him when she closed the door.

Jason didn't want to sit down or touch anything and he hoped like hell they'd sanitized the place after the last guy left. He flipped through a few magazines and then tossed them aside when the quiet of the room began to close in on him. Maybe a movie would speed the process along. Shit. What a mess.

He left the sample in a metal box in the wall and crept out of the office feeling as though he had just scored with a hooker. Jason felt a bit surreal returning to the office after jacking off to porn. He had forty-four emails waiting to answer and he'd promised Pace he'd be home to take Dillon to basketball practice. Jason rubbed his hands over his face and sighed. Looked like he was in for another all-nighter. Great.

Tarks was waiting in his office when he came in the next day, pissed because the prospect, who'd promised them exclusivity, had decided to solicit other bids. Jason spent the day on the phone sucking up to everyone at the client's office while polishing some pie-in-the-sky proposals he'd kind of saved for his new company. Just when he thought it couldn't get any worse, the phone rang and it did.

* * *

Mitchell had stayed home from school with a slight fever and Pace had put him in bed to rest. A stomach bug was going around school and she hoped he didn't start throwing up. Dillon played at a friend's house to keep germ contamination to a minimum. When she checked on Mitchell, he was asleep and a quick feel to his forehead told her the fever had gone down.

She'd just settled in front of the computer to answer emails when she heard the front door open. Pace glanced at the clock.

Four p.m. Nancy Palmore wouldn't drop Dillon off until five and it was way too early to be Jason, but she found him standing in the foyer when she came around from the kitchen. He just stood there, carrying his leather case as if waiting for an elevator. When he heard Pace and their eyes met, the look he gave her stopped Pace in her tracks.

"Jason, what's wrong? Why are you home so early?"

He looked at her, his brow furrowed, his knuckles white from gripping his bag tight. He didn't speak for a long time.

"Jas?" She moved toward him. He whipped his arm away before she could touch him. "What is it?"

He dropped his case and moved past her into the den. His head hung down and he had his hands on his hips as if he planned to give a half-time speech to a team getting their butts kicked. When he turned around, he looked…angry and perplexed, she'd probably have said.

"Dr. German's office called with my test results." His voice sounded quiet and very controlled.

"Okay…" The way he waited made Pace think they'd found cancer. He shook his head.

"They said I'm shooting blanks."

"What do you mean?" she asked stupidly, because this used to be his favorite way to describe his status after the vasectomy.

"I'm sterile, Pace. There's no way I got you pregnant."

CHAPTER 4

Caroline was right. Tori needed to do something about Colin. But what? The last time she suspected him of an affair—an extended affair—Pace had been in college and still so enamored of her father. She'd considered posing an ultimatum then, but there'd been so much to lose—his job, their life, her daughter. She'd never been able to shatter Pace the way her own mother had shattered her, forcing her father's hand and pushing him away for good. Tori grew up in the shadow of a father who, with his back against the wall, had chosen to start a whole new family. Colin would invariably select the same path; the man couldn't function alone.

Tori suspected he'd dabbled occasionally and dismissed his slips as normal male behavior—it certainly had been for her father—and much easier to stomach than lengthy affairs that posed a real threat to her marriage. But now that Caroline had pressured her to do something about Colin's behavior, she felt like a wish bone being pulled in two different directions.

When the phone rang at nine in the morning, she knew it was Caroline, checking in on her like she had every day since their lunch. Tori ended each call pledging to think about confronting him, think about keeping tabs on his schedule, think about protecting herself if his affair came to light. She was so tired of thinking about her options, when she really didn't have any, that she considered avoiding her calls. If it were anyone but Caroline, she would.

"No, before you ask, I haven't done anything since yesterday."

Caroline sighed with impatience and a little bit of the humor that had always been a part of their relationship. "Not even any thinking? Really, Tori, how much time does it take just to think about it?"

"More than I've got these days. The campaign is—"

"I'm talking about your life and all you can say is the campaign?" She wondered when Caroline's patience would expire. She'd never had much to begin with and it seemed today was the day. "The campaign isn't a person!"

"It's more demanding than a person has the right to be."

In the subsequent pause, Tori knew Caro tried to think of another tack to take, another phrase that would lead Tori to where she wanted her to go. "Doing nothing, ignoring his behavior, can't be one of your options."

"No, it's not one of *your* options."

"I swear, if you spent half as much energy fighting your husband as you do me, you'd be free of him already."

Why was Caroline so convinced she would be better off without Colin? Because really, whether or not he left her or she left him, she would be the one left alone. Did Caroline really not get it? "I know you want my freedom, Caro, but what matters is what I want."

"Exactly." Her voice softened and Tori imagined she'd slipped on what Ed called her sympathetic basset hound face. "What do you want, Tori? And before you answer I want you to think about it. What *you* want, not what's best for Colin or Pace or the campaign. What you want."

She couldn't have what she really wanted. She'd known that for years. "I want the fairy tale."

"Oh, honey." Tori heard Ed kiss Caroline's cheek before he left the house. She considered it a strike against her. "You've been living the fairy tale and it hasn't made you happy."

The fairy tale of their marriage had created her identity. She didn't know who or what she'd be without it. "Happiness is overrated."

When she heard Caroline snort, she thought she'd earned another twenty-four hour reprieve. "I called Paulina Hathaway."

"Caroline…"

"I had to talk to her anyway and it seemed like a good idea to ask about Heather."

Just hearing Heather's name felt like a twist of the knife in her heart. "I wish you'd leave this alone."

"He's taken her to Washington, Tor. Several times."

She didn't know if Caro spoke softly or if she could barely hear her through the ringing in her ears. "That doesn't mean anything."

"Really? What do interns normally do, other than collate paper and stuff envelopes all day? You're forgetting Bethany spent a summer working for Congressman Bartles. She got all excited when they finally let her answer the phone."

"Maybe Heather is more skilled than Bethany."

"Bethany was getting her masters at the time and I won't even bring up the brilliance of her thesis." Caro could brag about her daughter endlessly. "Heather hasn't even gotten her undergrad."

Tori rubbed her throbbing temple. "I don't want to argue with you about her qualifications."

"Your husband is having an affair with a twenty-year-old. If you don't want to believe me, that's fine. But you can't just ignore it. If Ed saw them and Colin's gallivanting around Washington with her, it is going to come out sooner or later. If you need proof, real concrete proof, then I wish you'd get it, because getting mad at me and thinking I'm crazy doesn't do anything to solve the problem."

The pounding in Tori's head would never cease if Caroline didn't leave her alone. The picking and nagging and rubbing Heather in her face! She almost slammed the phone down and vowed never to answer it again. "How am I supposed to get proof? You think I should follow him?"

"It doesn't have to be you and what you do with the proof is up to you, but at least you'd know for sure."

Tori didn't answer, but gave some excuse about being needed by the staff and hung up the phone.

Follow Colin? It seemed too absurd for her to consider. But Caro was right about her needing to protect herself. If rumors of Colin's affair started up, he'd deny it like he always did and she'd be forced to stand by him without evidence on her side.

* * *

Jason stood in his den, toy cars littered the floor, video games sat piled in the corner, and the painting he and Pace had picked out on their honeymoon hung over the mantle. He looked at his wife and it felt like he'd never seen her before.

"There has to be some kind of mistake," she said. "Either your test or mine is wrong."

It all sounded logical; medical science wasn't exact. "I made them go back and re-do the test. I'm sterile."

"Then my test is wrong."

"Didn't the nurse say blood tests aren't wrong?" He knew the answer. He'd thought of nothing else since he got the call about his sperm and headed home to confront Pace.

"Yes, but..." She came into the den and sat on the couch, sandwiching those nervous fingers between her knees. She looked up at him like a child, her eyes wide. "Jason, you can't possibly think I cheated on you."

"I don't want to think it, Pace, but I can't seem to find an explanation that doesn't come back to that."

She was up in an instant, her hands clutching his arms. "I've never cheated on you. I've never even considered it. Jason, we've talked about this before. You know how I feel about cheating."

"I know what you said."

They'd had a conversation about infidelity after one of her best friends found out her husband was having a long term affair with someone at his office. Jason and Pace had been shocked; they'd seemed like the perfect couple. After a few months of trying to work it out, their marriage ended in a nasty divorce. He and Pace had both agreed that cheating was a deal breaker, a bright neon line in the sand. So now, standing there facing her, he couldn't believe she did it or he couldn't believe she'd deny it faced with proof. He just couldn't believe...

"I didn't cheat on you. I would never..." She shook her head and didn't say anything else.

Mitchell screamed from somewhere in the house. "Mommy!" It was the kind of scream they both knew meant serious business.

Pace ran for the stairs and Jason followed behind. Mitchell sat up in bed, a Tupperware container between his hands, filled with vomit. The smell of it hit Jason's nostrils before he even saw it. Mitchell's eyes looked glassy and tired. He hated to vomit, hated to poop in public, hated to admit he had any sort of bodily functions that took place outside his own private world. When he saw his dad in the doorway, he looked confused and a little embarrassed.

"I threw up, Daddy." Jason's heart broke. His little man was down.

He moved to the bed and kissed his son's forehead while Pace emptied the container in the toilet and came back with a warm wash cloth. Mitchell leaned back against his pillows, closed his eyes, totally comforted by Pace. How could she have done this to them? He jerked the tie off his neck when he felt it strangling him.

Pace stayed with Mitchell, rubbing his belly, and when they both thought he'd fallen asleep, she tried to stand up so she and Jason could keep talking. "Mommy?" His voice sounded weak and pleading. "Don't go."

Pace looked at Jason. "I'm right here, baby. I'm not going anywhere."

Jason left them alone and went into their bedroom to change clothes. Once he'd thrown on his jeans and a t-shirt, he looked around their room at her stuff. Could there be a clue amongst her things? Had she left a note or something incriminating tucked away? With a glance down the hall toward Mitchell's room, he began opening the drawers of her dresser, moving aside bras and panties, shirts and shorts, looking for something that would tell him she'd been unfaithful, all the while thinking how unreal the whole idea of it seemed.

This was Pace, after all, the woman who'd walked away from a future paved in gold to marry him. Could that be the reason? Did she regret their life together? Was she bored? And what kind of idiot had he been for not even considering she'd had an affair when she turned up pregnant?

He found nothing in her dresser and moved into the closet. It smelled like her, the perfume she wore and the fancy soap she used at night in her bath. Jason felt like a hypocrite, looking through her stuff while she soothed their son, until he remembered the condescension he heard in the nurse's voice when he'd asked her to run the test again. He checked the pockets of her coats, the boxes of shoes—who needed this many shoes?—and found nothing. When he came out of the bedroom, he heard her singing the song she'd sung to the boys since they were babies.

He moved downstairs to her desk and the computer. She had over a hundred emails on her computer and a scroll down the list led nowhere. The drawers of her desk were filled with receipts and knick-knacks, stuff for the boys from school, old sunglasses. The only things he'd discovered were her packrat tendencies and that she owned too many shoes. He pushed away from the desk and went into the kitchen.

Jason always thought if Pace cheated, he'd bolt, come home and pack a bag. But there he stood with proof, undeniable proof that she'd had an affair and he kept trying to convince himself there'd been a mistake. If she cheated and got pregnant with some other guy's baby, would she be stupid enough to try and pass it off as his? She'd pressed him to have the vasectomy checked out. He whirled around and found her leaning against the doorway, staring at him with her arms tightly crossed, her fingers tapping away on her biceps.

"I'm calling Dr. Hidel's office. I'm going to make them re-do the test." She walked to Jason and stopped an arms length away. He wondered if she knew he'd been snooping through her stuff. "There's some kind of mistake, Jason. I didn't cheat on you."

He looked at her, her big brown eyes, her honey colored hair, and teenager's body. Any guy would be lucky to get their hands on her. She'd always been the prettiest person he'd ever known. Didn't her friend Sherry's husband admit, two six-packs into the night, that he'd pick Pace as his wife swap? He should have decked him instead of feeling proud.

"Call the doctor." What else could he say?

CHAPTER 5

Pace called the doctor and begged for an appointment, but they couldn't even squeeze her in until Friday. She couldn't bring herself to go into the whole sordid mess over the phone and decided it would have to be the end of the week. She couldn't believe the way Jason continued to look at her, like she'd had sex with every man on the block right under his nose.

Before she could say anything else, Nancy dropped off Dillon and Mitchell woke up and started vomiting again. Dillon peeked his head into Mitchell's room an hour later and said he and Dad were going to get dinner and that they'd bring something back for her. Couldn't Jason have come up to talk to her instead of sending Dillon in his place? He was deliberately avoiding her, hiding under that cool veneer he'd always used to keep people at bay. At the very least he should have checked on his son. Pace didn't have time to get worked up because, as soon as Dillon turned to leave, Mitchell dry-heaved into the bucket she held up to his mouth.

She spent the night on the floor of his room in a Scooby-Doo sleeping bag. By the next morning, her back was killing her, Dillon had made it on the bus, Mitchell felt better, and Jason barely spoke to her before leaving for work. By noon she'd started throwing up in the toilet. Life just kept getting better and better.

* * *

Jason kept thinking about when Pace first took him to meet her parents. He didn't have a clue how rich she was until they pulled into the drive of the Georgian mansion where her parents still live. He didn't feel worthy of mowing their lawn, much less dating their daughter. The house served as a glaring reminder, concrete evidence of everything he'd chosen not to see about her life—the designer labels on her clothes, her luxury car, her snotty friends. Pace belonged to a world he'd never seen and it scared him that they were so in sync and yet came from two completely different ends of the universe.

Her mother, Victoria Pace Whitfield, met them in the library, drink in hand, and perpetual smile on her face. He remembered meeting her and thinking she looked like the perfect Senator's wife, like a billboard advertisement for the American Dream. And now, sixteen years later, he felt the same way. She'd hated Jason from that very first day he'd walked in with sweaty palms and his heart in her daughter's hand. If he could have snatched it back from Pace as he'd faced the icy stare of her mother, he may have.

Pace had warned him about Tori. "She's not the warmest person, so don't expect a big hug and a welcome-to-the-family smile. She'll probably grill you."

"Grill me about what?" he'd naively asked. It wasn't like he had criminal record or anything.

"Everything," Pace explained. "Your parents, your siblings, your hometown, your goals, where you see yourself in five or ten years. Just don't be intimidated." Jason would never admit he'd been scared by the woman he still thought could wrestle secrets from third world terrorists. He'd never understood how his gentle, naïve wife had come from his mother-in-law.

Her dad had breezed in from the airport after a grueling session of Congress—Colin described every session as grueling—wearing a three-piece suit that probably cost more than Jason's car. He'd wondered, not for the first time, what the hell Pace saw in a guy like him. He had nothing in common with her dad. Colin was slick, from his perfectly styled hair and manicured nails to his tasseled loafers. He still cringed whenever he saw a man wearing loafers. It just seemed so wrong.

They'd had dinner at a table for twenty, just the four of them, eating duck and a whole bunch of food he'd never seen before and couldn't pronounce. He'd been politely cross-examined by Colin and Tori and probably written off as a phase.

Jason kept thinking about that night because it was a time in their relationship where a light bulb went off in his head. Before that night, Pace had been this petite girl with long, flyaway hair, big soulful eyes, and a really nice car. He knew her dad was a Senator, but he'd mostly blanked that out because he'd fallen in love with her sweetness. They'd made love like rabbits, eaten pizza for dinner twenty-two nights in a row, and she'd always kept him from taking everything too seriously. He'd loved her more than he thought he could ever love another person and then suddenly, after that night, he couldn't look at her the same.

He never thought their differences bothered Pace until now, as he sat at his desk wondering why his wife would cheat on him. Could this be another light bulb moment where he realized he wasn't enough for her? They hadn't exactly burned up the sheets lately, with his work and travel schedule, but he couldn't see Pace cheating for the thrill of cheap sex. And who the hell would it be? Someone in the neighborhood? Someone she met at school or at the grocery store? The gym?

Tarks called Jason into his office and, for once, he felt grateful for the distraction. He explained he was giving Jason another chance to prove himself. They'd been contacted by a prospect out of New York, a start-up company looking to build their headquarters, and he needed Jason to fly there next week and do the preliminary legwork. Jason couldn't care less about a new account and the thought of proving himself, after five years, made him want to toss Tarks by the lapels of his very expensive suit out the twentieth-story window. A new project, however, might keep him from thinking about Pace with a bevy of men.

By three o'clock, knee deep in zoning research, he felt strange not having talked to Pace. He wondered if she hadn't called because she felt guilty. He should feel guilty for not checking on Mitchell, but he still couldn't bring himself to pick up the phone and returned to his data on design constraints in the New York City suburb. Sometime later the phone rang. Jason answered without looking at the display and straightened in his seat when he recognized his wife's voice over the line. She sounded awful and explained she'd caught Mitchell's bug, but ecstatically announced she'd gotten her period. Overwhelmed with relief, Jason shoved files in his bag and left to go home early so she could rest.

* * *

Tori looked through the glass doors of Colin's office and wondered again if she was doing the right thing. She could see her reflection as she stood in the hallway and, for a moment, she stared at her image. With the two inches her boots added and the way her white hair rose above her forehead to curl against her cheek, she looked like a lighter, thinner version of Elizabeth Taylor in *Who's Afraid of Virginia Woolf?* How could she look so strong and yet feel so invisible?

The receptionist, an overweight and overeager employee, waved her through the door, jolting Tori out of her thoughts. "Mrs. Whitfield! What a nice surprise."

Her nameplate reminded Tori of her name. "Hello, Beverly. You're looking lovely today."

Her quick blush revealed no one had complimented her in awhile. "The Senator is out to lunch right now..." she looked down at the calendar on her desk, "...but he should be back soon. Would you like to wait in his office?"

Tori glanced at her watch and twitched her lips, acting as if she were pressed for time when, in fact, this charade was all she'd planned for the day. "Sure. I guess I can spare a few minutes."

"Can I bring you some coffee or a soft drink?"

Tori walked down the hall toward Colin's door. "I'll get it," she called over her shoulder.

She looked left and right over the tops of the cubicles and in the offices that lined the outer edges of the small space. Phones rang and people talked in muted voices, mostly men with their coats off and shirt sleeves rolled up to their elbows. She couldn't see Heather's dark head anywhere. She nearly ran into Trey while she scouted for Heather and didn't look where she was going.

Trey grabbed her arms to avoid a collision. "Tori? I didn't know you were here." As he flicked the blond hair from his eyes,

Tori couldn't help but smile at his handsome face and think about how different her grandchildren would look and behave if he and Pace had married.

"Oh, Trey, I'm sorry. I shouldn't be wandering around not looking where I'm going."

"I don't mind running into a beautiful woman." He flashed a devilish grin and she wondered why he wasn't the one bedding twenty-year-olds. Perhaps he did or perhaps he was too busy covering for Colin. "Were we expecting you?"

We. God, how the campaign made everyone feel territorial toward Colin. "I was in the neighborhood."

He wrapped an arm around her shoulders and led her down the hall toward Colin's office. "He'll be back soon. He's having lunch with some folks from the Chamber."

Tori couldn't explain her presence. Why didn't she think of an excuse before she came there? What had she planned to say if he'd been at his desk? "Is he worried about their support?"

Trey brushed off any suggestion of defeat. "He's not taking anything for granted."

She stopped him before they turned the corner and she wouldn't be able see the reception area. From where she'd paused she could see when the elevators opened. "Are you concerned about the man who intends to run against him? Does he really have a chance?"

"Not much of one, no." Trey excused himself after a woman poked her head out of an office and announced he had a call. "Make yourself comfortable, Tori. The old man will be back soon."

She didn't have to worry about loitering in the hallway, for as soon as Trey had disappeared, Colin pulled open the glass doors. She felt a weight lift off her shoulders when she realized he was alone. Tori knew the moment he saw her. His friendly grin turned serious and then snapped back into place as he walked toward her. He hadn't quite made it to her side when the glass doors opened again revealing Heather, the young and perky college student who had obviously taken a separate elevator to cover her and Colin's rendezvous. The way she looked, the confident way she carried herself, all but announced she'd had a productive lunch hour. The guilt on Colin's face was unmistakable. She could no longer pretend her husband wasn't having an affair.

"Tori?" Colin kissed her cheek when she turned her head away. "Did I know you were coming?"

She looked him dead in the eye. "I imagine you didn't have a clue."

CHAPTER 6

Pace called the doctor's office first thing Friday morning and told them she'd gotten her period and didn't need a follow up appointment. The nurse suggested she keep it, just to check things out. Pace felt better—she hadn't thrown up in eight hours—so she decided it couldn't hurt. Mitchell was back at school and, knock-on-wood, Dillon seemed to have dodged the bullet. The strain this whole ordeal had put on her marriage made her want to strangle the doctor and she wished she had her mother's bravado and could give him an earful at the appointment.

By the time the doctor arrived, Pace had waited over an hour in a freezing cold room wearing nothing more than a tissue paper gown. Her impatience, along with her meager temper, simmered at full boil. He swept in as if he'd graced her with his presence and glanced through her file.

"I'm sorry, Mrs. Kelly." He didn't even look at her. "First trimester miscarriage is very common. Spontaneous abortion occurs in women aged thirty-five and older twenty to thirty-five percent of the time, so you shouldn't feel as though this is a result of something you did." He lightly tapped her shoulder instructing Pace to lie down on the table. The nurse entered as he pulled out the stirrups. "We'll do a quick physical exam to check the womb."

Before she had a chance to explain that she'd never been pregnant, she was staring at the ceiling and he'd inserted the speculum. Her throat clamped tight when he began the examination.

"I can see the womb opening is closed and," his fingers pressed on her abdomen, "I can tell by the size of your uterus you've successfully miscarried. You can expect to bleed for a few days to a week." He extracted the speculum and instructed her to sit up. "That's good news, Mrs. Kelly. Your body's done the best it can with an improbable situation."

"Dr. Hidel," she finally managed to interject. He either had a tee time or a hot date for lunch. "I wasn't pregnant in the first place. There was some kind of mistake."

He made eye contact for the first time since he'd entered the room and whipped off his gloves before flipping open the file. "Nooo." He spoke to Pace like a toddler. "I'm looking at the blood results drawn just two weeks ago. Positive pregnancy." He flipped the file closed, discussion over. "There's no use beating yourself up about this and wondering why it happened. The most common cause of miscarriage is chromosomal abnormalities, which means the baby couldn't have survived outside the womb anyway. If you and your husband want to have another baby, give it at least six months and try again. Just be sure to take prenatal vitamins and folic acid."

"Dr. Hidel." Pace tried to use the same condescending tone he'd used with her, but only ended up sounding whiney. She couldn't believe the man who'd delivered her two children would speak to her that way. Didn't he remember how she and Jason cried when Dillon was born? Jason had hugged him in that awkward way men do and pumped his arm up and down so much the doctor kept slapping him on the shoulder to end the torture. Pace had watched the scene, blurry eyed, with her legs spread eagle, waiting for Dr. Hidel to stitch her back up, still reeling from having seen the whole delivery through the glare of his glasses after she'd declined the mirror.

"I wasn't pregnant," she insisted. "My husband had a vasectomy three years ago and, because of this scare, he had his sperm checked earlier this week. He's sterile. Which means there had to have been some kind of mistake."

"Mrs. Kelly…" He turned to look at the nurse, who, until moments before had been engrossed with straightening the counter, now listened raptly. "I don't know what happened between you and your husband, but you were pregnant when you came to see us..." he flipped open the chart again, "two weeks ago."

"No, I wasn't." Pace couldn't believe she'd recommended him dozens of times to friends for his compassion. "I came to see you because my periods were erratic and I'd been feeling tired and occasionally dizzy. But I wasn't pregnant, no matter what your test said." She tightened the tissue gown around her waist in order to muster some dignity. She felt glad to be sitting on the raised examination table because she wouldn't project much authority standing at her full five-feet-two in bare feet. "I want you to run another blood test and prove to me and my husband that I was never pregnant in the first place."

It seemed she'd finally gotten his attention, because of her request or the near hysterical tone it was delivered in she'd never know. He sat down on the stool and swiveled in her direction. "We can re-test the blood we drew at your last visit, but if we draw a sample today it will come back negative, as my physical examination confirmed. Would you like us to re-test the original draw?"

Was he an idiot or just hard of hearing? "Yes, I'd like you to re-test the original blood sample. As soon as possible, today, STAT, or whatever you people call it. I can't begin to tell you what this has done to my marriage."

"Okay, Mrs. Kelly. You can get dressed and I'll order a retest of the sample and put a rush on it."

Pace sighed and nodded her head. "Thank you, I appreciate it." He and the nurse left the room quickly, eager to discuss the lunatic patient with the rest of the staff she felt sure. She didn't care that she'd raised her voice. With the level of incompetence they'd displayed, she'd have to find a new doctor anyway.

When Pace came out of the room, back in her jeans and a sweater, the Doctor informed her that the lab had destroyed the initial specimen, as was their standard procedure after seven days.

"So there's no way to do a retest?" she asked in disbelief.

"Not on the original sample. And as I told you before, any blood we draw today will come back negative."

"So you can't tell me whether or not I was pregnant?"

He sighed, clearly ready to move on. With a quick glance at the nurse by his side he said, "According to your earlier test, and today's examination, I'd have to say you were pregnant and suffered a spontaneous abortion, otherwise called a miscarriage." He placed a conciliatory hand on her shoulder. She gripped her hands together to keep from flicking it off. "I'm sorry, Mrs. Kelly. If your bleeding persists for more than a week, please don't hesitate to contact the office."

Pace stared at him until he smiled weakly and turned away.

* * *

Jason thought the rough designs he dabbled with on the New York client looked good. The zoning laws for the area were strict, but forgiving and, after some research and a phone conversation, he learned the company founders liked cutting edge stuff. The project, as well as his relief at knowing Pace hadn't cheated on him, made him remember why he'd gotten into the business in the first place. He made arrangements to head to New York the following week to do an initial pitch and gather more information. He hated leaving town again, but he felt excited by the challenge of the deal.

Tarks checked on his progress during the day, but he didn't show him the preliminary work he'd done. Now that there wasn't a baby on the way, his plans to leave were back on track. The New York client could become his if he decided to go ahead with his plans to leave by spring. Thank God Don had talked him into accepting the offer on the farm.

After he returned from a quick trip to the sandwich shop in the lobby, he found the office humming. The Chicago client had called and committed to using their design, prompting some serious celebration amongst Tarks and the other partners. It seemed like the black cloud that had hung over Jason's head the last two weeks had disappeared and made him think of Pace. She didn't answer when he phoned, so he left a message for her to get a sitter and meet him for drinks and dinner when she could.

She e-mailed around three and said she'd meet him at The Barister, their favorite bar in Midtown, just around the corner from the office. Jason was anxious to tell her about work and to bounce his plans off her for the millionth time. They'd discussed his leaving and starting his own firm in the abstract, but he wanted to do it now, buoyed by the Chicago deal and his forthcoming bonus check. He needed Pace's support because a new firm would mean longer hours and a lot less money for awhile.

His usually punctual wife didn't arrive on time and just as Jason pulled out his phone to call her, she walked in, her cheeks a rosy pink from the cold. She didn't see Jason at first and wandered around the bar, flipping her head from side to side while her big brown eyes scanned the crowd. Jason watched her, his beautiful wife, and noticed a few heads turn in her direction as she weeded her way through the crowded bar to find him. She wore a red silk blouse, his favorite color on her, and he assumed she'd deliberately worn it for him.

He reached a hand out to grab her arm as she almost passed him by. "I didn't see you," she said with a breathy giggle.

He kissed her as she attempted to take off her coat and, with her arms stuck behind her, she stumbled into his chest. He didn't know why, but seeing her out at night, he felt like the young co-ed he'd once been, grateful to be in her sunny spotlight. He bit her bottom lip as he pulled back and her eyes widened in surprise. He had a sudden urge to press her against the bar and make out. "You look good, Pace."

She sat on the stool beside him, grinning. "I'll have whatever you're having."

They smiled at each other like a couple of teenagers. "Crown and ginger," he told the bartender. He reached out and tucked her hair behind her ear. He could feel the cold air on her skin.

"You're in a good mood." She took a sip when her drink arrived. "What's the occasion?"

"Well," he began with a laugh. "I know you don't want to hear this, Pace, but I'm just so damn relieved you're not pregnant." He watched her face fall and quickly added, "Not that

I wouldn't have loved our baby. That's not what I mean." He shook his head, dropped his forehead to hers. "Let me start over. I went a little nuts when I thought you'd cheated and I'm sorry."

She jerked back from him and knocked the guy behind her. "I didn't cheat on you, Jason."

"I know that, I know that *now*." He pulled her stool closer and leaned into her ear. "I couldn't stand the idea, the possibility..."

"There is no possibility. I wouldn't do that to you or to us."

"Exactly. So knowing that, and the fact that we secured the Chicago account today, puts me in a pretty good mood. And there's a prospect in New York that could be a big deal and one I could take with me to my new firm—now that you're not pregnant."

"Take with you? You mean..." She sipped and nodded and her eyes told him to go on.

"I think I'm ready to leave, Pace. I think it's time."

In her face he saw everything. Excitement, a little fear, and the pride that had always been there, even before he ever deserved it.

"Whenever you're ready. Baby, you know I'm behind you." She reached over and put her hand on his leg. After a quick squeeze, he could feel her fingers drumming away through his pants. "I'll help in any way I can. I can do your press kit and help design your new logo."

"We're going to pay out the ass for insurance until I can get my own policy in place."

"Are you trying to talk me out of supporting you? Because you can't." He stilled her fingers by covering her hand in his. The nervous patter was getting to him, despite her encouraging words. "You've always wanted to be on your own. We'll be fine, we'll scale back on Christmas—you know my parents always go overboard anyway—and we'll make due."

"There's been an offer on the farm, a decent one." Her brows furrowed, but she listened intently. "I told Don to draw up a contract."

She pulled herself upright and gripped the chair with her hands. "Jason, are you sure? I always thought you wanted to keep your grandfather's place?"

"For what, Pace? We're not moving back. I don't even have relatives in Belton anymore." That wasn't exactly true. He had a few aunts and uncles, several cousins scattered around the county. Most of them, well…all of them really, he'd never claimed as kin. "It was an investment, pure and simple, and it'll be a nice buffer for the first few years until the firm is up and running at a profit."

"I just hate to see you let it go. It's all you have left of your parents."

He snorted and put his hand on her leg. When she reached for his hand, he pulled her closer. The bar was loud and he wanted her to lean toward him again so he could see every muscle flick in her face, feel every twinge from her fingers. Didn't she know that she and the family they'd made were all he ever needed? "I never intended to keep it forever. Don said we should be able to close in a month, two max. That should put me on schedule for a spring grand opening."

"I'm proud of you, Jason, and if your clients don't follow you, they're just plain stupid."

He wound his fingers through hers. They sat so close he could feel her breath on his face, smell the whiskey as if he'd tasted it. He wished they were at home in bed so he could show her how grateful he felt for her support, how much he needed her. "I love you, Pace. We're not going to see much of each other until I get the business up and running."

She flashed a wicked grin and leaned in to whisper by his ear. "Then we'd better make the most of things now."

They finished their drinks and waited while the bartender closed their tab. People vied for their seats and they got knocked by elbows and shoulders. Jason pocketed his credit card, they made their way through the crowd to the door, and, without talking about where they'd go, they headed to the Southern cuisine restaurant they both loved. Jason delivered another drink to Pace while they waited for a table. When he asked her about the doctor's appointment, they got interrupted by Tate Jackson, an associate from Jason's firm. Tate was young, fresh from architecture school, and a big ass kisser. Jason hadn't made partner, mostly because he refused to kiss ass, but he'd been around long enough to qualify for some after-hours brownnosing. Thankfully the hostess arrived and saved them from Tate's drunken chatter.

They enjoyed the biscuits the waiter brought to the table while they waited for their food and Jason asked again about Pace's trip to the doctor. She stopped chewing and swallowed a piece of bread so big he could track its progress down her throat. He felt the fluffy biscuit turn to lead in his mouth as she stared wide-eyed at the table and gulped her water.

"It went fine," she finally said. In the soft lighting, it appeared as though all the color had drained from her cheeks.

He felt a tingling along his spine. "Are you sure?"

She laughed and flipped the knife on the table over and over again like a kid who couldn't sit still. "Yes, it was just a big misunderstanding. Apparently mistakes at the lab aren't that uncommon."

"That's pretty scary." He wondered if the doctor knew the hell they'd been through the last few days. "But you're okay? I mean, everything's normal?"

"Yep," she said with a bright smile. He watched her fingers tap away on her glass before she lifted it to her mouth. "Good as new."

As the waiter brought their food and Pace asked questions about the New York job, he couldn't help but feel as if something was a little bit off. He couldn't put his finger on it all through dinner as she chatted away about this and that. He forgot it completely when they got home and made love, but all weekend he couldn't shake the feeling she wasn't telling him something.

CHAPTER 7

Tori had had two drinks, one to calm her nerves and one for courage, before she picked up the phone to call Caroline. Even with a buzz, she felt sick about what she planned to do. She couldn't drink Colin's affair away or pretend it wasn't happening. Hadn't Caro said that all along? What did it say about her that she felt just as mad at Caroline for pressing her to act as she did at Colin for cheating? She blamed the alcohol as she dialed Caro's number.

Ed answered and in his voice she heard sympathy. The way he ushered Caroline on the phone spoke to his need to distance himself from the whole situation. If only Tori could distance herself too. Caroline sounded tired when she said hello. Tori envisioned them sitting in their den on the old brown couch, reading books or the newspaper. She could hear a news show on in the background as Caroline's earring banged against the receiver.

"Tori? What's wrong?"

"I'm ready, Caro. I'm ready for proof."

"What happened?"

She pictured Colin's face in her mind, his forced smile, the nervous twitching of his eye. At least he had the decency to feel guilty while his skin probably still held the warmth from his lover's touch. "Let's just say I can't ignore it any longer."

"Let me talk to Ed. I'll have a name for you by tomorrow." In the pause that followed, she felt sure Caroline waited for her to say thank you, but between the alcohol and the ache in her heart, she couldn't muster the words.

She heard Colin come in through the back door, talking to the maid, home early without Tori having to beg. Another admission of guilt.

"I'm proud of you, Tori," Caroline said. "I know this won't be easy, but you're doing the right thing for you."

If she were doing the right thing, gathering evidence, guilting her husband into coming home at a decent hour and thinking about her instead of his lover, then why did it feel so sickeningly wrong?

* * *

After the boys' Saturday basketball games, the Kelly's usually celebrated at the local pizza joint, dissecting each game, talking over every basket and missed opportunity, but this Saturday they decided to go home instead. Pace had the feeling Jason could tell she seemed troubled about something, even after she'd worked overtime trying to cover up her ping-pong emotions. She was suffering from an overwhelming sense of guilt at having lied to her husband, but at the same time and completely out of the blue, she felt a little down they wouldn't be having another baby.

She'd exhausted so much energy convincing herself the pregnancy was a symbol of God's faith in her and Jason's love, that when she saw the blood on her panties her first reaction had been panic—even though it undeniably cleared her of having committed adultery. And as much as she understood Jason's relief, she couldn't help but feel stung by his obvious joy that the whole thing had been a mistake.

But the guilt weighed on her. She'd spent all day Friday wondering how she would break the news to him that the doctor had insisted she'd had a miscarriage and the original blood sample had been destroyed. What she would say? How would she explain it? How would he react if she laughed it off? How would he react if she just blurted it out when she first saw him? Should she send him an email or phone him at work? As the minutes had stretched into hours, her indecision and confusion grew to become a hard fist of panic in her gut.

She'd decided not to mention it if he didn't ask. Why did he have to ask? It wasn't like his mind would ever wander to miscarriage. Hers hadn't gone there and she'd been the one who'd freaked out when she'd had a little spotting when she'd been eight weeks pregnant with Mitchell. As Pace had come crying out of the bathroom, Jason had kissed her forehead and told her to call the doctor and reassured her that it was probably nothing. It turned out to be nothing, but it hadn't even blipped on his radar. It wasn't like he'd been waiting for Pace to confirm his worst fears.

When he'd grabbed her in the bar and kissed her like he hadn't kissed her in so long and then confessed he'd gone crazy with the possibility she'd cheated, she knew she couldn't tell him what the doctor had said. Pace knew telling him would only cause Jason pain and further his suspicion. There wasn't any way to tell him the truth without Pace looking guilty and for both of their sakes, she had to lie. Pace never thought she'd lie to Jason about anything.

By Sunday, she felt desperate to put it all behind her and pretend it had never happened. Her guilt had started to recede and she figured that by the time he got back from New York, the whole nightmare would be a thing of the past. She knew he left in the morning, but beyond that she didn't know his plans.

"How long will you be gone?" she asked as she cleaned up the kitchen and he flipped through the Sunday paper.

After a pause he said, "Two, maybe three days."

"Will you be staying in the city?"

"They're in a suburb." He seemed absorbed in the sports page. Not a great time to engage him in conversation.

"You should try to see Adam while you're there."

"I doubt I'll have time."

"He's your brother, Jason. You haven't seen him or his kids in almost two years."

He folded the paper and swallowed the last of his coffee. When he lifted his eyes to hers, she couldn't tell what he was feeling. "I don't know, Pace. He's pretty bitter about the divorce. A visit from his happily married younger brother might not be a good thing."

"He could use a little support right now. Family matters most when times are bad."

"Not every family is as…involved as yours, Pace. We weren't the Waltons and we sure as hell aren't the Whitfields." He kissed her lips and hinted around about a quick getaway to the driving range.

Before she could respond, Dillon burst inside with blood dripping from a scrape on his knee. When she came back into the kitchen after doctoring him up, Jason had left a note that said he'd gone to hit golf balls.

Pace was reading in bed late Sunday night when Jason came into the bedroom holding a piece of paper in his hand. She didn't know what had gotten him so upset, but she could tell by the throbbing vein in his temple that he was furious even before he flicked the paper at her.

She carefully closed the book she was reading, a family saga that paled in comparison to whatever was going on with her husband, and reached for the paper with a sinking feeling in her gut. Her eyes widened with shock when she realized he'd printed the email her doctor sent late Friday afternoon after she'd insisted they forward her records. She should have deleted the darn thing, but it was too late now.

"What the hell is this?" Stupid question. Since he'd printed it out, he obviously read the nurse's damning comments about the doctor's insistence she'd had a miscarriage and that, despite her objections, the file would confirm his diagnosis. Pace didn't know who she felt more upset with—herself, for not deleting the email or Jason, for snooping through her stuff to find it.

"I asked for my records."

"Don't lie to me, Pace. That email says you were pregnant."

Shoot, shoot, shoot. "No, it says my records will reflect the doctor's reliance on faulty lab results."

"Bullshit. You said they admitted it was a misunderstanding." He shocked her with his language and practically shook with anger.

"They can't retest the original sample because the lab's already destroyed it. Without a new test, he insists on referring to my period as a miscarriage."

His eyes narrowed to absorb what she'd said, to figure out if she was lying to him again. "So we're back to square one."

"Jason…" She took a deep breath and wished she'd been more prepared for his assault. "I understand you're confused about what happened, but so am I. If there was anything I could do to prove to you that I wasn't pregnant, I would. But I can't, so you're just going to have to have a little faith in me, in our marriage, in the sacred vows we took, and try to get past this."

Her voice sounded pleading and pathetic, which was pretty appropriate because she basically begged for his belief and forgiveness. Perhaps she'd reacted to the way he looked at her, his hands on his hips, his mouth drawn into a tight line so that his dimple flashed mockingly. He walked to Pace's side of the bed and looked down at her in a way she'd only seen one other time, when she'd accidentally ran his car into the garage while talking on her cell.

"I'm sorry you're upset, Pace. I'm sorry I haven't been able to get past the fact that you were pregnant with another man's baby!" He screamed his last words so loud she swore the walls rattled. He'd so clearly embraced his anger, let it fester like a boil, and with nothing more than a gentle prod, it had exploded with a force neither one of them could have predicted.

She felt too shocked at his tone to return his anger. "You have got to be kidding me." She deliberately kept her voice down. "What do you think I do all day, Jason? Troll for men while the kids are in school?"

He shrugged his shoulders. "I never used to think so." He grabbed his pillow and headed for the door.

"Where are you going?"

He slammed the door shut behind him. Pace heard him move into the guest room and flick on the light. She got halfway across the room when the crack of another slamming door halted her progress. He was too upset to reason with and with all the yelling and door slamming, she felt sure the kids knew they were fighting. Heck, the neighbors probably knew they were fighting.

He'll cool off in New York, Pace told herself as she sat on the edge of the bed. He was angry, really angry, but once he got to New York and calmed down, he could think things through logically and he'd realize how ridiculous his accusations sounded. After an hour spent with her head tucked against her up-drawn knees, listening for any sign of movement next door, she finally reclined and slung her arm across his side of the bed. With her mind running a mile a minute, sleep seemed out of the question.

When the alarm rang at seven the next morning, the guest room was empty, his coffee mug sat empty on the counter, and his car wasn't in the garage. Jason had left town without saying goodbye.

CHAPTER 8

"You can't be serious," Tori said to Pace as they argued yet again about Thanksgiving. "You know that's out of the question. Why on earth would you even propose such a thing?"

Pace gave a dramatic sigh, as if she hadn't just suggested breaking the family's thirty-five year tradition. "Look, Mom, I just think it would be nice to have a small, casual Thanksgiving here at my house. Why is it so hard for you to understand that maybe I'd like to host Thanksgiving dinner? I *am* an adult."

Than act like it, Tori wanted to scream. "I've already bought the turkeys, arranged the photographer, made provisions for the staff to work in shifts, and decorated the house. I can't imagine going back and canceling everything now. It's too late to change the plans."

She could practically hear her daughter trying to figure out a way to change her mind in the hesitation before she cleared her throat and started again. "We're just so busy. Jason's out of town on work all the time and I'm trying to do some work on my own. It would be really nice to have a low key Thanksgiving instead of making such a production out of it."

Tori banked her mounting irritation. Didn't anyone appreciate the work that went into creating their picture perfect Thanksgiving? "It sounds as though you don't have the time or energy to host even the simplest meal. Thanksgiving at our house solves all your problems. You only have to show up."

"Fine." Pace, so accommodating and patient with everyone but Tori, hated not getting her way. "But it would be nice if, just this once, it wasn't so formal. The boys hate dressing up and I think it would be fun to shake things up a little."

Her naïve daughter had lived too long in the suburbs. "That would be perfectly fine if we didn't take our family Christmas picture before dinner. Can you imagine the reaction if our card went out with us all around the fire in jeans?" She laughed at the image in her mind. Pace and Jason may as well bring along their disobedient dog to slobber at their feet.

"I think it would be lovely and much more real."

"Reality has nothing to do with our image, Pace. For God's sake, it's like you've forgotten your upbringing." She waved an acknowledgement at the maid who tried to interrupt. Couldn't she see she was on the phone? "Now, what is this about you working?"

"I'm not, yet. I'm just feeling some things out."

"Do you need money?"

"No, Mother, I don't need money." Even through the phone Tori could tell Pace gritted her teeth.

"If you're bored, darling, the Junior League can always use your help. Sally Anderson was just asking about you the other day. She's in charge of the annual auction. I think you'd make a splendid chairperson."

"Don't volunteer me for the chairmanship, please. I'll never be that bored," she mumbled under her breath. Tori wondered if Pace knew how much her careless comments could sting. "And I'm not bored. I just want to use my brain for a few hours a day, that's all."

The maid came back looking as if she might pee on the floor if Tori didn't get off the phone. "Okay, darling, I must go. I'll see you Thanksgiving." She hung up the line and turned to face the young woman who'd started only weeks ago and whose name had escaped her. "Is this an emergency?"

The woman looked contrite before stepping forward with an envelope in her outstretched hand. "This was just delivered by messenger. It looks important."

Tori snatched it from her hand and waved her away. When the door closed and she felt sure she wouldn't be interrupted, she set the envelope on her desk and took a deep breath.

She never knew how easy it would be, like scheduling a haircut or having the house painted. Who knew how commonplace it had become for someone to have their spouse followed? Tori certainly didn't. For days she'd waited for the envelope to arrive. Waited and obsessed about what she'd discover. Well, that wasn't quite true. She felt pretty sure what she'd find inside the envelope. She tore it open with shaking fingers and let the pictures slip into her hand.

It felt like a slap to her face, a stinging blast that spun her head around and left her numb with pain. And she'd thought she could handle the truth. Nothing could have prepared her to see the man she'd married with another woman, see the way he'd clutched her, see the look on his face, the triumph and the unbridled pleasure. Had Tori ever seen him look at her like that?

Her knees gave out and she slid into a chair. Damn it, Caroline had been wrong. Knowing the truth didn't make it better, didn't make her feel protected and armed. Looking at images of Colin and his lover only made her feel dirty. How had Colin managed to smear her with dirt when he was the one who'd dug the hole that would bury them both?

* * *

New York sat under a foot of snow due to an early nor'easter and the dark, low lying clouds seemed to hover just out of Jason's reach. He felt like he was driving under a dirty piece of cotton and with the temperature so opposite the balmy sixties he'd left in Atlanta, he may as well have driven to the North Pole.

The town of Hardesty didn't look like much of a town, as far as he could tell, but more like a row of strip malls and restaurants. A squat clock tower anchored the downtown area and sat surrounded by old buildings that appeared more neglected than historic. From his research, he'd discovered the area's astronomical cost of living, with its proximity to the city and good schools, but the housing and architecture, or lack of it, left much to be desired. He pulled up in front of a 1970's brown brick building that held all the charm of a government building. The prospect of tearing the building down and starting over or adapting it for reuse made Jason forget the weather.

The site appeared level, the space adequate, and, as he glanced up and down Main Street, he knew that an updated building would spawn other improvements in town. He hurried inside, in a rush to beat the cold and to get started. The heat sang on full blast in the reception area and as he checked in with the girl at the desk, he shed his overcoat. The placard on the counter identified the girl as Deborah.

Deborah looked like a teenager, maybe twenty, and her buoyant breasts practically spilled out of her shirt. The temperature had peaked at thirty degrees and yet she wore the kind of strappy tank top his wife would put on in the summer. Jason couldn't get over her outfit and the amazing amount of skin she showed at the office. The only time Pace had breasts remotely close to the ones currently straining against the thin material before him had been when she was pregnant. The thought of Pace pregnant brought everything from home back to the front of his mind after he'd consciously buried it. When the girl smiled at him, he realized he was staring directly at her chest like a honing devise. He cleared his throat and looked away.

"You're probably wondering about my clothes," she said. Jason gawked at her blankly. He sure as hell didn't want to have a fashion discussion, especially after she caught him looking at her rack like a sixteen-year-old.

"They can't get the heat right in this building," she went on as if he'd answered instead of seating himself as far away from her desk as possible. "In order for the rest of the building to be comfortable, I have to suffer as if I'm working in the tropics." When she laughed, he noticed how pretty she was, with her dark hair and perfect smile. "I've threatened to wear a bikini to work if they don't fix it."

Just like that, an image of her in a thong and two tiny triangles flashed before his eyes. He glared at her again, God only knew the look on his face, and she lowered her eyes. When she glanced back at him and held his stare, he nervously grappled with the magazines on the table in front of him.

He tossed down last month's edition of *Money* and got to his feet when a man came out of a back hallway and introduced himself as Mark Bisbain, one of the managing directors he'd scheduled to meet and the one he'd spoken with over the phone. A tall man, Mark stood five inches over Jason's six feet, and sported a close cropped black beard. As he led him down the hall he'd just come from, Jason could feel the girl at the desk watching them, her eyes like a laser on the back of his head.

After a business lunch and three hours of meetings, he checked into a chain hotel near the interstate. Exhausted, he dragged his carry-on and briefcase over the threshold and lay down on the bed. Even though he felt beat, his eyes wouldn't stay closed. He stared at the ceiling, its grooved swirling pattern putting him in a trance, and thought of Pace.

He'd had a popcorn ceiling in his apartment in college when they'd met. The very first time they made love there, she'd commented on it. She made some silly remark about how a person could tell the quality of a building by looking at the ceiling and how she knew this without any of his fancy architecture classes. He'd laughed at her and she'd straddled him, leaned down, and ran her tongue over his one dimple. He'd never known anyone like her.

"I love this." Her voice had sounded like a purr. "It pops out when you smile, tastefully. Not at all like the ceiling."

God, he missed her. And hated himself for missing her too. He wanted to believe her, he had to if he wanted to stay in their marriage, but the way she'd acted... No matter how farfetched the idea of her cheating, he couldn't shake his suspicions.

With hours until bed and nothing to do, Jason called his brother and suggested they meet for dinner. They'd never been close, but after Pace's good-girl-knows-best guilt routine he didn't feel right about being in New York and not calling. Adam sounded glad to hear from him and they made plans to meet at some restaurant in Manhattan later in the week. He looked forward to seeing his brother, but worried what he'd say when Adam asked about Pace and the kids.

As he opened his bag and retrieved his shaving kit, his mind strayed back to Pace. She stayed at home at least six hours of every day all alone while he worked and the kids went to school. She certainly didn't have anyone looking over her shoulder. He examined his reflection in the mirror and wondered how he'd manage to put on a good face for Adam in the midst of all his heartache. If Pace had had an affair—or was having an affair— would he be like the guy from his office who caught his wife fucking a neighbor in the middle of the day? He turned on the shower and waited for the water to warm before stepping in the tub. Could he come home someday and find her in their bed with…who, damn it, who?

CHAPTER 9

Pace felt like her life had fallen apart and yet the days passed as if nothing had changed. The kids still got up and went to school, she still ran errands, the dog slept, ate, and pooped, and yet she couldn't deny the gaping hole in her heart.

Jason had been out of town since Monday. He'd called only twice since he left—once when Pace was in the shower—and he continued to speak to her as if she'd committed adultery. She had no idea when he'd come home, or if he planned to come home, and to top it all off her mother kept calling to pester her about Thanksgiving. Despite the fact that Pace had begged her to have a casual dinner, her mother still insisted on her typical elaborate affair, which meant they all had to dress for dinner. With Jason barely speaking to Pace, she could only imagine his reaction to having to spend the day in a suit and tie with her parents.

Why wouldn't he call or email? She'd much prefer yelling at each other over the eerie silence. She tried to act as normal as possible for the kids, but she had a hard time not hopping on a plane to find and confront him. They'd never gone this many days without communicating, even when Pace had worked and traveled.

She'd resisted calling Jason, but her pride had slowly evaporated into an aching need to hear his voice. To keep from reaching for the phone, she headed to the grocery store. Mitchell's class had planned a Thanksgiving feast and she'd volunteered to make pie. Just as she'd rounded the end of the canned goods aisle, she ran into Juliet.

"Pace," she said as their carts slid next to each other. "You still making pie, I hope?"

A quick scan of the contents of Pace's cart would've told her she planned to make pies. "That's why I'm here."

"Me too. I signed up for stuffing," she said as her eyes lingered on Pace's stomach. "How are you feeling?"

Pace felt startled by her question. The stomach bug she'd suffered through seemed like a lifetime ago. Did she look as emotionally wrecked as she felt? Did people know she and Jason were fighting? "Fine, why do you ask?"

When Juliet's eyes drifted back to Pace's midsection, it suddenly hit her—Sherry's visit, the pregnancy website, the rumor mill was up and running. "No reason." Juliet shrugged, but Pace couldn't help but notice the way her lips smirked. "You and Jason going to the Wilson's party Friday night?"

She'd forgotten about the Wilson's party. She'd already gotten a sitter and, before the nightmare began, had been looking forward to it. "Unless Jason gets in too late," she hedged, "we'll be there."

"Have you talked to Sherry?" Juliet asked as Pace scooted her cart ahead to let an elderly woman pass. "She thinks you're avoiding her."

Pace *had* been avoiding her, in hopes that she'd find someone else to serve as room mom, and because it felt dishonest not to confess her troubles to such a good friend. Maybe that hadn't been the wisest move, considering Sherry's suspicions. "No, but I need to call her. I'm sure they'll be at Greg and Melissa's on Friday."

Juliet's cell phone rang and she waved bye as she moved down the aisle. Pace picked up a few more items and headed home. The weight of everything she had to deal with—Jason's behavior, the rumor mill, having to isolate herself from everyone and act like nothing was wrong—made her want to scream and burst into tears on the short ride home. Before she carried the groceries into the house, she called Jason on his cell. It went straight into voice mail. No matter how much she wanted to reach out to him, she didn't know what to say. She hung up without a word and went inside.

Jason called that night as she made dinner for the boys. She felt pathetically glad to hear his voice, even though she could tell he was still mad. From the noise in the background, she assumed he was in a crowded restaurant or possibly a bar.

"Hey," he said. "How's it going?"

"Fine." She tried to swallow her jealousy that while he dined in some hip New York restaurant, she wallowed in guilt and ate grilled cheese and canned soup with the kids. "How's the meeting?"

"Good, promising." He paused and in the moment before he spoke Pace heard a female voice say his name. "Tell the kids I love them, will you? I've got to go."

Jason hung up before she could utter a response. Pace stood, her spatula frozen in mid-air, as the cheese popped on the griddle. She felt her limbs tingle with mortification and a painful stab of hurt. Did he call to check on the kids or to tell her he was getting even?

* * *

Jason looked over the crowded restaurant into his brother's face and couldn't believe how much he'd aged since he'd last seen him. He ran his hand over his hair, something he did constantly during the day, and wondered if in twelve years he'd feel more scalp than hair like Adam must when he touched his head.

Adam had always been better at everything than Jason; the perfect student, the standout athlete, the successful tax accountant—that was his rep back in Belton. But Jason's grades were higher and his athletic achievements would have outnumbered his brother's if he hadn't had to quit playing sports to get a job when his grandfather died. Adam's college education at NYU, along with their sister's duel degree from Michigan State, was why there hadn't been any money left for Jason. But living in Adam's perfect shadow had pushed Jason to bust his butt, that and wanting to get the hell out of his hometown.

"So, how's the senator's daughter?" Adam constantly referred to Pace as 'the senator's daughter' even though he knew it pissed Jason off. Adam's ex came from more money than the Whitfields, but Pace had always been a ray of sunshine compared to Lydia. Pace, with her optimistic attitude and quick smile, outshone just about everyone. Adam's taste in women had definitely changed considering the mousy brunette he'd brought along to dinner and introduced as, "My friend Candace."

"Pace is good." He picked through the bread basket and hoped his face didn't give anything away. Candace had gone to the restroom so Jason exacted his revenge. "How's Lydia?"

Adam cleared his throat as his eyes darted between Amelia and Jared, Jason's teenaged niece and nephew who sat slumped over their cell phones, texting. "Well, the same, I guess." He reached across the table and pulled out a roll. "Her new husband's a jackass, but what do you expect from a guy who makes his living directing off-Broadway plays?"

Jason looked at the kids. Thankfully they weren't paying any attention to their dad. Adam had lowered his voice, but the stage whisper only accentuated his bitterness, which seemed weird since he typically threw his accomplishments in Jason's face. "So they made it official?"

"Just an intimate ceremony for their hundred closest friends. She didn't even have the decency to tell me herself, just had her attorney call to work out the details for switching a couple of our weekends to accommodate the wedding and their honeymoon in Bali."

Lydia's bitchy attitude didn't surprise him, nor the fact that she put Adam through the ringer now that they'd divorced. Jason ran his hands through his hair and then purposely stopped. He didn't want to lose his hair. "Candace seems nice."

Amelia announced she had to pee and strutted off toward the restroom like a damn runway model. When she'd gotten Jason from the lobby as he'd talked to Pace, he'd been shocked by her appearance. She stood nearly as tall as him in her high-heeled boots and her clothes were…like that receptionist at Bisbain. He sure as hell didn't envy Adam.

"She's having a hard time with the divorce," Adam explained after Amelia disappeared around the corner. "Her mother's got her convinced I'm to blame for everything, like I made Lydia have an affair with her theatre teacher and leave our marriage, but Ame's always sided with her mother."

Jason tried to imagine him and Pace fighting over Dillon and Mitchell. If they got divorced, who would the boys live with? Pace, of course. He worked all day and traveled, but that hardly seemed fair since her behavior caused their split. She'd get to read the *Magic Treehouse* stories to Dillon and snuggle on the couch with Mitchell and his disgusting blanket, smell his kid scented hair, the grass and sweat smell that defined his youngest son. Would he be able to see them during the week or would he only get forty-eight hours on the weekends? Could he really picture them getting a divorce?

Adam stood up as Candace rejoined the table. "Candace is a gem," he said and she smiled up at him with her small, pointy teeth. Jason thought the whole night felt like a weird out of body experience. As the waiter approached to take their order, Jason asked for another drink and changed the subject. His big brother, the hero of the Kelly family, fat, balding, divorced, and dating a librarian. Jason wondered what his parents would think of Jason now compared to Adam and his screwed up life. Then he remembered the way he'd screamed at Pace and he knew they'd expect nothing less of him, the mistake that ruined their golden years.

After they'd dropped the kids at Lydia's, Jason heaved a sigh of relief when the cab pulled over and, after a chaste kiss on the lips, Adam deposited Candace with her doorman. Jason and Adam continued on to his apartment, a nondescript brick building in Brooklyn.

His new home couldn't have been farther from the Upper East Side apartment he'd shared with Lydia, where she now lived with her new husband. Jason looked around the main room and thought, *This could be my life*. A faded plaid sofa ran along a bare white wall, accompanied by a chair and matching ottoman. An ugly dining room table littered with papers completed the set. Everything seemed like it came from a garage sale.

Jason felt the sudden urge to talk to Adam about Pace and what he'd left behind at home. Adam lived out of town, his own marriage had ended in divorce after his wife cheated, and Jason felt pretty sure he'd get the sympathetic response he hoped for.

"Make yourself at home," Adam said. He carried two tumblers and a bottle of bourbon from the kitchen and dropped them on the coffee table. He asked about the business that brought Jason to New York as he poured them each half a glass.

"I'm meeting with a potential client." Jason accepted the glass from Adam's outstretched hand and sat on the couch. "I'm thinking of starting my own firm and hoping they'll follow." He didn't know what to make of his brother's blank stare. They'd never been close.

"Good for you," Adam said and chugged a hearty gulp. He sat back in the chair while the fake leather squealed in protest.

"I'm…Pace and I…we're having some trouble," Jason blurted out. He took a big sip and waited for a response from Adam, some sarcastic jab or smug look. His confused expression only fueled Jason's need to explain. "I think she may have had an affair and I'm thinking I should leave."

"Why?" Adam just sat there, holding his drink, his legs crossed at the ankles.

"She cheated." Jason knew he needed to say more and had planned to lay the whole story out for him. He thought they'd hack away at the details, then hack away at Pace. In some sick, perverted way, he'd looked forward to Adam admitting he never liked her. But Adam just sat there, waiting for Jason to explain, and now he worried Adam might side with her.

"She cheated," Adam repeated. "Are you sure?"

"Well, that's the problem. I'm not sure." So he told him about the pregnancy, his getting tested, her miscarriage, and the doctor's email.

"Why would she have pushed you to get tested if she'd cheated? Wouldn't she have tried to keep you away from having your sperm tested if she thought there was even a chance the baby belonged to someone else?"

The last thing Jason wanted to hear was logic. "What difference does it make? She lied to me. She was pregnant and even the doctor refused to call it anything other than a miscarriage."

Adam ran his hands over his face and then through the thinning hair on his head. He looked at Jason a long time before answering. "You'd better be sure before you do anything drastic."

Jason stood up and paced around the room before he turned to face his brother. "What do I have to do? Catch her in bed with someone? Jesus, this is the last thing I expected from you."

"Look, kid, don't get all worked up." Adam lifted his beefy hand in surrender. "I'm just saying you need to think this through before you do anything permanent. It sounds to me like you may have overreacted to something that could have a very simple explanation."

"I don't believe this. I thought you would understand. I thought you, of all people, would know what I'm going through."

Adam leaned forward to set his drink on the table and his chair crackled like a pop gun. "Jason, I get it, really, but…" He took a big breath and let it out slowly. "Look around. Does this look like a happy life? I'm alone in this shit-hole apartment, I barely see my kids, and when I do, I barely recognize them. The woman I'd planned to spend the rest of my life with is sleeping with her new husband in my old bed." He didn't get worked up about it like he did at the restaurant and his quiet resignation gave his words that much more power. "If I had a chance to have Lydia back, even after she left me and cheated, I'd do it in a heartbeat. I ignored all the signs she was unhappy, I ignored her pleas for attention, and even refused counseling when she admitted things weren't going well in our marriage."

"That's what I don't get," Jason said in a flurry of defensive anger. "There weren't any signs that things were going south. We were happy, at least I thought we were happy. I didn't look around and wonder what it would be like to be with someone else and I sure as hell didn't think Pace was. This whole thing came out of left field."

"So maybe the lab did make a mistake and she wasn't pregnant. It's not like that kind of stuff never happens."

Jason knew that was the most logical explanation, had said it to himself a thousand times, but the seed of doubt had wedged itself into his brain like a thorn in his ass. No matter what he did, no matter how he sat, he couldn't just forget it. "But what if she did cheat?"

Adam stared at Jason for a long time, his eyes unfocused. Everything about his brother—his sluggish movements, his unusually loud breathing, the way his lips fold downward at the corners—showed his resentment. "I don't think Pace would cheat on you, Jason. Not from what I've seen with my own eyes and not from what you've told me."

"I can't live with the idea that she cheated. I won't be blindsided when the truth comes out."

"I know how you feel." He waved his arm around the dingy apartment. "Lydia's affair felt like a sucker-punch. And by the time I got over being pissed, she and her lover were married."

The last thing Jason wanted to do was defend himself or discuss his feelings and talking about Adam's marriage to the super-bitch ranked even further down on his list. "Okay, so you fucked up your marriage. But this is different. At least you know for sure what happened. And just because Lydia's remarried—that doesn't mean your life is over. There're other women out there. What about Candace?"

Adam leaned forward and braced his elbows on his knees like he was letting Jason in on some big secret. "Do you have any idea what it's like to date? It sucks. Yeah, you get to sleep with different women, some of them are even halfway decent in bed, but I still end up back here every night alone. And everybody's got kids. I can't connect with my own kids. How the hell am I supposed to put up with somebody else's?"

Jason sat down as the bourbon and spicy chicken rolls inched up his throat. "I thought Candace was nice."

"She is nice, she's very nice. And despite her church-lady-like look, she loosens up in the sack. But I think I'm going to end it with her."

Jason tried not to wince as a visual of Adam and Candace having sex flashed in his mind. "Why?"

Adam sat back and took another sip. "Lydia and I…we kinda hooked up last weekend."

"Lydia? Your ex-wife Lydia?"

"We met to discuss the kids, same old shit, and ended up having a few drinks. Shared a cab back to my place."

"I don't get it."

"It was good, really good. I love her, I've always loved her, and I want her back."

"But she's married. She's married to the guy she cheated on you with."

"I plan to steal her back." Adam smiled, slapped his hand on his knee. "Look, kid. Take a lesson from your older brother. You've got a gorgeous wife—a Southern woman." He chuckled, took another sip. Jason noticed the way his hands shook and his slow, deliberate blinking. "That's where I went wrong. I married a Yankee." He pointed at Jason with his glass, sat back, and grinned. "Your kids still want to spend time with you, so before you fuck everything up, send your kids into therapy, and your wife into the arms of another man you'll end up hating for having everything you used to have, I'd think long and hard about what you plan to do." What started as a drunken lecture ended up sounding like stone cold sober good advice. "Take a really good look at me, Jason. I'm having an affair with my wife, hoping to steal her away from her new husband. Is this the future you want for yourself?"

CHAPTER 10

Tori sat on the pictures, ticking away like a bomb in her locked desk drawer. She spent two days in complete denial, pretending the pictures hadn't arrived, pretending she hadn't seen her husband with the twenty-year-old daughter of one of their oldest friends—a girl she'd talked him into hiring. Christ, after all this time, how had she convinced herself he'd changed?

Who had she been kidding? He would never change. If she thought there was a chance he'd end his ridiculous affair and beg her forgiveness, she wouldn't have kept the private detective on retainer. She'd hoped, that's all, she'd dared to hope that he'd come to understand how dangerous these little affairs were to his career and his legacy. To her legacy. If *she* knew he was having an affair, if Ed and Caroline and whoever else happened to spot them knew he was having an affair, how long would his secret stay buried?

And Caroline kept calling. At first Tori lied and said she hadn't heard anything from the detective. She eventually confessed to having the pictures.

"What are you going to do?" Caroline kept asking over and over and over again. Tori kept saying the same thing. "I don't know, I don't know, I don't know." Now she just avoided her calls.

She should have known she couldn't avoid her forever.

When Tori passed Caroline's house on her morning jog, Caro waited at the bottom of her drive wearing a green track suit and bright pink running shoes. The fact that Tori had never seen her in anything remotely close to an athletic outfit stopped her mid stride.

"Did you rob an elf?"

Caroline pulled herself up to her full five feet and threw her hands on her hips. "It's my walking suit. You're not the only one who can exercise."

Tori jogged in place and panted in the cool morning air. "When did you start exercising?"

"Today." She fell into step with Tori when she began to walk so her legs didn't cramp. "You've been avoiding me."

"No." She felt for her pulse and looked at her watch. She should have skirted Caroline's street altogether.

"You never could tell a decent lie."

"I'm a politician's wife." She quickened her pace and Caroline pumped her arms to keep up. "I practically lie for a living."

"You're confusing you with your husband." Caro reached for her arm and gasped. "Can you slow down just a bit? My legs aren't as long as yours."

She adjusted her speed to a near crawl and Caro smiled gratefully. Tori knew she was only trying to help, but it felt like an ambush. "Look, Caroline, I'm not going to do anything rash. Colin's out of town again and I'm thinking about how I should proceed." They turned the corner and tried not to breathe the exhaust from a passing trash truck. "He's actually been pretty decent lately. It may just be enough that he thinks I know what's going on."

"Enough for whom? You're his wife, for God's sake, not the checkout girl at the grocery store. There's nothing nice about infidelity."

"Will you keep your voice down, please?"

They both looked around. There wasn't a soul in sight, unless they counted the squirrels gathering nuts in the grass or the birds squawking in the branches above their heads. "Okay..."

"What do you want me to do?" Tori demanded. "I've confronted him before and it certainly didn't do any good. I've ignored it and let it run its course." That hadn't been easy, but Pace had been a teenager and Tori had been engrossed in keeping her stubborn, strong-willed daughter in line. The thought of confronting him now, when so much was at stake, went against all her instincts. "With the holidays around the corner and Colin gearing up for a fight…he needs to focus on re-election and me stirring things up with accusations and proof will only hamper his efforts."

"Do you hear yourself? *His* needs, *his* efforts. God, Tori." She threw her arms in the air. "I don't know how to get through to you."

"I also have Pace to think about."

"Pace? Pace needs a mother with a backbone and a solid dose of self-respect, not some driveling fool who follows her husband blindly." At Tori's scathing look, Caroline changed her tactics. "Look at how you raised her. She's strong and independent. God knows she's better adjusted than most of our kids. Look at Graham." Her son's drug use and stints in rehab were painful subjects. The fact that she'd brought it up made Tori realize just how determined Caro was to change her mind. "The holidays are the perfect time for Colin to see everything he's risking with his foolish behavior. Tell him you know, tell him you're leaving, and let him deal with Pace and the kids."

"Stop badgering me," Tori shouted. Caroline stepped back and her eyebrows shot beneath her bangs. They stared at each other as a car passed and a small v of geese flew overhead. "I know you're only trying to help, but I have to think about this. Pace adores her father and lately she and I have been picking at each other like we did when she was a teenager. She'd probably turn the whole thing around on me." She grabbed her foot and bent it back to stretch her thigh. She could feel every muscle in her body clenching. "This isn't new to me—Heather is new, her age—but his cheating isn't new. The only thing new is your pressure. Whatever I decide could affect the rest of my life. *My* life, Caro, not yours."

"I know that. You're right and I'm sorry." Caroline clutched Tori's arm and they started walking toward the Whitfield's street. "I love you, Tori. You've always been there for me, through the best and worst of times. All the stuff with Graham. You were my rock. You're so strong, so giving to the people you love. I've watched you prop that man up time and time again and he takes every bit you give him without ever giving anything back. I want to be a good friend to you and sitting back while he abuses you this way doesn't feel right."

Tori patted a hand over Caroline's grip. She'd never had a better friend, but she absolutely couldn't discuss this another minute longer. "You must love me to parade around in that get-up." She eyed her hideous track suit.

Caroline bumped her hip playfully. "The tag is in my pocket. I'm taking it back. This exercise thing is for the birds."

* * *

Jason called Friday afternoon from his office. He'd arrived back in Atlanta and had stopped by work for a few hours before heading to the house. To Pace's dismay, he made sure to mention he'd be home in time to go to the Wilson's party. She'd hoped to avoid it so they could talk and try to work things out. By the time he finally got home, the sitter had already arrived and they were spared an awkward reunion by the presence of a pimply faced fifteen-year-old.

The kids pitched a fit about Jason leaving again when he'd just gotten home and it didn't help matters when Pace suggested they skip it. Jason insisted, for some unknown reason, and the kids only calmed down when the sitter pulled out a DVD they'd been dying to see and promised popcorn and soda. Jason went upstairs to change his clothes while Pace tried to get the DVD started on the new machine and microwaved the popcorn.

After another plea from Mitchell for Jason to stay, they left the boys in the den, their noses pressed against the window panes and walked the two blocks to the Wilson's house in absolute silence. Pace kept waiting for Jason to say something about his trip, ask something about the week they'd spent without him, but he forged ahead. The only noise came from the passing cars, the sound of their shoes on the sidewalk, and the small puffs of air their breath made in the near forty-degree night. Jason looked everywhere—the darkened lawns and houses, the line of cars along the street—everywhere but at Pace.

"How was your trip?" she asked when it became clear he had no intention of talking.

"Good." He didn't glance at her but quickened his pace. So much for breaking the ice.

She'd replayed his phone call in her head a thousand times and considered herself the bigger person for letting it go. But she hadn't really let it go. Was his client a woman? Was it someone he met while traveling? Or could it have been the hostess telling him his table was ready? No matter how she tried to dismiss it, she couldn't stop wondering if he'd cheated on her while he'd been away.

Jason had said he'd be gone two or three days, but it took him five to return. *Stop thinking about it and reach for him.* Pace looked over. Jason's hands were stuffed into the front pockets of his jeans, a new pair she'd gotten him for his birthday, and his face expressed bored indifference. Just as she reached her hand out for his arm, they rounded the Wilson's drive and Jason disappeared inside the house to the hearty greeting of the men around a Friday night football game.

"Pace." Her friend Kimmy approached as soon as she'd shed her coat and looked around. Kimmy wore a low cut wrap dress that showed off her boobs. Rumor had it she'd had surgery. Pace wondered if the rumor of her pregnancy was still going strong. "I love your outfit," Kimmy said of her jeans and modest top. "I don't know how you stay so tiny."

"Metabolism, Kimmy. My mom's always been a size four." And as addicted to her thrice weekly runs as Pace was, or used to be before the drama of the pregnancy took all her energy. Regular exercise had always been the only thing she and her mom had agreed on. Pace helped herself to a cold beer from a cooler when it became apparent Jason wasn't going to make her favorite mixed drink and deliver it to her as he usually did.

When Kimmy leaned closer, Pace had a hard time not staring at her cleavage, poking out of her dress like two perfect snow globes. "Are you sure you should be drinking?" she asked in a whisper of her Mickey Mouse voice. The only thing that had saved Kimmy from coming across as a complete airhead had been her modest chest. Too late now.

Pace tried to look confused instead of offended. "What do you mean?"

"You know." Kimmy pointed to her stomach. "The baby."

Pace smiled indulgently and wished again Jason hadn't insisted they come to the party. "I'm not pregnant."

"Oh, well..." She seemed embarrassed. "Sherry said..."

Pace waved her hand in front of her face and laughed. "I told her I was doing research for a client. I should have known she'd head straight for the phone." Ha, ha. If only she could laugh it all away.

After two beers and small talk with just about everyone from the neighborhood, everyone who now knew she wasn't pregnant, Pace couldn't wait to go home. She scanned the crowd for Jason and found him playing pool in the basement with some guys she'd never seen him hang out with before—a group of six who typically drank until they couldn't stand and ended the night getting high.

Pete McAlister wrapped his arm around her shoulders when he caught her lingering in the doorway. His appreciation for single barrel scotch and beautiful women had gotten him into more than one fist fight at similar gatherings. "Well, now here's the prettiest girl in the neighborhood." He couldn't have delivered a more inappropriate comment considering...the situation.

Pace smiled weakly and wiggled out of his grasp. "Jason, I'm ready to go home whenever you are."

Jason leaned over the table and banked an impressive shot in the corner pocket. He'd taught her to play pool in college, in a dive bar her friends wouldn't go near. Their outings to the pool hall were some of her favorite memories. She'd never forget the feel of his body around hers, the way his breath had tickled her ear and sent shivers down her spine, the outrageous bets they'd made once she'd gotten the hang of the game.

He didn't lift his eyes from the table, didn't answer, but continued to play, making shot after shot. When he'd won the game, he turned to the men, completely ignoring his wife. "Who's next?"

The tension between them seemed obvious, but everyone in the room was either too polite to comment or too drunk to notice. Pace may as well have never entered the room, never spoken to her husband. She could feel her face flush and a lump form in her throat. With a lift of her brows, she turned and made for the spare bedroom to find her coat and slipped out of the house unnoticed. On the short walk home, she considered the possibility that Jason would never get over this debacle.

CHAPTER 11

Jason knew Pace was pissed. He knew how she would've looked if he'd bothered to glance at her, like a wounded animal he'd tried to run over with his car. He wouldn't allow himself to be swayed by her emotions. He couldn't.

He'd spent all night watching her and the men in the neighborhood. Most everyone's attention was on Kimmy Milsaps and her impressive addition to an otherwise unimpressive body, but that didn't keep him from looking for clues. Adam's warning kept echoing through his head, but he couldn't let go of his suspicions. He knew he needed to get over it, but the seed of doubt was still there, poking at his subconscious. One night spent feeling out the men in the neighborhood probably wouldn't lead to answers, but at least it felt somewhat constructive.

Pete's comment had been too obvious. The guy had a reputation as a leech and Jason knew Pace wouldn't go near him. Cheaters—the good ones anyway—were always the ones you least expected. He hadn't seen anyone looking at Pace like they'd been lovers, but he wasn't ready to give up yet. The more these guys drank, the better chance he'd have for someone to slip up. As soon as he felt sure Pace had left, he'd start the ball rolling. He couldn't leave until he'd uncovered every stone.

Greg slapped Jason on the back after his second victory. "You've sure got your game on tonight, Kelly." He filled Jason's glass with more bourbon. "You may need to use your winnings for a hotel room. If I'd ignored Melissa like that, I'd be sleeping in the yard."

"Women." Jason rolled his eyes and glanced around at the six men in the neighborhood most likely to cheat on their wives.

Greg, with his happy-go-lucky attitude and extra fifty pounds, didn't factor into the mix. The others, all around forty, big drinkers and even bigger talkers, topped his list.

Ken Mason ponied up a twenty for game number three and started with an impressive break considering he could barely stand. "I hear you knocked up your wife again, Kelly." He dropped a solid into the middle pocket. "Congrats."

How the fuck did this guy know about Pace's pregnancy? "You must've heard wrong." After Ken missed his shot, Jason slammed two stripes into opposite corners and then duffed an easy one to the middle.

Ken misfired a bank shot to the corner and used his stick to help him keep his balance. "I could've sworn Ginny said Pace was pregnant."

Jason took his shot and grinned. "You know how women like to talk." He swallowed a big gulp of whiskey and enjoyed the burn as it went down. *Damn Pace and her big mouth.* The cue ball sailed into the pocket instead of his last stripe. Shit. No way would he let this asshole take him.

"My wife keeps nagging me about having another," said Ben Wikowski. He didn't live in the neighborhood, but he wanted to. "I'd probably do it if she wouldn't get even bigger. That woman could kill me if she got on top." Ben stood all of five-six on a good day. Jason could probably rest his elbow on his head. "Your wife, Kelly, she could ride you all night long."

It took every ounce of self-restraint for Jason not to cram his stick up Ben's ass. What the hell did they say when he wasn't around? "And she does, Ben." His comment, spoken through gritted teeth, earned a big laugh and a few slaps on the back. After he finished off Ken, Jason glanced around at the remaining guys. If he wasn't good enough for a woman like Pace, these guys sure as hell weren't either. This exercise felt like a huge waste of time.

After they'd all disappeared to Ben's car for a joint, Jason left with new respect from the party crowd and little to go on. On the walk home, he considered hiring a private detective. He had no idea how to find one or how much it would cost, but how could he put a price tag on peace of mind? At the moment, with Ben's flippant comment bobbing around his head, he'd pay just about anything.

The house was dark and quiet when he arrived home. Pace had either gone to sleep or pretended to be when he came up to brush his teeth before heading to the guest room. He could see her tank top and knew she wore her favorite flannel pants. It'd been two weeks since they'd made love and even the sight of her naked shoulder made him hard. In a strange twist of fate, now that he didn't know if she'd been faithful, he wanted her like he did when they'd first met and he'd thought he'd never be good enough for the senator's daughter. What the hell was wrong with him?

* * *

When Colin called from Washington, Tori heard the familiar sounds of the rotunda, the echoing drumfire of shoes on marble that told her he was on the move from one meeting to another. Now that she knew what he'd been up to, and with whom, she was convinced he called her when she'd hear in his voice and in the background the pressure he felt. Of course he felt pressured. Imagine trying to make important decisions for their state, wage war against a novice challenger, and bed a school girl. Who wouldn't feel overwhelmed?

"How is it going?" she asked as she checked her image in the mirror. She pulled the loose skin around her eyes toward her hairline and contemplated a lift.

"Crazy. This country is changing, Tor. So fast it scares me sometimes."

That's right, she told herself. He had to have these philosophical conversations with his wife, someone born of the same generation as him, someone who had the experience and mental capacity to understand what he said, who could put his words in the context of the past and what looked to be the future. Certainly his teenaged lover hadn't paid much attention to the state of the nation when she'd been in high school.

"Problems with the bill?"

"They're ram-rodding their own version through without even considering our side of the issue. It's like dealing with a bunch of kindergarten bullies."

Tori had to bite her tongue from suggesting he use his girlfriend to mediate the argument. Surely she spoke their language. "Keep fighting the good fight, Colin. That's all you can do."

He paused on the line and in that moment she heard muffled laughter and heels clicking on the marble floor. "Is something wrong, Tori? You don't sound like yourself."

She dropped her hand away from her face. She didn't need a lift. "There's nothing wrong with me."

His affair had nothing to do with her. She pushed away from the bathroom and walked to the window. It looked like rain. She wanted nothing more than to slip between the sheets of their bed, take a sleeping pill, and drift into oblivion. The only thing that stopped her was the certainty that nothing would have changed when she woke up.

"I'll be home later in the week; it just depends on the progress we make. If we make any progress at all."

She wished he'd stay away longer. It was so much easier to resist him when he wasn't around. "Take your time."

Again a pause where she wondered, not for the first time, what he thought.

"I miss you, Tori."

She wanted so badly to say the same. *I miss me, too.* Except the me she missed was the person she had been before he cheated, the one who wasn't so jaded, so cynical about life and love. She had to wonder which of her he missed, too.

CHAPTER 12

Pace could no longer pretend her life remained normal. She felt like she'd been sucker punched and everyone could see the bruise on her face. Her neighborhood friends kept calling, discretely asking how she felt, asking about Jason, asking about their plans for the holidays, like they expected her and Jason to announce their divorce any day. And judging by his behavior, she wouldn't be surprised if they did.

She couldn't even think about her and Jason not being married. Not that they couldn't get divorced—of course she knew it could happen—but she couldn't even picture it. She equated it to thinking of her parents having sex. She knew they did it. She had her mom's long fingers and her dad's nose, but the image of it, thank goodness, refused to form in her mind.

She deliberately put it all away for a little while and met her friend Amanda for lunch. Concentrating on something other than her disintegrating marriage seemed just what she needed. Amanda already sat at the table dressed in a dark suit and sexy stilettos, the same combination of power and womanhood Pace had always associated with her former boss.

Amanda looked at her watch as the hostess pulled out Pace's chair. "I was wondering if you'd show up."

"Parking was a nightmare." She smiled as Amanda raised her brows. Pace felt relieved to spend time with someone outside of her daily bubble.

"It wouldn't be if you didn't drive a tank." She reached across the table and squeezed her hand. "It's good to see you, Pace."

"You too. You look good."

"Do I?" she asked smugly. "Maybe it has a little something to do with this." She picked up her water goblet and wiggled her fingers. On her ring finger perched a startlingly large diamond solitaire.

"Oh, my gosh." Pace grabbed her hand as soon as she put her glass down. "Is this what I think it is?"

"Um huh. Close your mouth before people start to stare."

Pace had always thought of Amanda as a devout professional woman, a corporate communications legend whose main goal had been to break the glass ceiling. She never thought she'd get married, never knew she even considered it an option. "Who the heck are you marrying?"

"His name's Paul Bryner. He's an investment banker with Shores & Littleman. He's worth millions."

"Well, that certainly explains the rock." Pace sat back in her chair to stare at the woman who suddenly seemed like a stranger. Amanda had teased her unmercifully about her devotion to Jason and when she'd decided to quit work and stay home with the kids, in Amanda's eyes Pace had committed an act of mutiny. "I guess I need to keep an eye out for flying pigs."

Amanda laughed and the throaty depths of it caused several men around them to turn in their direction. Her confidence and lack of inhibition had always made her the center of attention. "What can I say? I'm in love."

"With his millions or with him?"

"Don't be so cynical. He's an amazing man. One ex-wife and, thank God, no children."

Amanda ordered a salad when the waiter came to the table and Pace did the same. She felt too surprised about Amanda's announcement to even care about food.

"How old is he? Where did you meet? When's the wedding?"

"Oh, Pace, the journalist in you is showing," she said. "He's forty-five, we met at a visitor's bureau function, and the wedding is in two months. We're having a small ceremony on the island of Nevis, with a fabulous after party when we return." She eyed Pace's current ensemble of pants and a sweater and pursed her lips. "We'll have to go shopping."

"Well, to say I'm shocked would be an understatement."

"You're not the only one. When I called my mother, she cried."

Amanda's Korean-born mother could barely speak English. She didn't drive and had never worked outside the home. "I guess you're back in the will."

"Exciting, isn't it? One-third share of a nineteen-seventies split level in Northern Virginia." She sighed dramatically. "Imagine the possibilities."

"And here I thought you wanted to talk about me doing some work for you." Although thrilled for her friend, Pace suffered a pang of sorrow that the work wouldn't come her way. It seemed like the only thing she had to look forward to.

"I do. Paul's accepted an overseas assignment for a year and he wants me to go with him. I'm taking a leave of absence."

Pace sat stunned by Amanda's announcement. Somehow the thought of her leaving work for a year was more surprising than her engagement. "Have you ever thought of giving a person some warning before you hit them over the head? A leave of absence?"

Amanda's expression turned serious. "I'm surprised myself, but…" She drew her shoulders up in an uncharacteristically self-conscious gesture. "I'm scared shitless, if you want to know the truth. I figure if I'm going to do this, I may as well give it my all."

The insecurity she saw on Amanda's face suddenly made her want to cry. The strongest woman she knew had put it all on the line for love and at the same time Pace walked a dangerous tight rope. She willed herself to get a grip on her emotions.

"Obviously I can't leave without someone on board to pick up the slack." She quickly returned to business, any hint of doubt gone. "I talked to Jerry and he's not going to get a replacement considering the company's budget shortfall, but he's asked John Stephenson to absorb most of my job while I'm gone. John was hesitant at first, as any person would be who doesn't want to work an eighty hour week, but then I thought of you." She smiled like the Cheshire cat. "Problem solved."

"What kind of commitment are you talking about? I thought a few freelance assignments were all you wanted."

"It's up to John, but considering he's immersed in marketing, I'd say he'll take as much as you can give him. I'd imagine he'll want you to come into the office one day a week and work on as many clients as you think you can handle."

Pace's mind raced. She hadn't expected to dive back into the deep end. But with all the drama going on at home, maybe a distraction like Amanda described would be just what she needed. "It sounds doable, but I'm going to need specifics."

Amanda slapped the table with her hand as if she'd sealed a deal. "I'll set up a meeting with John after Thanksgiving to get the ball rolling. I don't leave until mid-January."

"Great."

"What?" Amanda asked as her brow furrowed.

"Nothing. I'm just...impressed, that's all." Pace placed her napkin on her lap as the waiter delivered the salads. "You obviously love Paul a lot."

"I do." She took a bite of salad and chewed thoughtfully. "We've taken some precautions after what happened to his first marriage and that makes me feel a little better."

"Precautions?"

"Marriage therapy. Couples counseling," she said when Pace stared at her blankly. "Surely you've heard of it?"

"Well, of course I've heard of it, but you're not even married yet."

She smiled slyly and Pace sensed a glimpse of the old Amanda. "We like to think of it as preventative medicine." She stopped eating and stared at Pace. "Not everyone meets their soul mate in college. What's with the face?"

Obviously she couldn't hide her feelings. No wonder she went into print journalism instead of broadcast. "I'm just...Jason and I..." She looked down at the napkin on her lap as her eyes filled with tears. "We're having some problems."

Amanda carefully placed her fork in her bowl of spring lettuce and grimaced. "The golden couple is having problems on the eve of my marriage. Why do I feel like fate is tapping me on the shoulder?" She placed her elbows on the table and laced her fingers together. "Tell me it's not serious."

Pace told her everything, the blood test, his tests, the phone call, everything. She hated bursting Amanda's happiness bubble, but it felt so good to share her problems with someone else, someone who wouldn't judge her.

"So did you?" she asked when Pace finally took a breath.

"Cheat on Jason? No, of course not. But I don't know how to prove I didn't and now we're in this weird place where each one of us is wondering about the other. Jason's just so proud, I don't know if he'll be able to let it go."

Amanda waved a hand in front of her face. "All men are proud. I know you like to think Jason is the standard, Pace, but really. Can't he use a little common sense?"

"I'm not just saying that." Amanda scrunched up her face in disbelief, urging Pace to justify her comment. She searched her memory bank for the best example. "When we were in college, he had this professor who was ready to quit. Rumor had it he'd been caught with a student and they weren't renewing his contract when the semester was over. Jason was very serious about school. He studied all the time, went to class every day."

"So did I," Amanda said.

"One day about midway through the semester, Jason turned in a paper. I remember he'd stressed out for weeks about finishing this paper, making it perfect. He turned it in and the professor handed it right back, told Jason he didn't need to grade it because he'd watched him in class and he knew Jason deserved an A."

"Well, I'd say good for Jason."

"Yeah, that's what I said. You know what he said?"

Amanda shrugged her shoulders and looked around. Pace had lost her already. "He was angry. He spent all that time researching, studying, putting the paper together, and the guy didn't even take the time to read it and grade him accordingly."

"So Jason's a stickler for the rules, so what?"

"So every day he studied for this class. Every day. He memorized chapters, made flash cards, everything he could think of to immerse himself in the lessons, even after the professor had made it perfectly clear he wouldn't be grading anything as long as the students showed up and at least acted like they paid attention."

"So your husband's a freak."

"Exactly. And if he thinks I cheated on him and there's no way to prove I didn't, he can't just forget about it and move on."

Amanda fished through her bag for what Pace assumed would be a tissue, the same bag Pace had admired in a paparazzi photo of a celebrity in *People*, and handed her a business card. "Here." She picked up her fork.

"What's this?" The card said Raymond T. Falcon, LMFT, with an in-town address.

"Dr. Falcon was our counselor."

"You think we need a marriage counselor?"

"You don't?"

Of course they did, she just couldn't imagine Jason's reaction if she suggested it. "What's he like?"

"Mid-thirties, kinda cute if you like the academic type, although to my great disappointment, he never wore a cardigan or a sweater vest." She shook her head at the waiter as he took their plates and asked if they'd like anything else. "You're at an impasse, Pace. He doesn't believe you and you're pissed and beginning to question him. It's a nasty cycle. Dr. Falcon can help you."

Marriage therapy? It was the last thing she expected Amanda to suggest and yet it made perfect sense. She knew they couldn't stay in the weird limbo they were in forever and if they didn't do something soon, she feared they were headed for divorce.

* * *

When Jason phoned home one afternoon to ask Pace if she'd called a plumber about the leaky bathroom shower, she didn't answer. His imagination immediately jumped to thoughts of her with another man—in their home, in their bed, in a seedy hotel room, in her car behind an abandoned warehouse. He'd never been the jealous type, well…not really and certainly not lately, but he couldn't stop thinking about her cheating on him.

At least Dillon had basketball practice that night so he didn't have to slink around the house feeling guilty. Pace had started hovering around him, watching him at dinner, and she seemed unusually disappointed when he went downstairs to his office to work after dinner instead of dealing with their marriage. He couldn't face the expectant look she gave him when he came home each night from work and couldn't face her disappointment when he busied himself with work or chores until she gave in and went to bed.

Dillon had eaten by the time he got home and Pace had made him a sandwich to take to practice. She'd grown up dining in the best restaurants in the city and now she made sandwiches for her family. Jason couldn't help but wonder if she felt unhappy with their life and the little luxury he managed to provide.

After practice he sent Dillon to shower and went upstairs in the quiet house. Mitchell had already gone to bed. He could see the neon green from his nightlight glowing under his closed door. When Jason peeked inside, he found him sound asleep with the teddy bear his aunt had sent at his birth tucked under his chin. Jason pulled the covers over him where he'd kicked them off and ran a hand over the cowlick on his forehead. When Mitchell's hand twitched, Jason imagined his youngest son dreaming about building a Lego fortress or chasing after Cooper.

He crept out of Mitchell's room, closed the door behind him, and went into his darkened bedroom. He found Pace in the tub when he went in to use the bathroom. He'd assumed she'd gone to bed and was surprised to see her. She'd pulled her hair up and the heat from the water had turned her face pink with color. His eyes were drawn to the swell of her breasts above the water line and he fought the urge to strip down and join her.

"Oh!" Her head snapped up when he opened the door. "I didn't hear you come in."

Obviously, or maybe she'd deliberately tried to make him suffer. He dismissed the thought immediately. Pace didn't have a devious bone in her body and she'd never understood his powerful need for her. He turned to leave before he did or said something he'd regret, but not before she called his name. He didn't turn around, he couldn't, but stood at the threshold staring into their bedroom and listening as drops of water fell from her body as she wiggled in the tub.

"Where's Dillon?" she asked.

"He's in the shower. I'll put him to bed."

"We need to talk, Jason," she said. "After he's asleep, we need to talk."

He sat on the couch in the den, flicking one by one through the television channels when Pace came downstairs wearing her flannel pajamas and tank top. His stomach cramped as she eased onto the arm of the couch. Did she intend to confess?

"Jason." When she touched his arm, the heat from her skin went straight through him. He hit the power button on the remote and plunged the room into silence. He pretended to be annoyed, but he couldn't wait to hear what she had to say.

"I had lunch with Amanda today."

Lunch with her man-hating former boss couldn't lead to anything good.

"She's getting married."

It took him a minute to process what she'd said and when he met her eyes he knew they were both thinking the same thought. "Amanda's already married," he said. "To her career."

When she smiled down at him, it felt like someone had reached inside his chest and twisted his heart in their fist. He wanted his wife back so badly it hurt.

"I know. She completely floored me, too." She ran her hands through the damp ends of her hair, then clamped them together in her lap. "She said her and her fiancé saw a marriage counselor and she gave me his card."

Son of a bitch. "You told Amanda."

"I didn't mean to, but she could tell I was upset about something and it just came out."

If Pace had been looking for someone who'd encourage her behavior, she'd picked the right person. "A counselor?" The idea of it made him want to puke. "Why? So we can argue with each other for a hundred bucks an hour?"

"So we can talk about our situation with someone objective, who might be able to help us get past this...this place we're in right now." She reached for his arm again and he could tell she planned to put on the full court press. "We can't go on like this forever, Jas. I'm not happy, you're not happy, the kids are going to catch on pretty soon." She let her hand fall and straightened her shoulders, causing the tank to stretch across her breasts. "If this guy can help us, I'm willing to try."

Shit. If he said no, he'd look like a complete jackass...But counseling? He remembered Adam saying he'd refused counseling and now he was trying to steal his wife away from her new husband.

He stared at the darkened television and tried to imagine talking to some stranger about their problems. Pace started stroking her hand down the arm of his sweatshirt, up and down, up and down, like he'd seen her do with Cooper to calm him down. Except her touch had the opposite reaction. When he turned to look at her, she smiled and raised her brows pleadingly. Jason lifted her hand from his arm and linked their fingers. That simple connection caused her smile to fade and even in the muted light he could see the shock in her eyes. Before he even knew how it happened, Pace slithered into his lap and they were kissing as if not to do so would be the end of them both.

She snaked her hands under his sweatshirt and raked her nails down his back, pulsing against him. He lifted her tank and drew her nipple into his mouth, eliciting a gasping moan that snapped his control. He couldn't get close enough, touch enough of her skin, draw her clothes away and plunge inside of her fast enough. Her frantic movements told Jason she felt as eager as he did and only incited his need further. He flipped her onto her back and yanked her pants to her knees.

She put the palms of her hands on his chest and pushed him back. "Jason, wait."

"No, no, no, baby, I can't wait." Christ, he was begging her, fumbling with the button on his jeans. Why did she just lay there? Couldn't she help him? Couldn't she see the way his hands shook?

"Jason." The sound of her voice, the harsh way she said his name, had him sitting back on his heels.

"What?"

She propped up on her elbows, shook the damp hair out of her face. Her naked chest taunted him as she tried to catch her breath. "Does this mean you believe me?"

Fuck. What the hell did he say to that? Yes meant he had no more doubts and he could fuck her until neither one of them remembered what the hell they'd fought about. No would be more truthful, since he still wasn't a hundred percent sure, but that would end this—.

"That's what I thought." She sat up and pushed him away.

"Pace, wait."

She tried to get up, but he grabbed her arm and pulled her back down on the couch.

"No, you wait. I love you, Jason, and I've never slept with another man or wanted to sleep with another man since the day we met. If you don't believe that, or me, I think we need to see the counselor."

Christ. He walked right into that one. He tugged his shirt back down as Pace stood to pull her pants up and jerk her arms back into her tank. "This isn't a question of love, Pace. You know I love you."

"But you don't believe me?"

"It's not that I don't believe you, it's that I can't forget that you were pregnant."

"Jason, I wasn't pregnant. I believe that with all my heart."

"You think the doctor's lying?"

"I think he made a mistake," she said. "I think the lab made a mistake."

"That's an awful lot of mistakes."

She looked at him, her eyes narrow, her skin still flushed from his touch. "You're making a bigger one, Jason, if you think I'd cheat on you."

"What the hell is that supposed to mean?"

"It means I can't live like this." She threw her arms into the air. "I can't be with you until you believe me or figure out how to get past your insecurity."

He nearly jumped out of his skin. "My insecurity!"

"Do you really think I'd let another man touch me, Jason?" She pointed down at the couch where one of the cushions had fallen onto the floor. "After what just happened, do you really think I would?"

"I sure as hell hope not because I'd kill him."

She took a deep breath and let her shoulders sag. "What if Dr. Falcon can help us?" She righted the couch, sat down, and pulled him down next to her, reached for his hand. He wanted her so badly he vibrated with need. "Will you please give this a try? Please?"

He couldn't say no, not when he could still taste her on his tongue. Damn it, he couldn't catch a break. "Fine." He pulled his hand away and reached for the remote. "Whatever." He shrugged and turned the TV back on. Pace stood up, sighed, and passed in front of him on her way up the stairs.

Shit. He should have just said yes.

CHAPTER 13

Dr. Falcon's office was located in Midtown, in a cluster of office condos off Peachtree Street, a good forty minutes from home, not including traffic. Jason could make it in ten from his office, but Pace would be lucky to make it home in time to get the kids off the bus. He'd hit the nail on the head regarding the doctor's hourly wage. If therapy didn't work, they could probably buy a car for what they might spend.

Pace had waited in the small reception area for ten minutes before Jason walked in. He left for work most mornings before Pace got up and the sight of him in his charcoal suit, so handsome, even with the scowl on his face, had her longing. Their groping encounter on the couch nights ago had only made things worse. As soon as the kids went to bed, they avoided one another as much as possible.

He'd gotten a haircut earlier in the day and when he sat in the chair beside her, Pace could see little clips of hair on his collar. She thought back to the day he first met her parents. When she'd opened the door to him at her apartment, she'd nearly fallen over with surprise.

"You cut your hair." She'd reached out to touch his newly shorn locks. She could no longer twist her fingers around the ends. "Why?"

He'd shrugged uncomfortably. "I didn't want to meet your parents looking like a shaggy dog." He'd looked nervous and it made her worry about her mother pouncing on him when they arrived. Her parents had already asked about Jason's family. Neither of them had ever heard of his hometown.

Later that night, when they made love in his apartment back in Athens, when she ran her fingers over his head, she felt like she was with a stranger. "I feel like I'm cheating on my boyfriend." They'd both laughed. They sure weren't laughing now.

"How long have you been waiting?" he asked as they filled out paperwork on clip boards.

Pace tried to catch a glimpse of what he wrote. "Not long."

"I've got a conference call at three, so I can't be here forever."

Only a few minutes after they'd returned their paperwork to the receptionist, Dr. Falcon greeted them and led them to his office. It was pretty sparse, with a desk, two chairs, and a love seat, diplomas and certificates on the wall. A plum tree outside his window had deep purple leaves that seemed to wave at them in the breeze. Amanda's description of Dr. Falcon was dead on, except she forgot to mention his unassuming good looks. She really had fallen in love.

Dr. Falcon sat on one of the chairs and faced them on the couch. His jeans and golf shirt made Pace feel overdressed in her slacks and cashmere sweater. Inappropriate nervous laughter bubbled up her throat, but a sideways glance at Jason, at his skeptical profile, tamped it down fast.

"So," Dr. Falcon began, "I've read over your paperwork and what I typically do at the first session is let you both explain why you've come to see me, sort of assess the situation as it stands today, and then see what you'd like to get out of our time together." He reached for a legal pad and ballpoint pen from his desk. "But before I ask you questions, do you have any questions of me, about my background or training?"

Jason and Pace looked at each other briefly, then back at the doctor. "My friend Amanda Potts recommended you, Dr. Falcon."

He seemed appeased by Pace's answer and smiled at them. When he asked Jason to tell him why he'd come, Jason squirmed in his seat. "Well," he cleared his throat and flipped the end of his tie. "Pace was pregnant and there's no way I was the father."

"No way?"

"I had a vasectomy and I had it rechecked after she found out she was pregnant."

Pace sighed audibly and Dr. Falcon zeroed in on her. "Pace, would you like to explain why you're here?"

"I wasn't pregnant." She explained the details briefly. If he *had* read the papers they'd filled out, it wouldn't have been news.

"I see." He scribbled something on the pad. She couldn't see what he'd put down. "So, there's been a loss of trust on both sides."

"Both sides?" Jason asked.

"I'd imagine you're questioning your trust in your wife and that she's questioning your faith in her." He scribbled again and looked up, smiled, and pushed his little round glasses up the bridge of his nose. "What has your relationship been like since the doctor called?"

They both switched positions on the couch and Pace shoved her sleeves up her arms. Neither answered right away. "Not good," she said when it became obvious Jason wasn't going to respond.

"Have you discussed the situation calmly, are you fighting openly, has there been an accusation of cheating?"

When Jason snorted, she felt embarrassment flush her cheeks at the thought of revealing the private details of their life to a stranger. "There's nothing to discuss or fight about until she admits she had an affair or her doctor admits a mistake."

Clearly her husband didn't have the same reservations. "I didn't cheat on you, Jason."

Dr. Falcon skillfully moved them past their blocking point. "Can you tell me about your relationship prior to the supposed pregnancy?"

"It was good," she said, all embarrassment gone. There'd never been anything embarrassing about their love. "Really good."

"Jason?" Dr. Falcon prodded.

He shrugged. "I thought it was good, but if she was cheating...I can't be sure of anything."

Dr. Falcon jotted something on his paper and seemed to study his work before looking at them in turn. "I think you've come to me at the right time. It's important to discover what led you here, not just the pregnancy or supposed pregnancy," he said when Pace opened her mouth to interject, "but other factors in your past and present that may cause you both to question the other's actions and reactions to this particular situation. I think it would be best to see you both individually, and as a couple, on a weekly basis."

"Three sessions a week?" Jason asked. Pace could see him calculating the expense in his head.

"Three total, two for each of you." He got up and went behind his desk, but didn't sit down. "You've got a complex situation here, Mr. and Mrs. Kelly. Without proof, for either of you, we're going to have to work especially hard at rebuilding your trust in each other."

"Dr. Falcon," Pace said. "We've got two small boys. They're going to figure out something's going on, but we don't know what to tell them."

"How old?"

"Five and seven." Images of the boys flashed through her mind. The temperature had dropped since this morning and she hoped Mitchell remembered to wear his sock cap. They'd be getting off the bus soon.

"I find it best for parents to tell kids that age that mommy and daddy are having problems, but that you're working on them. Be sure to tell them your problems are private and not for discussion with friends. That way, if they have questions, they'll come to you."

* * *

"So what do you think?" Pace asked Jason as they exited Dr. Falcon's building. A blast of cold air hit them in the face and blew her jacket open. Jason noticed she wore the necklace he gave her for their seventh anniversary, the sterling silver heart.

He blew out a big breath and contemplated his answer. This kind of stuff, talking about the past and about his feelings, made him desperately uncomfortable. He didn't understand guys like

Dr. Falcon. In some sick way, he had to enjoy putting people on edge; maybe it made him feel really good about his own life to pick other people's problems apart.

"I think this is going to cost a fortune." He watched Pace's expression quickly turn from hopeful to hurt and had to stifle the urge to apologize. "I know that's not what you want to hear, but I just don't see how this is going to help." When she stared at him blankly, he looked at his watch and said, "I've got to go." He walked away toward his car without saying goodbye.

As he pulled out of the lot, he glanced over and saw Pace sitting in her SUV. She hadn't started the car; she just sat in the driver's seat with her eyes closed and her head bowed like she was praying. Jason turned onto Peachtree Street and into traffic, pushing on the gas harder than necessary. He'd do anything to distance himself from her pain.

He felt like a schmuck, going to see a counselor, watching Pace look at him so expectantly, waiting for him to say, "It's okay, honey, I believe you." He wished like hell he could just say it and move on, but he couldn't let it go. What kind of fool would he be if he turned his back on that kind of evidence?

He pulled into the office lot and looked at the clock. Ten minutes until three. As he sat in the parked car, he thought about when he'd left for their session. When he'd told his secretary he'd be out of the office, she'd questioned his whereabouts. "I'm meeting my wife," he'd explained. She had the nerve to lift her brows suggestively. Ha. When he'd first gotten a job as an intern with another big firm in town, he and Pace used to meet for lunch as often as they could. They'd smile at each other like a couple of kids playing at being grown ups and they pretty much were. Jason never thought they'd meet in the middle of the day for marriage counseling.

That night the boys started fighting over Lego's. When Jason heard Pace send them to their rooms as he changed his clothes, Dillon slammed his door and, through the wall, Jason heard him mutter, "I hate her," about his mother. Jason stormed into his room before Dillon even had time to fling himself onto his twin bed. It still had the dinosaur bedspread he'd begged for when he was four.

"I don't ever want to hear you say something like that about your mother again. Do you understand me, young man?"

Instead of lowering his eyes and mumbling, "Yes, Sir," like he usually did when he got in trouble, Dillon stared at his father and shouted, "Why not? You can't stand to be around her either."

Jason felt like he'd been slapped by his seven-year-old. He didn't know who felt more shocked—Dillon, for standing up to his dad, or Jason, that Dillon had figured out how he felt. He and Pace obviously hadn't done such a great job keeping their problems from the kids. "Mitchell?" Jason called through Dillon's open doorway. "Come in your brother's room for just a minute." When he turned to yell downstairs for Pace, he found her standing at the threshold.

"What's going on?" she asked.

Mitchell pushed past her and joined Dillon on the bed, their little legs dangling from the sides, nowhere near the ground. "We need to have a talk, guys." Pace came into the room and stood beside him, her eyes wide as a doe. Thank God she'd asked the therapist how to handle the kids.

"Look." Jason ran a hand through his hair. How the hell was he supposed to shatter their world? "I know you guys know Mommy and Daddy haven't been getting along lately." Dillon blinked his eyes quickly and Mitchell looked down at his lap. Jason paused and cleared his throat. He couldn't turn back now. "We want you to know we're working on our problems and that it's okay to be confused and upset about our…disagreement. But you have to respect and listen to Mommy and Daddy just like you always have. That doesn't change. And if you have any questions or want to talk about what's going on, you need to ask us. This is a private family matter and you're not to discuss this with your friends."

"Are you getting divorced?" Dillon asked with the saddest expression Jason had ever seen on his face. He wanted to tell him no, if only to stop his chin from quivering.

"I don't think so, buddy."

He could see Pace fidgeting out of the corner of his eye. She'd twisted the dishrag she'd carried up from the kitchen between her fists.

Dillon turned his head to look at her for the first time since she'd entered the room. "Why can't you just say you're sorry?"

For a minute, Jason thought his son knew his mom had been with someone and that he might know who. He almost dropped to his knees and shouted, "Who is it, Dillon? Who was Mommy with?"

"I..." Pace stuttered, took a step toward the boys, and then stopped. "Why should Mommy apologize?"

"Daddy's mad at you," Dillon said. "Whatever you did, just apologize and he'll forgive you."

Jason heard her sigh, long and hard, before she said, "It's not that simple, Dil." Her voice sounded high and soft and he knew she was about to cry. And that was the last thing the boys needed to see.

"You guys wash up for dinner, okay?" Jason ushered Pace into the hallway and down the steps. He expected her to go into the kitchen. He could hear the oven timer beeping and saw a pot on the stovetop with steam hissing out, but she headed into the hall bath and closed the door. Even with the water running full blast into the sink, he could hear her crying.

CHAPTER 14

Tori hung up the phone without leaving another message. Pace didn't answer and had obviously ignored her mother's earlier voicemails. It wasn't like Pace to pout for so long and over something as ridiculous as Thanksgiving. Pace's immature behavior was the last thing Tori needed on her plate right now, but she couldn't help but worry there was something else going on.

She'd decided to hold off confronting Colin until after Thanksgiving. He came back from Washington, chipper as ever, and shifted right into pre-campaign mode, expecting Tori to do the same. Her schedule became packed with luncheon, speaker, and hostess duties she normally would have declined. She only wished she had the commitment to the campaign necessary to ensure Colin's victory. She'd always been an important part of his success, with her family name and contacts, but after twenty years in the Senate, he'd eclipsed her and, with everything else that she'd discovered, she felt especially vulnerable.

He came in late one night as Tori read an old favorite in the den and sipped a brandy.

"You're up late." He joined her on the couch. He looked exhausted as he pecked her cheek. She had to remind herself not to recoil. He'd been more touchy-feely than ever. It should have been her first clue. They hadn't made love in weeks, but not because he hadn't tried. How in the hell was she supposed to perform for him knowing he'd compare her body to a twenty-year-old? In her prime she'd have given Heather or anyone else a run for their money, but now...

"Would you like a drink?" she asked.

"No." He pulled off his tie and absently wrapped it around his hand. "Buddy Ellison was pouring 'em strong at dinner." He looked at Tori and smiled. "We missed you. Judy said she hasn't seen you in ages."

"I couldn't stomach another fundraising dinner. I hope you passed along my apologies."

He looked at her solemnly. "You're not up for this round, are you, Tor?"

She used to be his biggest fan, his most ardent supporter, even through the worst of times. She used to think it mattered. "I'll get there, Colin."

He reached over, lifted the cover of her book, and grinned. "You reading that again?"

She couldn't help but smile. He did pay attention, sometimes. "You know it's my favorite."

"But you know how it ends." He leaned back against the cushions and she caught a faint whiff of his cologne. "I don't see the point."

"It's soothing and familiar." Tori shrugged uncomfortably when she realized he stared at her. Was he going to try to seduce her again and would she have the strength to refuse?

He scooted closer and ran his hand over her sweater and along the side of her breast. "So is this."

She tried to visualize the pictures to harden her reserve, but his charm, the boyish grin he used on her when all else failed, was hard to resist. She thought of everything he'd put on the line for a piece of ass: his career, their marriage, her sanity. And then there was her biggest fear of all: what if he was with this girl for more than just sex? After years of putting up with his slips, she couldn't believe he'd put her in such a vulnerable position at a time when he needed her the most. "You're dead on your feet."

"I've got stamina to spare."

She looked at him and something in her glare stopped him as he'd reached behind her to pull her into him. "Are you sure?"

He stared at her like he could see into her heart. Tori would have sworn at that moment he knew the gig was up. She felt sure he'd admit it if she asked, but she just stared at him. Why didn't she ask? What was she so afraid of? This certainly wasn't the first time.

His face remained unreadable and she could feel the power shift back to her. In so many ways he was still the innocent boy she married. Would he leave her? she wondered for the first time in ages. And what would she do if he did?

He let her go and looked away. "I suppose sleep will do me some good." His knees cracked as he stood up and walked slowly out of the room. He paused and turned to face her at the door. "You coming along?"

She felt as though he was asking about more than just bed. "I'll be up in a minute."

* * *

I'm in therapy. We're in therapy. Pace kept repeating those words to herself, as reassurance or to acknowledge an impossibility she wasn't sure, but she couldn't seem to stop. She passed her neighbor in the car, her son in the backseat with a balloon from the local grocery store, and envied her the innocence of mundane life where her biggest worry had been what to make for dinner. Pace wondered if her marriage would last through the end of the year or heck, the end of the month.

Thanksgiving was next week and she'd agreed to attend yet another over-the-top celebration at her parents' house. Jason hadn't even gotten upset when she'd mentioned it, like the thing he dreaded for a full year seemed completely unimportant. He kept shutting her out by working late and barely speaking to her when he finally made it home. She couldn't stand the quiet at night after the kids went to bed. Neither one of them slept well. He'd moved back into their room after the scene with the kids and they spent their nights trying hard not to touch each other in bed. Just a brush of his skin left her aching. Pace felt sure a day spent with her mother would pull them even farther apart. Her mother with her super detection powers had always been able to see right through her, read her moods with a look. Would she be able to fake happiness for hours on end with the people who, other than her husband, knew her better than anyone?

She arrived early for her individual appointment with Dr. Falcon. He wanted to see her first and she couldn't help but think he was going to badger her to into admitting an affair. She flipped through a magazine in the waiting room and tried to keep her mind off the unknown behind the door down the hall. She stared at the geometric pattern in the rug, the leather seats in the waiting room, and the variety of reading material—*Atlanta Magazine, Better Homes & Gardens, Fortune*—and couldn't visualize Amanda sitting in this very same space, ready to bare her soul to a stranger. Or maybe Pace was the one who couldn't imagine baring her soul.

If her mother knew she was at a therapist's office, about to discuss "family matters," she'd probably drag her from the building or threaten to do bodily harm if she didn't leave. One thing the Whitfields never did was talk about family. Dr. Falcon cut her pondering short when he emerged from the back hall, sans the client the receptionist told her he was with. She felt a little disappointed at not getting to see another one of his patients.

"Mrs. Kelly." He shook her hand with both of his as if they were old friends. After a few of these appointments they probably would be. He wore jeans and a blue button down rolled up at the sleeves. Pace thought he looked like a runner, with his long gait and lean build. A picture of a kid sat on his desk, but he didn't wear a wedding ring. Great, she thought. Advice from an unmarried father. When she sat on the same couch she'd shared with Jason, it felt too big and she wished she'd sat in the other chair. When Dr. Falcon sat down and smiled at her, she figured it was too late to switch seats.

"How are things at home?" he asked. She could feel a lump rise in her throat. How in the world was he going to help her when she couldn't get her emotions in check?

"Okay, I guess. The same." She cleared her throat and tossed her coat on the adjoining seat cushion. "Actually the kids asked if we're getting divorced. We aren't doing such a great job hiding our problems."

"And what did you say?"

"Jason told them what you said, that we're dealing with things and to keep it private."

"Were you there when he talked to them?"

"Yes."

"And how did they take it?"

Pace shrugged. He could probably attribute meaning to his son's every move, but her boys didn't open up about much, except their devotion to PlayStation and their mutual hatred of girls. "They've been quiet since our talk, but it's only been a few days."

"Any behavior changes at home or notes from teachers?"

"No, not really. My son asked why I don't just apologize so Daddy can forgive me." The memory of it, sobbing in the bathroom and the uncomfortable dinner afterwards, brought back the lump. When she'd come out of the bathroom that night, they'd all been sitting at the table, like the perfect family waiting to be served. Jason had taken the casserole from the oven and turned off the beans from the stove. The look he gave her was the most tender since their whole ordeal began. "I told him it's not that simple."

"No, it's not." Pace noticed the yellow pad on his lap again. "Do you feel you have anything to apologize to Jason for?"

Why did she feel shocked at the blunt question? He didn't know her, didn't know she'd never cheat on Jason. "No, Dr. Falcon, I don't." Irritation snapped her out of her weepy state. "I didn't cheat on my husband."

He nodded his head, stared at her through his tiny little glasses as if waiting for her to say more. "And how does it feel when he accuses you of cheating?"

Pace sighed, but what she really wanted to do was scream, *"How do you think it makes me feel?"* "It hurts. I'd never cheat on him. Ever. And yet he seems to think I did and, without a guilty conscience, continue to lie about it. I hate it that he has so little faith in me, in us, and what we have together."

She looked out the window at the leaves of the plum tree, so bold against the gray day, and thought about how to explain her husband to Dr. Falcon. He and Jason would have their time together, unless Jason refused to come, but even if he did come, she wondered how honest he'd be.

"Dr. Falcon, this thing with Jason, it's complicated. Deep down I know he doesn't believe I cheated on him. It's just, well....he's not jealous, that wouldn't be the right term, but..." She tried not to sound naïve or like a know-it-all, but she needed him to understand her tender-hearted, frustrating, multi-faceted Jason. "His parents basically abandoned him. What we have together—our family—it's his foundation. So for him to be unsure about me..." How could she explain that she knew how he felt, that she understood, despite hating it, the way he'd been acting? "He's so hurt."

"What about you?"

"I'm hurt, too. I understand how he feels about the test results and the fact that I lied about what the doctor said, but I won't admit to something I didn't do."

He scribbled something down on the paper. The sound of it echoing in the otherwise quiet room was like nails on a blackboard.

"Tell me about your background."

Oh, God. She'd expected the question and the subsequent clutch in her gut... "I'm an only child. My parents are...wealthy and pretty well known around town."

"Well known in what way?"

She tapped her fingers on the soft brown fabric of the sofa arm. "My father is a United States Senator and has been for over twenty years."

He didn't ask her father's name, but since the state's only other senator had been newly elected, he had to know his identity. "So, tell me what it was like growing up the only child of well known parents."

Pace wiped her clammy palms on her pants and sat on her hands to keep from tapping. She'd already noticed Dr. Falcon glancing at her nervous fingers. She knew she'd have to talk about her parents and yet she looked around the room for signs of her mother or some sort of recording device. Dr. Falcon must have sensed her hesitation because he said, "Often times a person's background and family are keys to unlocking what's going on in their current relationships. You just told me why you think Jason's having such a hard time with this. I'll remind you again that anything you tell me stays with me, inside these four walls."

His reassurance should've made her feel more at ease, but it didn't. She was about to break the cardinal rule of political life. But her marriage meant more to her than upsetting her parents. "It was insulating. I was out of the spotlight, but I went to the most selective private schools and they kept me inside the bubble of a small circle of acquaintances. College was like a wake up call," she said with all the delight she'd felt at finally being free. "I'd never been around so many people with so many different lifestyles and experiences. I thought everyone went skiing over the Christmas holidays and flew to Europe in the summer."

"Is that where you met Jason? In college?"

"Yes." The party, the night they spent talking until dawn, the single white flower he'd brought her the next day flashed through her mind. She never tired of thinking about or telling that story.

"What was your parents' reaction to your dating Jason?"

How could Pace describe her mother's horror? "My mother was already planning my wedding with my high school boyfriend. No one but Trey would ever be good enough in her mind, certainly not Jason. I only made it worse by refusing to come home for summer break."

"Did you?"

"It was the first time I'd gone against them. Even my father got involved and he never got involved."

"What did your father do?"

"He said he'd buy me a new car if I came home, said we'd go to Spain for two weeks, and that he'd arrange for me to intern at his best friend's law firm." She could still hear her mother's voice in the background, spilling out more promises for him to recite. "When I wouldn't budge, they demanded I bring him home so they could meet him properly."

Dr. Falcon's eyes flicked to the wall clock over the door and back to Pace so fast she couldn't be sure he'd ever looked away. "And how did that go?"

"It was dreadful. My mother peppered him with questions, practically rolled her eyes in his face, and brought up my lineage. She actually used the word lineage whenever she could. We couldn't get out of there fast enough."

"And yet you married."

"Their worst nightmare, or at least my mother's."

"What about your father?"

Pace thought of her funny, charismatic father and how he went along with whatever her mother asked him to do and still did. "He just wants me to be happy. He loves Jason and has always made him feel a part of the family. My father wasn't born into money like my mother was. He put himself through college and law school, fought hard for everything he accomplished. He and Jason are very much alike in that way."

At this Dr. Falcon shifted ever so slightly in his seat, but Pace noticed. He wore his mask of objectivity well and this was the first time she'd seen it slip. "So your father defers to your mother?"

"Habitually."

His eyes flicked to the wall clock again and, after noting something on the pad, he scratched his chin. "We're running short on time, but I think we've got a lot to work with here. Are you and Jason planning to come in together on Friday?"

"Unless you scare him off during his session."

* * *

Jason found Pace going through a box of old photos the night of her first therapy session. "What are you doing?"

He'd startled her, he could tell from the way she whipped her head around and swiped at a tear leaking from the corner of her eye.

"Nothing." She gathered the pictures and frantically shoved them back into one of the many photo boxes she kept in the basement.

He stuffed his hands in his pockets to keep from reaching for her. He'd seen the pictures; shots from college when they'd first met. He dreaded going to see Dr. Falcon the next day and seeing her walk down memory lane made him dread it even more. The last thing he wanted to do was rehash the past. His dinner with Adam had been enough.

The afternoon of the appointment he was knee deep in drawings and emails with the New York client. Their list of questions about the process and their options kept him busy and responding to each one made him feel bogged under. Spending an hour he didn't have in therapy pissed him off. His secretary lifted her brows again as he left; the whole office probably thought he was having an affair.

Dr. Falcon opened his door right at three and ushered him inside with a wave. Jason couldn't stand the guy's casual greeting, like they were friends and he'd purposefully stopped work in the middle of the day to hang out with him. Just because Pace thought Falcon could magically make their marriage all better he was forced to sit in detention like a scolded child three times a week. The whole thing felt like a huge waste of time and money.

He sat in the chair opposite Dr. Falcon without taking off his coat. He didn't consider their meeting a friendly chat and he couldn't wait to get out of there. He could tell by the look on the doctor's face he was judging him on his appearance, his scowl, and whatever information Pace had supplied in their individual session. God only knew what she'd told him. Falcon's intense focus made Jason want to punch him in the face.

"How are you doing, Jason? Can I take you coat?"

He hated it that he called him Jason as if they were pals. "I'm fine, thanks." When he realized he'd gripped the arms of the chair in a white knuckle hold, he deliberately relaxed and dropped his hands over the sides.

"I understand you and Pace spoke to your sons about what's going on?"

Jason nodded and when Falcon continued to stare at him, he knew the session wouldn't be quick. "It wasn't easy. Dillon, our oldest, I find him watching us together. I guess he's looking for clues."

"It's very hard on children to realize their parents might not always be together. Be sure to keep the lines of communication open with both of them if you think they want to talk or ask questions. Sometimes the best answer to give is, 'I don't know.' They appreciate your honesty."

"I guess so." He began to sweat in the warm office and stood up to shed his coat. He tossed it on the couch, sat down in the chair, and checked his watch.

"Pace told me you and she met in college. Can you tell me about that?"

"What do you want to know?"

"How did you meet?"

Jason stared at him without blinking. "I thought you said she told you how we met."

"I'd like to hear you tell me."

Christ. A hundred bucks an hour for this? "We met at a party."

"What was your first impression of her?" Falcon asked.

Jason sighed and thought back. The first time he saw her she was...stunning. Smiling, laughing, hopping around the room from girl to boy without a self-conscious bone in her tiny little body. He'd wanted to scoop her up and put her in his pocket. He knew right then he had to talk to her, had to find a way to draw her over to where he stood watching. "I thought she was beautiful. She looked classy, but...approachable."

"And you approached her?"

"She came up to me. I'd been staring at her and she called me on it."

"And?"

"And we started talking." Dr. Falcon lifted his brows, expected more information. Damn, what did it matter? "The band cranked it up a notch, so we went outside. After awhile, we went to the intramural fields by the river to talk."

"What did you talk about?"

Jason shrugged, thinking of that long ago night. Most of what he remembered was how pretty she looked in the moonlight and how she really listened. When he kissed her, she tasted like strawberries. "Stuff, school, our majors, where we were from, the usual when you first meet someone."

"And you were smitten?"

Smitten? What the hell? "I wanted to see her again."

"Did you?"

"We're married, aren't we?" He couldn't do this for an hour.

"Did you know her father was a senator the night you met?"

"I'm sure she told you I didn't."

"Jason…" He leaned forward in his seat. Jason pictured Falcon's college professor coaching him in dealing with reluctant patients. "Whatever Pace told me in our session, I can't repeat. It's important for me to understand your relationship, from the very beginning and progressing to what's brought you here. I promise you that although these questions may seem random or tedious, they're relevant."

Jason imagined him quietly lecturing the kid whose picture sat atop his desk, that conciliatory tone droning on and on about what the kid did wrong and why it was wrong and did he understand why he couldn't do it again. "No, I didn't know her father was a senator when we met." He fought the urge to smirk and say, "*Happy?*"

"How did you find out? Did she tell you eventually?"

"My roommate razzed me about it the next day." He could still see his face, hung-over, sitting on the couch in his briefs when Jason walked in the next morning. "Dude," he'd said. "You've got some kinda balls."

"Did you approach her about the fact that she hadn't said anything?"

Accuse her was more like it. "I mentioned it."

"Mentioned it how?"

Jason gritted his teeth. He knew Pace told him he'd yelled at her. "I thought she was messing with me, ya know, using me to make some rich frat boy jealous or just trying to rebel." He'd nearly ruined it that morning, letting his insecurity and pride get the best of him. He'd never forget the way she looked that day when he'd said those things, like a little wounded bird. He'd mangled the flower he'd brought her in his fist.

"Did she try to hide your relationship from her friends, sneak around to be with you?"

"No, no one at school. Once we cleared the air about why she hadn't said anything, we started dating. We were together all the time."

"How did you feel once you knew who her parents were, once you knew about her background?"

Naïve and insecure, but he'd never admit that. "Everyone knew who she was, how she'd grown up. I guess I felt luckier, more independent, and a little intimidated." Jason propped his leg on his knee. "She didn't tell her parents right away. She seemed a little scared of them and now that I know them I understand why. Her mom's a snob and her dad…let's just say he hates me."

"How did you feel about being kept a secret?"

Jason shrugged. Admitting he didn't like it wouldn't do much good. "I figured she knew best how to deal with her parents. Her ex kept calling from Yale. Prick wouldn't leave her alone. She didn't tell him about us either because she knew it would get back to her parents and she wasn't ready to deal with them yet."

"You weren't intimidated enough to back out of the relationship?"

"We were in love. Completely in love. It never felt like something either one of us had a choice in."

Falcon jotted something down on his notepad and shifted focus. "Tell me about your family, your parents, siblings."

"My parents died…" Jason had to search his brain for the date. They'd never really been around, so the amount of time they'd been gone didn't really register. "Eight years ago."

"An accident?" Falcon asked.

He shook his head as the heavy weight of the past settled on his chest. "My dad died first. He'd battled cancer for years. He was seventy-three. My mom basically died of a broken heart. She stopped eating, stopped taking her meds. She only lasted three months without him."

"So your parents were older."

"My mom had me when she was forty-six." The big mistake, she'd always said.

"Siblings?"

"My sister Cami's fifty-one. My brother, Adam, he's forty-seven."

Falcon noted it all down and tapped his pen on the pad. "Quite a big age gap between you and your siblings. You're…" he rifled through a file on his desk, "…thirty-five?"

Jason nodded and glanced at his watch again. Thirty minutes to go.

"What was it like having a sister and brother so much older than you?"

He shrugged, shifted positions in the chair. He had a feeling no matter how or where he sat in this office he wouldn't be comfortable. "I never really knew my sister. She was out of the house when I was two."

"And now?"

"She lives in Minnesota with her husband. They've got four kids and a grandchild. We exchange Christmas cards."

"And your brother?"

"Adam's in New York. He's an accountant, two kids, divorced. I just saw him last week when I was in town, but before then it'd been two years. I guess you could say we're not really close."

"Where did you grow up?"

"Belton, Georgia." When Falcon cocked his head, Jason said, "It's an hour-and-a-half from nowhere, little town with one stop light, two churches, and a diner that closes at eight. No one's ever heard of it."

Dr. Falcon smiled at his description of the town that had held him captive for years. "What did your parents do?"

"They both worked for the junior college two towns over. My mom was a secretary in the English department and my dad ran the science lab."

"Were you close to your parents when they were alive?"

"No." What the hell did this have to do with him and Pace? "Why?"

Jason could feel his muscles tense. He hated talking about his parents. He tried to remember what he used to tell people when they'd ask why his parents weren't around. It had been so long he couldn't recall what he used to say. "When my brother got out of college, I was nine or ten, my parents retired. They'd saved to get Cami and Adam through college and had both put in thirty years. They wanted to travel, see the country. So they did, as often as possible."

"Did you go with them?"

"No. I was in school and couldn't have cared less about exploring the US in an RV." And he'd never been asked.

"Who did you stay with?"

"My grandfather. He was ninety, died at ninety-six. I think they wanted me to take care of him more than him to take care of me."

Dr. Falcon sat up in his chair and uncrossed his legs. "How did that feel, being left to care for your aging grandfather when you were just a child?"

"It sucked. He couldn't drive, so I had to catch rides for sports, rarely saw my friends who lived farther away than I could ride my bike. We used to eat charity meals when the food my mom left ran out and we couldn't get to the grocery store."

"How long would your parents be gone?"

Jason's eyes shifted to the window, where he noticed it had started to rain, as he thought back to their absences. "A month or two, sometimes longer."

Dr. Falcon wrote something down on the pad. When he raised his head, his brow furrowed and disapproval was written all over his face. "Tell me about your grandfather."

"He was a crotchety old son of a bitch. He chewed snuff all day long and carried an old tin can around to spit in." To this day Jason couldn't stand the smell of tobacco. "He liked to play cards, poker usually, and he told the same stories over and over again. He'd get real confused, called me Adam most of the time."

"How did you do in school?"

"Good. I liked school, the order and structure of it. Besides, I knew there wouldn't be any money for college and I couldn't wait to get the hell out of town. An academic scholarship was my only hope."

"Did you get one?"

"Nope. And my parents made too much money for me to qualify for financial aid." Not that they'd spent a dime on him. "I found a mason jar filled with cash on my grandfather's property one day. By the time he died, I'd found six in all. Over six thousand dollars. No one seemed to know they existed, so I used the money to pay for my first year and a half. I got a loan for the rest."

"So school was important to you?"

Jason wanted to slap the pity right off his face. Dr. Falcon's parents probably paid for graduate school. "It was my only option." He sat up in his seat and got to the point. At the rate they were going, Jason would likely pay for Falcon's kid's education, too. "Look, Dr. Falcon. I'm sure there's some reason for all these questions, but what I'd really like to talk about is my marriage and what you can do to prove to me that my wife didn't sleep with some other guy."

He sighed and tapped the end of his pen against the yellow legal pad on his lap. "Jason, there may never be proof one way or the other. You've lost faith in each other and rebuilding that trust is pretty much the same as if one of you cheated."

Jason looked at him, with his khaki pants and sweater, his little round glasses, and the picture of his son on his desk. Pace had said he was widowed. He'd felt grief and had to deal with it because his wife wasn't ever coming back. "Do you think she cheated?"

"It's not what I think that matters."

Jason sat back and rapped his fingers on the chair's arm. He needed some answers. "I've gone through her stuff, her drawers, her purse, her emails. I've even looked through the trash a few times. I go over the phone bill with a fine tooth comb, have looked over past phone bills. I've done a history on her internet searches, looked through her calendar…" Jason shook his head. "Nothing. There's no evidence she cheated. I've been reading some stuff, on the internet." He shrugged, felt embarrassed to admit he'd researched infidelity. "Most of the stuff I've found says a marriage can't be fixed after one partner has cheated if the cheating partner isn't willing to admit to the affair. But if she's telling the truth and the affair didn't happen, if it was just a huge mistake, she won't ever admit to it."

"I can't imagine she would if she didn't do it. What would be the point?"

"So what do we do?"

Dr. Falcon looked at Jason, cocked his head to the side like he was trying to think of a way to say what he wanted to say. "You need to decide if you believe her. If you can accept that she wasn't pregnant, that she didn't cheat on you, you can begin to move past this and get on with your marriage." Falcon leaned forward and braced his elbows on his knees. "But things won't go back to the way they were just because you say you believe her. She's lost faith in you, just as you've lost faith in her. Your absolutes are gone. You'd be starting from a new place and building back to where you were, to where you can both trust and love again without questioning."

"What if I can't do it?" Even though everything seemed to point to her innocence, Jason still wasn't sure he could believe her and living in the boggy middle ground was driving him crazy.

"If you didn't want to be in this marriage, if you truly didn't believe her, you wouldn't be sitting here right now. You'd never have agreed to therapy, you wouldn't be living under the same roof. Admitting you love your wife, that you want to be with her, that you want your family to be whole again, it doesn't make you weak, Jason. It makes you human."

CHAPTER 15

Since his individual session with Dr. Falcon, Jason seemed more withdrawn than ever. Pace was dying to know what they'd discussed and what had left him so troubled. She quickly dismissed the notion that they'd spent the entire hour bashing her and women in general. It was therapy, she reminded herself, not boys' night out.

She knew he had a lot on his plate right now, with the jobs in Chicago and New York, but he'd never holed up in his office like he had lately. The boys had given up trying to lure him out at night and usually ended up playing quietly in one of their rooms. Their conduct since the big chat had been exemplary, as if their behavior had anything to do with their marriage troubles. They all pretended like everything was the same as it used to be. Pace was beginning to forget how things used to be.

She and the kids arrived at her parents' house Thanksgiving Day without Jason, who planned to come straight from the airport. She hadn't let her parents know about his plans, as she didn't learn of them until the day before when he finally managed to tell her his schedule. She felt upset he'd been gone all week, although she had to admit it was easier to keep the peace at home when he was away. If only the kids didn't keep looking at her as if she was the reason Daddy was never home. Her only hope for keeping her mother's suspicions at bay was to ply her with alcohol.

"Pace," her mother called as the housekeeper led them into the den. They'd already gotten their Christmas tree up and decorated. "Just who are these two handsome young men you've brought with you?" Tori leaned down to fix both of their crooked ties.

"Grandma, it's us," Mitchell said. Dillon tried to loosen the tie she'd just tightened.

"Well, I almost didn't recognize you two, all suited up." She glanced at Pace and raised her palms. With her alabaster hair and red dress, she looked like she came straight from Santa's workroom. Pace felt distressed to see she hadn't started drinking. "Where's Jason?"

"He'll be here soon." Pace put the wrapped present from the boys in her hands. "Business," she said to Tori's arched brows and accusing look. She'd always tried to make trouble between them. "Here, the boys made this for you."

Tori feigned surprise and opened it with much adulation. The homemade ornament with their picture wouldn't ever grace the Whitfield's professionally decorated tree. The boys usually made one for Pace and the fact that they wanted to give it to Grandma spoke volumes as to their feelings.

"Where's Dad?" Pace hoped to distract the boys from the fact that Grandma hadn't placed the ornament on the tree, but set it back in the box on a side table.

"He's changing." She furrowed her brows, still as brown as they'd always been, despite the lightness of her hair. She was the only woman Pace knew who defined the term striking. "He insisted on going to the gym this morning. I swear he's obsessed."

Pace found it odd that she would criticize his choosing to exercise when, between the two of them, she was the one obsessed. She'd nagged him for years to work out. Why couldn't she cut him a break?

"Who wants to color?" Tori asked the boys. Dillon stared at Pace pleadingly. He'd complained the whole ride over that he didn't want to go because there wasn't anything to do at their house and because Grandma treated them like babies.

"Mom, the boys aren't really in to coloring." Pace stood behind Dillon and grabbed his shoulders. He was getting so big, almost up to her chest. She'd had to buy him a new suit for the day. "Why don't you guys see if there's a football game on in the study?"

They ran out as fast as they could over Tori's sigh. "Pace, football on Thanksgiving?"

"It's what ninety-nine percent of Americans do on Thanksgiving Day. I'm sure Dad's got some statistical research to back me up."

Tori moved to stand in front of her daughter, her perfect cupid's bow mouth set in a stubborn line. "You've lost weight." She slanted Pace's face toward the light from the Palladian window. "And you've got shadows under your eyes." She dropped her hands. "What's going on with you? Are you sick?"

What did it take, five, six minutes for her to notice? "No, I'm not sick. I've been busy and the weather's been so cold…" She shrugged her shoulders, moved away from the light. She ran her finger over an ugly table lamp. "Is this new?"

"Pace." Tori turned her around. Fooling her mother was like trying to fool God. "What is it?"

"Nothing, Mom. Jeez, just drop it, okay? I'm fine."

Tori walked to the bar. "Do you want a drink?"

Thank God. "Yes, I'd love one."

As she made them both a martini, Pace realized she'd starting viewing her parents' marriage differently since seeing Dr. Falcon. His words kept bouncing around her head. Once they'd gotten into it, she started thinking he was zoning in on her mother's bossiness as a way to get Pace to confess to a secret affair or at least some manipulative behavior. She got angry and asked why he wouldn't even consider the possibility there was a mistake at the lab. His answer nearly brought her to her knees.

"Pace," he'd said, with what seemed like genuine compassion. "If there was a mistake at the lab and you were never pregnant, chances are, you'll never be able to prove it. The only way to deal with healing your marriage is to rebuild trust as if you did have an affair. Whether you did or not, Jason thinks you did. That's all that matters now."

Hearing what she'd panicked about since the whole ordeal started, knowing he was right, didn't make her feel any better. It just made her numb. If Jason really thought she'd had an affair, he wouldn't ever get over it. Pace thought she'd find an ally at therapy, someone who could see her side and help Jason see it too, but instead she felt like she wouldn't ever find someone who believed her.

"Is it strong?" Pace asked when Tori handed her the martini glass.

"What do you think?" Tori sipped her freshly made drink and sat in her favorite chair. She carefully placed her glass on a beaded holiday coaster. Pace felt a strange affinity with the olive she'd pierced with a toothpick in the shape of a sword. She sat on the couch facing her beautiful mother. Pace's friends used to tell her how lucky she was. "Your mother's so pretty, Pace, so young and cool. I wish my mom was hip like yours." They had no idea Pace would have done anything to have an ordinary, cookie baking, PTA mom. Tori micromanaged every aspect of Pace's life—from forcing her to take years of piano even though she had no talent or inclination to forcing her to ask disgusting Alex Barneby to the club's Sadie Hawkins dance because he came from a good family. Pace took a small sip and tried to let go of the bitterness. She didn't need to get drunk and say something she'd regret.

Fortunately, her father waltzed into the room and scooped Pace into a huge hug. The familiar scent of his aftershave, the feel of his strong arms around her, made her want to cry. She hung on extra long when he would have pulled back. No matter what happened between her and Jason and with her mother, her father loved her.

"Darling," he said to Tori when Pace took her seat. He sipped Tori's drink before kissing her on the cheek like a precious possession. Pace knew he thought of Tori as an untouchable diamond, worth more than he could ever pay. She needed to remember that her father's behavior—his groveling to meet her every demand—had always been his choice.

"Where's my son-in-law? I saw the kids in the study and they said he wasn't here."

"He's flying in from Chicago this afternoon. He'll be here in a little while." He raised his brows at Tori. *Just because she keeps you on a short leash doesn't mean I have to do the same for my husband*, Pace wanted to shout. She put her drink down. A few more sips of that and she wouldn't be able to stop herself. She only hoped Jason was in the right frame of mind to pretend everything was fine for a few hours.

Colin sat on the opposite end of the couch and crossed his legs. Jason hated it when he sat like that. He said it wasn't manly. "Your mother tells me you're going to start working again."

"Freelancing from home."

Tori cleared her throat. "If you need extra money, sweetheart, you know all you have to do is ask."

Thank God Jason wasn't around to hear her quip about money. He hated it when they offered to help out. "There're strings attached, Pace," he always said. "And I won't be their puppet."

"We don't need money, Mom. I like to work and now that Mitchell's in school, it gives me something to do."

"How is Jason's business?"

"Busy, which is why he isn't here yet. He's got a couple of big projects going on right now."

"Colin?" Tori gave her husband a saccharine sweet smile, one that clearly meant he was about to be dismissed. "Why don't you go check on the boys so Pace and I can have a few minutes to talk?"

He nodded, hopped up from the couch, and sauntered into the foyer toward the study. They both knew they wouldn't see him again until they went looking for him. "Subtle, Mom. Why don't you just tell Dad you'd like to grill me for minute?" Pace resented the way she treated her dad and yet they never talked about it. Was it any wonder she'd ended up in therapy?

She was granted a reprieve from Tori's questions by the highly unexpected appearance of Trey Conway, her father's campaign manager and Pace's high school boyfriend.

"Trey?"

His Italian suit seemed nearly iridescent in the sunlight and Pace could only imagine the look on her face as he moved to embrace her in a hug. "Pace, you look beautiful as always." He held her at arms length. "I see your mother didn't mention I was coming."

To describe Trey as handsome would be like calling Georgia's summers balmy. He'd always been as smooth as he was good looking and all Pace could think when she saw him was why, why, why did he have to be there today of all days? Jason couldn't stand Trey. He'd hated him in college, hated that he now worked for her father, and hated that he was forced to deal with someone she'd once had a relationship with, no matter how many years had passed. Jason conjured up some of his grandfather's favorite sayings when talking about Trey. He'd called him slicker than snot on a doorknob, useless as tits on a bull, and, her personal favorite, that Trey thought the sun came up just to hear him crow. The fact that he described Trey in those terms only exemplified the differences between them. Her father loved Trey and she knew her mother had had high hopes they'd eventually marry. "No, she didn't. How are you?"

"I'm very well. Tori." He gave her mother a kiss on her cheek and she beamed under his spell. "You're the picture of holiday cheer."

"I'm glad you could join us, especially considering Colin is the reason you're not sailing the Mediterranean with your parents."

"And miss an invitation to the legendary Whitfield Thanksgiving?"

"What's going on with the campaign?" Pace asked. Her father's senate bid was usually nothing more than a forgone conclusion.

Trey returned his eyes to her after accepting a drink from her mother. "There's a young state senator from Gainesville who's going to announce his candidacy before Christmas." He took a sip and winked. "We've got a lot of work to do."

"Daddy hasn't had serious opposition in awhile. Are you worried?"

Trey shrugged as if the suggestion were ridiculous. "He's young and spouts off about change and the next generation as if your father's two decades in Congress mean nothing. We're...adjusting our strategy, that's all."

"Mrs. Whitfield?" The housekeeper said from the doorway. "May I see you for a moment?"

"Certainly." She rested a hand on both of their arms. "I'll just be a moment."

Pace watched her leave and sat down. Trey followed suit.

"So, how have you been?" Trey asked.

"Good. I was just telling my parents about some freelancing I'll be doing after the first of the year."

He eyed her suggestively over the lip of the ruby red tumbler her mother pulled out every year for the holidays. "I never could see you happy as a suburban housewife."

It was a jab, one he volleyed whenever she saw him, and one she expected. She knew Jason's feelings about Trey were mutual. "I am happy, I just want something of my own now that Mitchell's in kindergarten."

"Ahhh, the children. Are they here?"

"In the den watching football. We let them out of their cages on major holidays."

"Pace…" He reached his arm along the sofa and touched the ends of her hair.

She tilted her head out of his reach. She should have taken a seat in the chair where he wouldn't be tempted to pull one of his stunts. "What are you doing?"

He reached for her hair again and shrugged when she stood up. "It looks like you've dipped the ends in gold."

"Pace." It was Jason, standing in the archway. From the look on his face, he'd witnessed Trey's attempt at flattery. Shoot.

"Jason." She walked toward him on unsteady legs and reminded herself she had nothing to feel guilty for. "You're back early."

"I went standby." He breezed past her and whispered as she reached him, "Surprised?" He stood in front of Trey, but didn't offer his hand.

"Jason, you remember Trey Conway?"

They looked like two prize fighters, eyeing each other from their respective corners. Trey, the blonde golden boy and Jason, her dark knight. It would have been funny if it wasn't so...not funny.

"Jason," Trey said jovially. He couldn't resist stoking the fire. "Glad you could join us."

"Am I interrupting?"

Pace grabbed Jason by the arm and ushered him to the bar. "Don't be silly. Let me get you a drink."

Tori came back in and engaged Trey in some conversation that, from the snippets Pace overheard, involved the club and one of Pace's old sorority sisters. Jason stood next to her, quietly furious, nearly quaking with anger. When she poured him a bourbon, he nudged her aside and poured more. It splashed over the sides of the tumbler when he threw in three cubes of ice.

"How was your trip?" Good Lord, she sounded guilty. *Get a grip, Pace.*

"Fine." He looked over her shoulder at Trey and she wouldn't have been surprised to see him vaporize under the intensity of Jason's gaze. When he zoned back in on Pace, he flicked his eyes over her like he was checking to see if she looked disheveled. "Keeping busy while I've been away?"

There was no mistaking what he implied. "Jason...that was nothing. You know how Trey likes to flirt."

"Actually, Pace, I don't. Why don't you enlighten me?"

The boys rushed in to greet their father. They dragged Jason toward the study where one of their favorite singers was performing the halftime show. Pace felt both relieved he was gone and upset she couldn't defend herself. She knew she shouldn't, but as she glared at her mother practically salivating at Trey's feet, she blamed her for causing yet another rift in her marriage.

* * *

Colin walked up to Jason and handed him another drink that could have singed the hair from his body. He could always count on a good buzz at the Whitfield house. At dinner, after a lengthy blessing from Colin, the staff presented them with a picture-perfect turkey. Jason was usually bothered by the overabundance of food for their small gatherings, but today he didn't care. He needed food to stem the alcohol in his otherwise empty system. All he could think about was his wife and her ex and the possibility that she'd had an affair with him.

Pace sat next to him, quiet as a mouse, while her former boyfriend and possible lover sat across from them filling in the awkward breaks in conversation. He'd expected Pace to overcompensate in front of her parents, but she just sat there, moving food around her plate. Guilty, was all he could think. She was guilty as sin and uncomfortable with the fact that her husband and lover were sitting at the same table.

He'd actually spent the better part of his business trip thinking about their marriage and all the things Adam and Dr. Falcon had said before he'd left. He came home early because he wanted to talk to Pace, maybe pull her outside in her parent's garden and tell her that he was willing to move beyond their stalemate. Jesus, what a fool he'd been.

"So, Jason," Colin began his usual interrogation. After all the years he and Pace had been together, his father-in-law's tone and questions still pissed him off. "Pace tells us you've got two big projects going on right now."

"Yes, Sir. I just came from Chicago and I'm heading to New York tomorrow."

The kids groaned and Dillon actually dropped his fork onto the china. "Dad, you just got back."

"I know, bud, but I've got to go. I'll be home Saturday."

"The game," he said with a huge smile. Obviously Pace hadn't told them they'd have to skip their planned trip to the Georgia-Georgia Tech game.

"I don't think we're going to make it this year, guys." The look on their faces was enough to make him want to change his flight right then.

"Why don't you come up with us?" Trey said to Pace. "There's a big group going up early, some guys from the club and their wives. You know most of them." Before Jason could tell him what to do with his offer, Pace flashed Jason a sheepish look and said, "We're going with some neighbors, thanks."

He stared at her profile. It never occurred to him that she'd go without him.

"Becky called yesterday to see if we were going." She shrugged and looked down at her plate. "They've got a tailgate with tons of kids. The boys will have fun."

"Great." Jason glanced up to find Tori staring at him. If she expected him to make a scene, she was going to be disappointed. "You guys will have a great time."

"Daddy, I want you to come," Mitchell whined.

"I won't be back in time, but it sounds like you'll have fun. Just bring back a victory."

The topic of football led Colin to a story about meeting a former professional player running for Congress, which led to another Washington insider story, and had Jason reaching for his wine. His father-in-law didn't know when to turn it off and Jason wished he'd just shut the fuck up. If he started in on one of his anecdotes where he, as chairman of the ethics committee, had to ride in and save the day, Jason would get up and leave. He found himself sneaking glances at Pace and Trey. They looked so good together it made him sick. Trey was the perfect match for the senator's daughter and had never missed the chance to mention that Jason was way out of her league. When they'd first met, at some barbeque Pace insisted he attend back in college, Trey actually had the nerve to tell him to enjoy her while he had the chance, that he'd be there for her when she'd finished slumming. The only reason Jason hadn't punched him was because, for some stupid reason, he didn't want to embarrass his girlfriend. He should have broken his nose.

Of all the people he'd been trying to imagine her cheating with, he never even thought about Trey Conway. How many times had he made comments to Jason about how tight they were growing up, about how much in love they were in high school, about how close he was to the Whitfields' and to Colin especially? How many times had Jason walked in on him with his hands on Pace in some seemingly innocuous way, seen him watching her at social functions, listened to him talk to their friends about the good old days when they were a couple? Trey was an asshole with a capital A and Jason would have, before seeing them together, said he was the least likely candidate for an affair with Pace because he'd always been so obvious with his intentions and she'd always laughed him off.

And now they were going to be at the game in Athens together, able to socialize, or whatever they were doing, right under his nose. Every decision he'd made on the plane ride back, every vow to forget about the pregnancy test and the email from her doctor, went up in smoke as he watched the two of them together. Seeing Trey there, at the table, in his in-law's house on Thanksgiving, felt like salt in a gaping wound. It was time to call in the cavalry and he didn't mean Dr. Falcon.

Jason got home Saturday a good five hours before Pace and the kids got back from the game. He'd torn the house apart looking for evidence against her. By the time he got home, he'd convinced himself she was having an affair with Trey and, although he didn't find anything at home, he couldn't stop searching for the truth. He ran a finger over the number he'd scrawled on a notepad: Frank DeAngelo, Private Detective. According to DeAngelo's web page, he specialized in infidelity. Photos, reports, twenty-four hour surveillance. What a way to spend your days and nights.

As Jason looked over his website, he thought about what a huge step this would be, what a breach of trust it would feel like to their marriage. But if hiring a private detective proved she wasn't having an affair, he'd live with the consequences if Pace ever found out. He really hoped she didn't find out. DeAngelo's fees list read like a take out menu: one price for half-day surveillance, extra fees for travel and unexpected expenses, hourly fees where everything was a la carte, and there was even a GPS option, the most economical choice of all. He wouldn't have been surprised to find a link to coupons for buy-one-get-one-free or fifty percent off for those unfortunate bastards in a second or third marriage.

Frank DeAngelo didn't sound gruff and world weary like Jason had imagined, but normal, like an accountant. He listened while Jason told him about their situation, practically congratulated him on narrowing the suspects down to one, and suggested the GPS option with a couple of half-day surveillances for a time when he'd be out of town. When DeAngelo advised him to look on his website for the signs of infidelity, a staggering list of nearly forty items, Jason could only attribute six, most of which were pretty random. The six out of forty seemed too small to really matter, but the pregnancy, her lies, and Trey Conway tipped the scales and, before he knew it, he'd agreed to send DeAngelo a thousand dollar retainer. A little peace of mind was putting a serious dent in his wallet.

CHAPTER 16

"What is it, Tor? I'm swamped right now."

Tori heard the irritation in her husband's voice, even through the background noise that reminded her of the early days of his first campaign. She vividly remembered the sense of anticipation they woke to every morning, sometimes on the floor where they'd either passed out or made love the night before when the passion of what they were doing needed a release. This was why she hadn't told him she knew about Heather, despite her vow to confront him after Thanksgiving, and why his affair made complete sense. The long hours, the infectious sense of doing something important, the way everyone banded together. It was hero worship and, for the first time, Tori could understand why a young woman like Heather would be drawn to Colin. At that very moment, she convinced herself his affair was an offshoot of the campaign and not a real threat to their marriage.

"I'm sorry to bother you at the office, but we've barely seen each other in days. I need to talk to you."

"I don't know when I'll be able to slip away. Trey's arranged a handful of interviews and that's on top of everything else."

She suppressed a sigh of impatience. It was difficult to understand his tunnel vision when she was outside the tunnel. "I'll wait up for you then. It's important."

It was after midnight when Colin came home. She could tell by the sound of his footsteps in the hall he was tired and he confirmed it when he entered the bedroom with his coat in his hand and his shoulders slumped. For the first time in a long time, she thought he looked old.

"Hey." He squeezed her foot under the blanket and threw his coat over the chair. "I didn't think you'd still be up."

She closed her book and took off her reading glasses. "You look exhausted."

"It's a good kind of exhausted." He unbuttoned his shirt and headed into the closet. When he emerged pulling a t-shirt over his head and wearing pajama pants, she felt a stir of desire. Competition, it seemed, was good for both of them.

"I'm worried about Pace."

Colin cocked his head to her great irritation. *We only have one daughter*, she wanted to scream. Couldn't he focus on anything but the campaign? "What about Pace? She looked fine at Thanksgiving."

"She looked the exact opposite of fine at Thanksgiving." She pulled back the duvet and stood up to plead her case. "Didn't you notice the bags under her eyes and the way she and Jason were together?"

"No."

She sighed dramatically and was reminded of her daughter's theatrics. Pace obviously got her flair for the dramatic from her mother. "There's something going on between the two of them, I know it."

"Okay…" He went into the bathroom to brush his teeth and she followed.

"I need you to talk to her, see what you can find out."

"Me?"

Toothpaste pooled at the corner of his mouth and he looked like an overgrown child. "You know she won't talk to me," Tori pleaded. "She'll think I'm interfering."

He spit into the sink and wiped his mouth. "Then why do you think she'll talk to me?"

She'd spent so many years insisting Colin take an active role in his daughter's life, scheduling time for them to spend together, arranging dinners and lunches out, buying special gifts for Colin to give to Pace, all in an effort to make up for her own lack of a father. But in doing so, she'd somehow managed to diminish her standing in Pace's life. "She adores you." She let him pass and they faced each other with the bed between them. "A little prodding from you will seem like nothing more than fatherly concern. She'll tell you what's going on."

"I don't think so, Tor." He pulled back the covers and got into bed. "We don't talk about stuff like that."

"Which will make her more compelled to put you at ease or empty her conscience. Please, Colin. I'm really worried."

"Honey, I don't know that I can fit this in right now. I'm going back to Washington at the end of the week and with the campaign…"

"Colin, you know I wouldn't ask if I didn't think our daughter was in trouble. I've come to accept Jason into the family, but if he's making her unhappy…"

"Okay, okay. I'll call her and set up a lunch." He slipped down under the covers and let out a big breath as if she'd asked him to negotiate a peace treaty. "But I don't think she'll tell me what's wrong—if there even is something wrong."

She got into bed and turned out the light. Too wound up to sleep, she stared up at the tray ceiling and watched the fan spin round and round. "There's something wrong, alright. I just don't know what it is."

* * *

Pace was surprised to see Sherry at her door Tuesday morning, her daughter Katie on her hip, a knowing look in her eyes. "Can I come in?" she asked when Pace just stood at the door.

"Yes, of course." Pace moved out of the way and followed her as she headed for the kitchen. It was a mess, dishes piled high in the sink, the boys' breakfast plates still on the table, the coffee pot off, but not cleaned out. She'd spent so much time obsessing about Jason that she couldn't seem to get anything done.

Things had been better between them before Thanksgiving. Before Trey and his antics. Trey had cornered her outside the bathroom and asked if there was trouble in paradise, like a breakdown in her marriage was something she'd discuss with him or joke about. And of course Jason had seen them coming out of the small passage together, another encounter Trey may or may not have orchestrated that she was left to explain. It was hard to explain something to someone who avoided speaking to you.

Sherry looked around at the mess and then set Katie down at the only free spot at the table and pulled a container full of cheese cubes and applesauce from her bag. "Well, I guess I shouldn't worry about Katie mucking up your usually pristine house. What the hell is going on with you, Pace?"

Pace leaned against the sink in her pajamas—flannel pants, tank top, and old sweatshirt—and wondered how to answer. Was Sherry mad because she hadn't called her in awhile or that she didn't immediately step up and agree to be room mom when no one else would? "What do you mean?"

Sherry let out a big breath as she scanned Pace from her slippers to her bed-head. "You look like shit, you totally avoided me at the Wilson's party, and I haven't heard from you in weeks. What gives?"

"Nothing." Pace tried to think of an excuse that would keep her off her back. Her foggy mind went blank. "I've been busy." Her attire and the state of the house proved Pace a liar. She was sick of pretending nothing was wrong. She'd rather Sherry think she'd turned into a lazy slob.

"You haven't returned my calls."

"Did you call?" Truth was, she hadn't exactly checked the machine or answered the phone in awhile.

"About a million times. Pace, honey, what's wrong? Are you sick?"

The last time Sherry had wanted to know what was wrong she thought she was pregnant. Now she didn't know what she was. "No, I'm not sick."

"Then what is it?"

"Nothing." What else could she say?

Sherry looked at her, picked up Katie's spoon when it fell onto the floor, and rinsed it off at the sink before passing it back to her daughter. Pace could tell by the look on Sherry's face she wasn't done with her interrogation. "Seems like Jason's working all the time lately."

"He's busy, yes." Where was this going?

"Honey." She turned Pace to face her. She was pretty, with her blond hair and dark blue eyes. They looked brown sometimes when the light wasn't bright. "Are you and Jason having problems?"

Pace knew this was coming. She knew the phone lines had been burning up with gossip that the Kelly marriage was on the rocks. She'd gotten snide looks at the grocery store, heard the whispers when her back was turned at school or at the bus stop, but hearing Sherry say it made her want to throw up. She'd lie to her if she could, tell her straight to her face that she was wrong, nothing was wrong, make her feel ashamed for asking. She wasn't sure how much longer she'd be able to sustain the facade. The truth, in its own damning way, seemed like the easy way out.

"Why would you ask me that?" Pace turned her back to Sherry and walked into the den. When she sank onto the couch, Sherry took a seat in Jason's favorite chair and cast quick, but worried glances between Pace and Katie, who still sat the table chomping away.

"My sister said she saw you and Jason coming out of a therapist's office. A marriage therapist."

Of course, in a city of millions, Pace couldn't go anywhere without being seen. And yet Jason believed she'd pulled off a secret affair?

"What happened?" Sherry asked.

Pace shrugged and didn't say anything. She wanted to tell her, but she didn't want to tell her. It seemed like everyone already knew, but telling Sherry would confirm the rumors and start in motion something she might not be able to stop. "I don't want to talk about it, Sherry. I can't."

Sherry stared at her for a moment, then asked, "Is there anything I can do? Do you need anything?"

"I know it's all over the neighborhood. I'd appreciate it if you didn't talk about it, would appreciate you encouraging everyone else to butt out."

"People are worried," Sherry said. "I'm worried."

"There's no need. Whatever is going to happen will happen with or without the whole neighborhood being in on the dirty little details."

"I won't tell anyone the details if you just want to talk." She frowned at Pace. "You really look like you could use a friend."

She could use a friend. She'd tried calling Amanda, not that she was the most sympathetic of her friends or that she was in any place to hear about her marriage troubles, but she already knew. It wouldn't seem like she was doing something wrong in discussing it with someone who already knew and was familiar with their therapist. Amanda had been out of town, with Paul she'd assumed.

"Is Jason cheating on you?"

The surprise on her face was probably vivid and, for some reason, she almost laughed. When Katie screamed to get down, Sherry snapped up and brought her into the den. "You don't have to answer, Pace. Just know I'm here for you if you need me."

Pace stood up and hoped Sherry would take the hint she wanted her to leave. "I hope you'll keep this between us."

"Yes, of course I will." Sherry stopped at the door and turned to face her. "Please call me if you need anything, to talk or get out for awhile."

Pace appreciated her offer and told her so before she went. She knew what Sherry thought as she loaded up her daughter in her new minivan. "Glad it's not me," she probably said to herself as she headed back home to her nice little life.

Pace waited at the soccer field for Mitchell and Sherry's son Stetson to finish with practice. Winter had taken a three day reprieve as it sometimes did in the South and the mid-sixty degree temperatures had brought everyone back outside. As the boys dribbled balls between cones, Pace walked to the playground to check on Dillon and his friend Jack. They swung from the swings and giggled like a couple of girls. She smiled at their innocence and silently thanked Sherry for letting Jack come along.

She and Dillon usually kicked a ball around or she helped him with his homework during practice, but lately he'd asked to sit in the car and read. Normally she'd have been thrilled he wanted to read, but she knew it wasn't a newfound love of books that had instigated his request. He didn't like to be around her one-on-one anymore. She heard him laugh as he pumped his legs on the swing and physically ached for her loss. Of all the things this mistake had cost her, she never imagined it would include the carefree laughter of her children.

As she turned back toward the playing field, she spotted Lynda Daniels, an old neighbor who had moved to a smaller house after her divorce. Lynda sat on a bench while her two daughters played in the sandbox. She'd cheated on her husband with a contractor they'd hired to update their kitchen. Her affair, the discovery, and subsequent divorce had been fodder for months and spread like wildfire through the neighborhood and school. Lynda had been ostracized by friends, acquaintances, and even strangers.

More shocking than the affair was that it was her, seemingly the least likely person in the neighborhood to cheat. Lynda was understatedly pretty, with the kind of classic looks and dress of conservative, yet stylish women. Her husband was a big time stockbroker and if either of them were to cheat, he certainly seemed more likely. Pace remembered hearing absurd stories about how she and the contractor spent their time together, most unsubstantiated and probably untrue.

Pace fell into the acquaintance category with Lynda, their kids having spent a year in kindergarten together. She stared at her now. Lynda wrote something in what looked like a journal, glancing occasionally at the girls. She seemed peaceful and healthy, not at all like the gaunt woman who used to slink around town after her affair became public knowledge. Pace had heard from someone she was still with the contractor.

Lynda turned her head and saw her staring from where she'd leaned against the fence. *Caught*, Pace thought and stood upright. She knew Lynda recognized her, she could see on her face and in her eyes that she expected Pace to turn around and pretend she didn't know who she was. A few weeks ago, she probably would have. But now, looking at her, knowing she'd survived what Pace was in the middle of, she couldn't ignore her. She walked to the bench and cleared her throat.

"Hey, Lynda." Pace brought her hand to her chest. "I'm Pace Kelly. We live in Hidden Forrest and my son Dillon was in your daughter's class at Parkside."

Lynda gave her a weak, skeptical smile. Without an invitation, Pace took a seat on the bench at the opposite end where she sat. "How have you been?"

She watched Lynda take a breath, with her eyes on her girls, and let it out slowly. "I'm fine, Pace. How are you?"

For such a simple phrase, one usually devoid of meaning, she'd packed a punch into *fine*. Pace had never passed along gossip about Lynda, but she sure did hear enough about it to feel guilty. "I'm…" She paused and while she struggled with how to answer, a fine line built between her brows. What the heck was she doing? She didn't know this woman, she didn't owe her anything that her own fine wouldn't cover, but somehow… Pace shrugged and turned her head toward Dillon as he and Jack jumped off the swings and ran for the monkey bars. She could feel Lynda's eyes on her like a heat lamp. "I'm okay. Are your girls doing well at Loring?"

Lynda looked at her warily. "Yes, Loring's a good school. They've adjusted to everything very well."

Why was she talking to her? What did she hope to gain from reaching out? "Parkside's the same. We lost some good teachers this year to the new school. Mrs. Brennon left." Lynda stared at her like she was crazy, like she couldn't care less that her daughter's kindergarten teacher wasn't teaching at the school her kids didn't attend anymore. "Your girls look good, happy."

"They are. We are." Lynda turned her head to look her in the eye. Pace twisted her clasped hands in her lap. "It was a rough couple of years, but we're doing better now."

Pace smiled weakly. "I'm glad to hear it."

"Mommy," her youngest daughter interrupted. "Can we go over to the swing set?"

"Sure, sweetie. I'll be right there."

As her daughters ran off toward the two swings Dillon and Jack had abandoned, Pace felt the weight of Lynda's stare. "Heard things haven't been so good with you lately." Pace felt the blood drain from her face and her hands began to shake in her lap. She stared at Lynda, looking for the sarcasm her comment should have been delivered with, but there wasn't anything on her face that gave her away. Lynda shrugged. "I still keep in touch with a few of the old neighbors. Seems like you're their latest victim."

"Oh, I..." What could she say? It wasn't like they were in the same boat. Lynda cheated on her husband and Pace hadn't, but she felt a strange affinity with the woman who shared the bench with her, like she was the only person in the world who could sympathize with her current situation. "Things aren't so good right now."

Lynda glanced down at her journal, closed it, and looked around for her daughters. "People don't understand what goes on in someone's marriage. They think everybody's biggest worry is what to have for dinner." She peeked at Pace and whatever she saw on her face kept her talking. "I was lonely. He worked all the time and when he wasn't working he was playing golf or out with the boys. It's no excuse, but...Steve paid attention to me. We talked about stuff, he listened to what I had to say." Lynda flashed a wicked grin. "He still does. Nobody understands what it's like to fall in love, really in love, when you're not in a position to do it. Leaving Ben wasn't nearly as hard as dealing with the women in the neighborhood."

Pace didn't know what the bigger revelation was, that Lynda knew all about her marital problems or that dealing with the gossip had been harder than ending her marriage. "I'm glad you're doing better, Lynda, but I...things are different for me. I didn't cheat on Jason and I haven't fallen in love with anyone. I still love my husband and want to be with him."

Lynda laid a hand over Pace's and looked at her like she was a naive fool. "It doesn't make any difference to other people what you did, if you did it, or if you're happier now. People you thought were your friends, thought would stand by you, use your life and your problems to be center stage for awhile…and it hurts." She pulled her hand away and tucked her journal into a bag by her feet. "But trust me, when it's all over, you'll know who your real friends are."

Pace heard the kids chant the end of practice cheer and stood up with Lynda. When she glanced back at the field, she saw two of her neighbors huddled together talking. When they noticed Pace watching, they looked away. Lynda's gaze followed. "Good luck," she said and walked away toward her girls and her new and improved life.

* * *

The puppy got out of the backyard occasionally and he'd been gone for awhile before Jason realized he hadn't heard any barking or scratching at the door. When he went to investigate, he found the gate wide open. Shit. He grabbed the leash, told the kids to tell Mommy he'd gone to look for the dog and not to leave the house. On his second trip around the block, he saw Glen Early in his driveway, watering a bush that looked dead.

"Glen?" Jason watched the water arc from the hose to the driveway before Glen smiled and shut it off. "Cooper's on the run again. Have you seen him?"

Glen ambled toward where Jason stood on the sidewalk. "No, but I've only been out here for a few minutes. How long's he been gone?"

Jason scanned the street with his eyes. The sky was getting dark and the streetlights had just come on. There was no telling where Cooper had wandered off to. The kids would be frantic if he came home without the dog. "Not sure. If you see him, would you give me a shout?"

"No problem." Jason turned to continue his search when he felt Glen's hand on his arm. "Listen, Kelly." Glen ducked his head and seemed embarrassed. "I heard about you and your wife. You need anything, just let me know."

Jason couldn't have been more shocked if Glen had sprayed him in the face with the hose that dangled by his side. He stared at Glen, completely thunderstruck. Glen looked at him, waited for some sort of response, but Jason couldn't think of anything to say. After a brief nod Jason walked away.

What the fuck? How the hell did Glen Early know about their marriage problems? He stormed home, no longer bothering to look for the dog. Stupid dog wanted to wander around, let him figure out how to get home.

Cooper sat on the front porch when he got there, panting and wet up to his trunk. "Stupid dog." Jason opened the door a crack to call the boys. "Guys!" They came running. "Cooper's been in the creek. I need you guys to give him a bath. Go turn on the shower in Mommy and Daddy's bathroom and I'll carry him in."

Once he'd gotten both boys and the dog in the shower and changed his shirt, Jason went in search of Pace. He found her in the laundry room, humming and folding clothes like June Cleaver. He said her name loudly, and she turned around, surprised, clutching a pair of Mitchell's underwear to her chest.

"Jason, you scared me."

"Glen Early just told me he was sorry about me and my wife." Her already pale face lost all its color. "How the hell does Glen know we're having problems?"

"I…" She let out a defeated sigh. "It's around the neighborhood. Sherry told me everybody knows."

"You told Sherry? Jesus, Pace, why don't you just put it on a billboard?"

"I didn't tell her. Her sister saw us leaving Dr. Falcon's office and she put two-and-two together."

Jason stared at his wife, pallid, withdrawn, guilty. "How does *everybody* know?"

"I don't know." She looked back at her neat stacks of laundry. One for her, one for him, one for Dillon, and one for Mitchell. She put the underwear on top of Mitchell's pile and returned his stare. "It probably started at the Wilson's party."

He looked at her and he couldn't believe what she'd implied. "You're blaming me?"

"I'm not blaming anyone. I'm just trying to piece it together."

"Great." He banged his fist against the sink. "That's just fucking great."

Pace gave a startled gasp and blinked with surprise. She gripped the washer as she stepped back. He rarely cussed in front of her and he usually kept his explosive temper on simmer. "The boys are in the shower with Cooper. I'll be back later."

"Jason, wait. Please don't go. We need to talk about this."

He turned around and stared at her. She stood in the hallway, her arms crossed over her chest, and batted her big brown eyes. His little Tinker Bell. How could she stand everyone knowing their business? How could she seem so calm?

"Why doesn't this bother you? How can you stand the fact that everyone is talking about us?"

"It does bother me, but I don't know what to do about it. I asked Sherry not discuss it with anyone."

"Sherry has the biggest mouth in the neighborhood!"

Her arms dropped to her sides and her hands balled into fists. "Jason, I don't know how to stop the gossip any more than I know how to convince you I've been faithful."

"So I guess I'm the one with the problem." He whirled around and kicked the dog's squeaky toy across the kitchen on his way to the garage.

"Where are you going?"

He didn't answer, grabbed his keys from the counter in the kitchen, and peeled out of the driveway. He headed west along a series of back roads that led into the less populated parts of town. Horse farms and pockets of wild, undeveloped land dotted the route. The temperature had dropped into the low fifties, but Jason kept the window down, hoping the cool, clean air would clear away his confusion.

He didn't give a shit what people thought, but he knew that if everyone was talking about them, it would get back to the boys. He sure as hell didn't want them to hear the gossip. He'd grown up listening to people whisper behind his back. *"There's that poor Kelly boy whose parents took off and left him."*

The gossip had come to a head in the sixth grade when big mouth Johnny Thompson thought it'd be funny to call him an orphan. Jason had shoved Johnny hard in the chest only to have the world's biggest eighth grader slam his head into the edge of an open locker. He'd bled like a stuck pig, but somehow managed to land a punch along Johnny's jaw before getting peeled apart by Mr. Stephens and sent to the principal's office. Jason gripped the steering wheel with one hand and fingered the scar at his hairline with the other. The only good thing that came out of the ordeal had been the end of the whispers and a sympathy French kiss from Susan Littleby.

He hadn't told anyone but Adam about their problems and Pace had told Amanda and now one of the biggest busybodies in the neighborhood. It felt like another betrayal. If she needed someone to talk to, wasn't that why they were seeing Dr. Falcon? Why the hell was he shoveling out three hundred bucks a week?

CHAPTER 17

Jason stayed gone for hours. Pace heard the garage door raise and lower at one in the morning, but he never came upstairs. As she lay in the semi-darkness, the full moon casting weird shadows through the plantation shutters, she wondered if she should go find him, try to talk it out. What would she say? He was mad at her because people knew or thought they knew their private business, but she wasn't to blame for that.

Pace had just started to not be so skeptical about their future, but after Thanksgiving with Trey and now the neighbors, she was back to wondering how they'd survive. She tossed and turned in bed and at three, she flipped back the covers and went downstairs. She was going for water, she told herself as she peeked into the open guest room door and saw the neatly made bed. She paused at the base of the stairs and glanced into the den. The TV was on with the volume down low and Jason sat in his chair, his feet crossed on the ottoman. He'd fallen asleep and his head hung half on his shoulder and half on his chest. His neck was going to kill him in the morning.

Pace walked silently over the carpet to stand before him and watch the gentle up and down of his chest. He looked so much like Dillon when he slept, his lips pouted, his hands folded over his chest. *Oh, Jason, what's happening to us?* She didn't want water, she didn't want to go back upstairs and crawl into that damn empty bed. She just wanted to curl up next to him and lay her head on his chest, feel his breath on her skin. He slept a step away from where she stood and it felt like he was a million miles away. Pace pulled the throw from the back of the couch and gently placed it over him and cut off the TV. With one last look, she headed back upstairs because what she wanted really didn't seem to matter anymore.

Her father called and asked Pace to meet him for lunch at the Ritz. It was something they used to do a lot, their father-daughter outings he'd called it, but they hadn't made time for it in over a year. She instantly assumed her mother had put him up to it after the disastrous Thanksgiving dinner, but she never considered turning him down. Pace needed a good dose of fatherly love right now, especially since Jason was out-of-town again and barely speaking to her thanks to Glen Early.

Colin had arrived on time and sat at his regular table, tucked in a corner along the restaurant's wall of windows and thick panel curtains. He was so handsome, her dad, even more so now that his hair was peppered with silver. He stood up as Pace approached the table, ushered the host away, and pulled her chair out himself.

"Sweetheart, I'm glad you could join me." He kissed her cheek before taking his seat and straightening his tie. "I wasn't sure you'd come with everything you've got going on right now."

"I'd never turn you down, Daddy. You know that."

"Well, I'd hoped not." After the waiter left with their drink order, Colin turned to Pace, his expression grim. "Tell me what's going on with you and Jason." She felt stunned at his bluntness. Their conversations had always meandered from topic to topic, even when one of them had an agenda. She was about to say, "Nothing," when he held up his hand to stop her. "Don't tell me nothing because I have eyes, my darling daughter. You're hurting."

Oh, God. She wanted to crawl in his lap and cry all over his expensive suit, damn the restaurant diners and propriety. He must have seen the stricken look on her face because he covered her hand in his and patted it lightly before letting go.

"We're...working through something, Daddy. It's...complicated."

He chuckled and took a sip of his water. "Yes, marriage is rather complicated, isn't it?" He stared at Pace for a long moment before speaking. In that pause, she thought he was going to tell her something, some secret that would make it all okay, something that would lead her down the path of redemption with Jason. "Pace, honey, your mother and I are worried about you. We've always been so proud of you, making your way through life, forging ahead on your own. We want you to know that if you need us, if you need support—of any kind— we're here for you. We don't want you to feel like you don't have options."

Pace sat back in her chair and stared out the window. She watched cars creep along Lenox Road and a few people leave the mall across the street, but nothing registered but what her father had just implied. Her parents had endured the ups and downs of marriage for almost four decades. If she wasn't mistaken, her father had just told her it was okay to leave her husband if she decided to—that not only was it an option, but one he would support. "I'm not sure I understand what you're saying."

"Sweetheart, you know we love Jason."

The picture he'd begun to paint came into startlingly clear focus. And it was ugly. Pace was upset with her husband, but she sure didn't want her parents to blame him. Their tenuous marriage might not withstand that kind of pressure. "I know you tolerate him, for my sake."

"Honey..."

"Look, Dad, I love Jason. We're going through something right now, something hard, but I have absolutely no intention of leaving him. None. If Mom wants to take this opportunity to push me in that direction, she's going to be very disappointed."

The waiter arrived with their food, Pace's favorite crab cake sandwich with apple slaw, and she couldn't have eaten if she'd had a gun to her head. Her father had no problem talking about divorce amid bites of his rare filet as if they were discussing the weather. "We're not encouraging you to do anything. It was very clear at Thanksgiving that you're not happy." He blotted the corners of his mouth with his napkin and nodded to a passing patron. "As I was saying, you know we love Jason, but if he hurts you or makes you unhappy, we're going to side with you, every time."

Could Pace have alienated anyone else while she was at it? Her father's only goal was to console her, to let her know he cared. "I'm sorry, Daddy. I didn't mean to suggest an ill motive." Her father loved her, offered his unconditional support as he'd always done, and she threw accusations in his face while he tried to soothe her. "I'll be fine. We'll be fine."

"That's all we want for you, Pace."

They finished their meal in silence. She moved food around her plate and thought about the nose dive her life had taken. She was playing right into her mother's hands. If she didn't snap out of it and take control, she'd end up spending the rest of her days dodging appropriate suitors from good families deemed worthy by her mother. She could actually envision her mother assigning points based on ex-wives, children, country club memberships, and board connections to the area's finest private schools.

As Pace left the restaurant, through the luxurious lobby where she'd spent quite a bit of time in her youth, with her father at the table awaiting another appointment, she felt…exhausted. She was exhausted from worry, exhausted from half-truths and dimmed explanations. What Pace wanted, what she really wanted, was to crawl into bed with her husband, the man who promised to love her, who did love her despite his misgivings, the man whose pride was wounded and who was hurting as much as she was. When he got back from his trip, she was going to throw herself at him. She'd taunt and tease and badger and do whatever she had to do to get him into bed. They needed each other right now.

She'd thought her father could solve her problems, appease them with his understanding words and comfort, but the only person who could comfort her was Jason. She needed her husband more than ever.

* * *

Jason stopped by the office before heading home from the airport. It was late and he needed to get home; he'd been gone for three days, but was anxious to check his email and see if there was any word from the private detective who, according to Jason's instructions, was supposed to trail Pace this week while he'd been gone.

After he logged onto the computer, he found a recent email from Frank DeAngelo containing a detailed description of Pace's whereabouts and the people she'd encountered on each day of surveillance. Day one was pretty standard stuff: grocery store, dry cleaner, neighbor's house. Day two was a meeting in Midtown with two people, a man and a woman. Jason's fingers started to tingle as he clicked on the attached image, only to realize it was a work meeting when he saw Amanda and a man he sort of recognized from Pace's old office. DeAngelo's report stated the lunch lasted a little over an hour and it appeared to be some type of business transaction, with files passed around and Pace leaving alone. Day three she had lunch at the Ritz with an older man. DeAngelo reported they kissed and hugged when she arrived and then did a lot of hand patting. Son of a bitch. An older man couldn't have been Trey, but who the hell could it have been? He clicked on the image and blew out a big breath when he recognized his father-in-law. The picture showed them in the Café, huddled together at an intimate table as if sharing gossip. Pace didn't look particularly thrilled to be there, which seemed odd considering she worshiped the ground her father walked on. He checked the photo carefully, made sure Trey wasn't lurking in the background, waiting for Pace to finish and lure her away to one of the hotel's luxury suites. Trey was nowhere in sight and the report stated she left after forty-five minutes and went straight home.

Jason felt relieved and…guilty, very guilty for having her followed. If Pace was having an affair and he'd been gone for three whole days, wouldn't she have made time to see her lover while the coast was clear? The attached bill for DeAngelo's services, a whopping three grand, made him wonder if his money would have been better spent with Dr. Falcon, whom he hadn't seen in weeks.

He was about to flip off the computer when he saw an email from Bisbain, his client in New York.

Dear Jason,

I've attached the latest notes from Mr. Bisbain and Mr. Thompson from your recent meeting. Mr. Bisbain would like for you to look them over and let him know if there is anything that needs amending.

On a personal note, you looked really tired when you were here last week. I hope you're getting some much needed rest and staying warm in this cold weather.

Hope to see you soon,
Deborah☺

He reread the email sent from the receptionist. It sounded so inappropriate, her using his first name and yet calling her employers by their formal names, actually including a personal note commenting on how he'd looked at the meeting. He'd never had someone behave so unprofessionally and yet it made him feel guilty instead of mad. Had he provoked her somehow? Did she know what a distraction she was whenever he saw her?

She was twenty-three. She'd told him the last time he saw her when she was smoking outside the building when he'd come in. "You'd think at twenty-three I'd know better than to do this," she'd said with a lift of her shoulders. "I'm quitting." She'd stomped on the half-smoked cigarette. "I'm down to two a day."

A twenty-three-year-old knock-out sent him personal notes where, if he wasn't mistaken, she was flirting. In her last email, she'd commented on the tie he wore on his first trip to New York. He'd been tempted to write back that he'd be sure to thank his wife, who'd bought the tie, but instead he'd let it go. And so the emails continued.

Had he given off signals that his marriage was on shaky ground? Had he looked as lonely as he felt? Was she desperate? He couldn't respond to the email, couldn't lead her to think he wanted any sort of personal relationship with her, but if he were being honest, he'd have to admit he felt a little thrilled at the attention. He and Pace, for all intents and purposes, were no better than roommates.

He'd woken up in the middle of the night before he'd left and wandered into their bedroom. He'd stood at the door and watched her sleep, her arm tucked under her pillow and her hair all around her face. He'd thought back to the first time they'd woken up together, in his tiny apartment on that squeaky double bed he'd had. He'd woken up first and watched her eyes open, watched her confusion change to delight when she saw him. Her cheeks had turned red even as she'd smiled. She'd looked like he felt when he'd woken up and found her in his bed, like he'd had the best dream and realized it wasn't a dream.

Jason had wanted so badly to kiss her, to rub his hands under her gown and be inside her before she fully woke up. But he'd just watched her sleep and went back to the guest room. It wasn't just the sex he missed and he *really* missed the sex. He missed Pace and everything they'd had together.

He'd been thinking about what Dr. Falcon said. He needed to decide. He may never have proof and he sure as hell couldn't spend three grand a week having her followed every time he left town. He wanted to believe her and Falcon was right—Jason wouldn't be in therapy or living with Pace if he really thought she'd cheated. Trey was just up to his old bullshit and Jason had played right into his hands. He should send DeAngelo's bill to Trey.

At one point during a session with Dr. Falcon, not long after Pace had discovered he was widowed with a kid, when Jason asked him if he thought she'd cheated, he really thought he was going to call him a selfish bastard because he was throwing away something Falcon would kill to have back. He saw it on his face, in a quick look and an impatient gesture before he collected himself and told Jason to decide. As he stared at the computer screen, where a young girl's attempt at flattery made him confused, he was ready to put it all behind him and start over. There was never really an alternative.

CHAPTER 18

Pace heard the garage open from their bedroom just above it, felt the floor vibrate as if she was standing on an electric razor, and took a deep breath. It was after nine on a Thursday night and the kids were in bed and sound asleep. She looked at her reflection in the mirror and hoped her attempt at seduction would work. She ran her hand over her stomach and felt it glide over the silk negligee that was Jason's favorite, watched the red material shimmy in the dimmed light.

She'd lit candles and the scent of black current lingered in the air, hopeful and sexy. *Please*, she silently prayed as the door downstairs opened and closed, his footsteps moved to the stairs, slow with the weight of his carry on. If he didn't wander into their bedroom to see what smelled good, he should at least have to unpack.

Pace stood by the bed as candlelight flickered over the room. The door was cracked, waiting, inviting. First she saw his fingers, the tapered ends pushing open the door, then all of him. He looked a little bit dangerous standing in the near dark, his expression unreadable. He didn't enter the room or move away, but just stood there in the doorway with his suit coat folded over one arm, his tie loosened, the top button undone. He set his suitcase down and stared at her.

What did he think? Could he see her heart rapping beneath the thin material? Could he hear the breath enter and exit her lungs as if she waited for a punch? Could he see the tremble in her hands and legs?

He stepped inside the room and then turned to close the door. She thought she heard the click of the lock, but couldn't be sure what she heard over the drum beat of her heart. He walked toward her, slowly, and stopped in front of her. The light flickered over the angles of his face, slid off the slick black ends of his hair. He had just a hint of a shadow on his chin and Pace knew if he gave her the chance, she'd feel the scrape of his whiskers on her skin. He tossed his jacket over the footboard. Her eyelids dropped as his fingers snaked through her hair, as he pulled her into him, into the long length of him, and into his kiss. With one gentle brush of his lips, everything from the past month rolled away like a stone down a steep hill. It was like every kiss they'd ever shared and unlike any other.

They trembled, both of them, their lips hovering, their eyes locked like a couple of gunslingers waiting for the other to make their move. When he said her name, it sounded like a promise whispered in the dark. Pace wrapped her arms around his waist and held him tight.

She ached to feel his skin against hers, taste his flesh, take him inside of her. She could smell the aftershave on his skin, some hotel shampoo in his hair, and as she removed his tie and unbuttoned his shirt, she felt his heart hammer beneath her palms. This was what she'd needed, what she'd missed. Pace didn't want the understanding words of her father, her neighbor's support, or her kids' perfect behavior. She needed Jason. He was all she'd ever needed.

"Pace." He pushed her back against the bed and she thrilled at the intensity of his need. How had she forgotten his hunger? They'd never gone so long without making love, not in all the years they'd been together and they were both ravenous. His touch felt urgent and yet gentle; hurried, but not frantic. Every kiss, every sigh erased all the harsh words they'd said and the veiled accusations. The feel of his breath on her skin, the taste of him, the rough brush of his stubble, brought such pleasure and relief as he fed her with his body. She'd worried all night that if he came to her, they'd fumble or be awkward with each other. She'd worried for nothing.

When Pace's head began to clear and she opened her eyes, Jason had wedged his face between her neck and shoulder, his breath panting in rhythm with her pulse. She ran her hands through his hair and smiled. Her body felt alive and weightless and she could have drifted off to sleep with very little effort. Relief felt like a tidal wave washing over her, leaving her breathless and void of energy. When he tried to move off of her, she gripped him tight. "No, don't leave me yet."

Her husband, her lover, her whole world, lay trapped in the hold of her arms and legs. "I'm not leaving you." In his words, Pace heard a vow of forever, one she had feared would never come.

When she woke, they lay tangled together. Maybe they were both afraid if they let go during the night, the other would slip away. Pace immediately worried that their night together, the hours they'd spent loving each other, wouldn't mean any more to him than a physical release. But when he opened his eyes and she saw in the clear green depths the love she'd always known was there, she started to cry with relief.

"Baby." He kissed away her tears. "I love you, Pace." And then he did, even when they heard the boys waking up, the shuffle of their feet down the hall, the jostling of the knob that Jason had so rightly locked the night before. He loved her and she loved him in return. Her heart, at long blessed last, was whole again.

* * *

Pace sprawled beneath Jason, her legs crossed in a vise against his ass. Her skin looked flushed and her mouth swollen from his. He'd always liked to watch her face after they made love. It was her face he'd noticed first, the big soulful eyes, the flawless skin, the little cleft in her chin. She had only grown more beautiful and he recognized her beauty in their children.

She groaned and stretched her arms above her head before threading her fingers through his hair. "I guess we should get up, get the boys ready for school." But he didn't want to leave the bed or leave her body. She didn't let him go right away, just shifted to look at the clock.

"Urrrrr," she said and dropped her legs, slowly untangled her hands from his hair. Jason didn't move off of her. "It's later than

I thought." They stared at each other. "Are we okay?" she whispered.

Jason nodded and watched her eyes close in relief. She clutched his shoulders and he rolled over to bring her on top of him. He wished they had more time and he was about to say, "Fuck it," when they heard a knock on the door.

"Daddy? Mommy?" It was Mitchell, his voice froggy from sleep. "Are you getting up?"

"I'll be right out, bud," Pace called over Jason's shoulder. She looked back at Jason, her face serious. "I love you so much, Jason. I've missed you so much."

"I know, baby." Jason sat up so they were facing each other. "I'm working through it."

She cupped his cheek with her hand and rubbed her thumb over his chin. He could see in the morning light he'd scratched the delicate skin of her neck. "I'd never let another man touch me, Jason. It's only ever been you."

He believed her. For the first time in weeks, when she said she didn't cheat on him, he believed her completely. He never thought they'd get back to this place, no matter how boggy it still felt, but he was relieved to have come this far.

* * *

Colin's talk with Pace must have changed something because she sounded normal when Tori talked to her, happy even. The fact that she'd called meant things were good. Tori felt more relieved than she thought she'd be. It was like pulling teeth to get information out of Colin about their lunch. "She seemed fine to me," he'd said with a shrug. Colin could barely give her ten minutes when he came in afterward to change and head back out for a dinner she'd opted out of. "I told her we'd support her no matter what she decides about her marriage."

"Did you actually suggest she leave her marriage?" She couldn't believe he'd insinuate that's what they wanted. Jason hadn't been her first choice for Pace, certainly hadn't even been in the running, but to recommend divorce...

"I told her we'd be there for her, no matter what."

"What did she say? Is that what she's thinking?"

He came out of the closet in his tux and asked her to help with his tie. He'd never been able to do it alone. "She said they were going through something, so I guess you were right. Ouch, Tor. Not so tight." He was lucky she hadn't strangled him with it. Whatever he'd said, whatever they were going through must have passed because Pace seemed back to normal.

There was a time, back when they were dating, that she would have done anything to get Pace away from Jason. She and Pace fought during that time more than they ever had and, considering the amount of fighting they'd done while Pace lived at home, it was amazing they still spoke to one another.

Jason had been wrong for her from the beginning, with his cocky attitude and nomadic background. She'd hoped and prayed their dating had been Pace's idea of rebellion. Until they married. God, what a nightmare. Her only child, a daughter no less, betrothed to an absolute nobody with less potential than her fingernail. But he'd proved her wrong. She imagined his degree in architecture only masked his true identity an artistic drifter, but he'd quickly advanced in his field and now worked with a man she'd heard some call a master. She wouldn't go so far to say that she was proud to have him as a son-in-law, but he'd certainly exceeded her expectations, both in making Pace happy and with his career.

If they just didn't live in the suburbs. Tori had been thrilled when they'd decided to stay in Atlanta when they could have settled anywhere in the country, but she'd never understood why they choose their cookie-cutter neighborhood amid chain restaurants and strip malls. Practically everyone else Pace had grown up with lived in town and belonged to the club. It was a little embarrassing to announce where her daughter had chosen to live, as if she couldn't make enough of herself to afford their area. But if that was the worst of it, Tori knew she'd gotten pretty lucky.

Colin had been gone quite a bit lately, stumping through the state and back and forth to Washington, so avoiding her confrontation with him had been pretty easy. If only it was as easy to avoid Caroline. She kept calling, but thanks to the birth of Bethany's third child, she'd been out-of-town and more than a little preoccupied.

She thought Colin had possibly ended his affair or at least she'd hoped he had. They'd made love twice since she'd received the pictures and if he seemed distracted, Tori felt certain it was a result of the campaign and a surge by his recently-announced challenger in a poll. The more Colin reached out to her, the more he insisted she attend this function or that function either with him or in his place, the more she realized her fears of him leaving were unfounded. He needed her, in his heart and in his political corner. His campaign, the very thing that had caused his infidelity over the years, seemed to have sucked her back into his life. She tried very hard to feel grateful.

CHAPTER 19

Jason felt like a two ton weight had fallen off his shoulders. He and Pace were back to normal, for the most part. He never realized how quiet the house had been in the last month until the boys returned to their boisterous selves, wrestling, fighting, and laughing. It was so damn good to hear them laugh again. Even the dog seemed to have calmed down.

He grabbed Pace from behind Saturday afternoon while she was doing the dishes and kissed her neck. "What do you say we sneak off to the bedroom?" He looked around the corner at the boys watching cartoons in the den. "They'll never notice."

He could feel her heart pounding beneath his fingers and saw her pulse jump along her neck. She had the sexiest neck, all soft and slender. Everything about her was soft and slender. "Jason…"

When she turned around to face him, he could tell it wouldn't take much for her to agree. He smiled as he stared at her, remembering.

"What are you smiling at?" she asked.

"I was just thinking about the last time we made love in the middle of the day."

A little line formed between her brows and then the corners of her mouth twitched. "The closet."

Jason nodded. "The closet." A year ago, maybe, Mitchell had started waking up in the middle of the night and calling for them. He had sonar, Jason used to think. Every time he'd reached for Pace, had worked them both up into a frenzy, Mitchell either sauntered into the room or started howling from down the hall. Jason had come home early one afternoon because he seriously thought they'd never make love again. Pace was going through the kids' closets, pulling out clothes that didn't fit, rearranging toys and blankets. He'd found her in Mitchell's tiny walk in closet, up on a step latter, her shirt rising over the waistband of her pants as she reached for something on the top shelf. She screamed when he startled her, screamed again as he made her come. Her feet never did touch the ground.

Jason pulled her away from the kitchen amidst her half-hearted protests. "The bed, now. And neither one of us is leaving until we absolutely have to."

They were halfway up the stairs when the phone rang and she sagged back into his chest. "I'll get it," he said and turned Pace in his arms to look her in the eye. "You'd better be naked in bed when I get there."

He heard her jog up the stairs giggling as he answered the phone in the kitchen.

"Just the man I was looking for."

The nasally sound of Frank DeAngelo's voice was the last thing Jason expected to hear on the other end of the line. "DeAngelo?" He glanced behind him toward the empty staircase. "I thought I asked you not to call me at home."

"No choice, Mr. Kelly. I need to speak with you about something important."

Jason positioned his body so he stood by the kitchen pantry door, the only spot where he had a clear view of the stairs and into the den where the boys still sat in front of the television. He peeked up the stairs, relieved to find no sign of Pace. She'd probably gotten naked by now. "I got your email and I've authorized payment. Was there a problem with the card?"

He coughed into the receiver and Jason pulled the phone away from his ear. "Card's fine, but there is a problem. It's about the fee. I'm afraid it's going to be a little more than we discussed. Well," he said with a chuckle, "quite a bit more."

"You've already sent the invoice. How can the fee be more than we discussed?"

"I've got some more pictures. You're going to want to see them, but you're going to have to pay for them first."

"More pictures? Why didn't you send them with the invoice?" Why was Jason treating this like a business transaction gone wrong? More pictures meant more evidence against Pace. "What's in the pictures?"

"Like I said, Kelly. You pay first."

Shit. He'd figured out how to hide the three grand, but more… "How much?"

"I'd say they're worth at least fifty."

"Fifty *thousand*?" Jason rechecked the stairwell for Pace after almost screaming into the phone. "You're out of your mind."

"Figure I could get more on the open market. Your choice."

Mitchell came into the kitchen and opened the refrigerator to graze. "What are you talking about?" Mitchell handed Jason a Gogurt and he opened it with his teeth, smiled, and ushered him back into the den. Neither one of them remembered he wasn't allowed to eat out there. "What open market?"

"You didn't tell me who I was following. Your wife's Senator Whitfield's daughter. I almost didn't catch it at first, but I sure am glad I went out on a limb after their fancy lunch at the Ritz."

"I'm not paying you fifty thousand for something I haven't seen."

"I'll give you a preview, but it has to be in person. And you'd better bring the cash."

"When?"

"Three o'clock. There's a diner on the corner of Cypress Street and Sixth."

"Today?" Jason wiped his sweaty palm on his jeans and ran his fingers through his hair. "I can't get fifty thousand dollars in cash today."

"Hey, I'm giving you three hours to figure it out. So figure it out. Three o'clock. Don't be late."

He gave Pace a lame excuse about a work emergency and made it to the bank two minutes before they closed. He was willing to beg, borrow, or steal the money, but on the way to the bank he remembered the escrow check from the Belton farmer he'd deposited just a week and a half ago. Fate, certainly a cruel twist of it, seemed to have a hand in the twenty-five thousand dollar cashiers check sitting on the dash of his car as he pulled into the dump on the corner of Cypress and Sixth. It wasn't enough, but hopefully DeAngelo would accept it as down payment or a good faith investment until he closed on the land at the end of the month. Jason prayed it would work because it was all he could get.

DeAngelo sat alone in a booth near the back of the diner along a filthy stretch of wood paneling that looked like it had come right out of a 1970's basement. He acknowledged his approach by sitting up and slinging an arm along the red vinyl back. "You're punctual."

Jason slid into the seat across from him. "Where are the pictures?"

DeAngelo's eyes darted to the lone waitress, picking at her nails behind the counter and flirting with a customer who resembled a gang member. "Show me the cash."

Jason pulled the envelope with the cashier's check from his back pocket and slid it across the table, but didn't let go when DeAngelo tried to yank it from his grasp. "The pictures."

The detective cocked his head and pulled a letter size envelope from the inside pocket of his coat. "These are just a preview." Jason snatched it from his hand and pushed the cashier's check out of DeAngelo's reach. "And they're copies."

Jason's hands were shaking as he removed the black and white photographs of what he assumed were Pace and Trey from the envelope.

Shock. That was the first emotion he registered when he was able to think at all. DeAngelo must have gone for the shock factor when he decided to place the particular photo on top of the stack. It took a moment to recognize Colin's naked ass thrusting into someone who was definitely not his wife. He flipped through the rest quickly, just to be sure there weren't any of Pace and felt both relieved and disgusted to realize they were all of his father-in-law.

"You think I'm going to pay fifty grand for this?" He shoved the pictures back into the envelope and flung them across the table.

"Aren't you?" DeAngelo seemed almost cocky as he carefully folded the envelope and placed it back in his pocket. He linked his fingers together on the tabletop.

"Those are disturbing, DeAngelo, but they don't concern me."

His brows shot up. "Your father-in-law is banging some cheap whore and it doesn't concern you?" He laughed and for some reason Jason noticed his perfect teeth. They must have been capped. "I'm sure your wife would be very interested in these pictures. I'm sure the senator's wife and his constituents would be very interested in these pictures. Oh, wait a minute." He held a hand mockingly over his mouth. "I'll bet the press would be interested in these, too."

Jason sat back and stared at the sleazy private detective who'd found his wife innocent and who'd condemned him to hell. He was right, of course he was right. While Jason personally didn't give a damn that his father-in-law, chairman of the congressional ethics committee, had the morals of a horny teenager, Pace sure as hell did. And so did his kids. And so did Tori. Fuck.

"I want all copies and originals, including your camera's memory card." DeAngelo nodded without a second thought and Jason knew he was getting played. But what the hell else was he supposed to do?

"Hand over the check."

Jason released it from his grip and saw he'd smeared the ink on the bank's logo.

"This is only twenty-five," DeAngelo said under his breath. "I said fifty."

It's also my future. "It's all I could get my hands on with such short notice. I'll have the rest in a few weeks."

"Weeks?" DeAngelo laughed and tapped the check against his open palm. "I've already asked around, kid. I could get twice what I'm asking you. If you don't have the cash, the deal's off."

Panic, swift and sharp as a knife blade, filled his gut and had Jason grabbing DeAngelo by the sleeve of his coat as he pushed his considerable girth from the booth. "Wait a minute. Just wait a damn minute."

"I don't have a minute." DeAngelo yanked his arm free and straightened his coat. "And I sure as hell don't have weeks." He threw the check onto the table and a five dollar bill for the cup of coffee he hadn't touched and sauntered to the door with surprising speed for someone his size. How in the hell did he blend in with a crowd? Jason wondered as he watched him get into his late model sedan and pull out into traffic.

The waitress, ready to collect her money, came up to the table. "What can I get for you, honey?" She swiped the five and the cup in one swoop.

A do over, Jason wanted to say.

A big fat mulligan.

Jason felt dirty as he drove to the Whitfield estate, like the detective's sleaze had smeared all over him, on his hands, under his fingernails, like even if he'd tried to pretend he didn't know what was coming, there'd be no way to hide the truth. He had to warn Colin, but the thought of admitting what he'd done—to Pace and inadvertently to her father—made Jason nauseous. He felt like he'd played a part the Whitfields had created for him years ago: total fuck-up and good-for-nothing son-in-law. It may have taken sixteen years to shine in his role, but he sure as hell outdid himself.

The house looked as it always did, perfectly manicured in the late afternoon sun. There sat the trellis he'd tried to climb up to get to Pace's room one night and had almost killed himself. He never admitted to her he'd tried to sneak in, but failed, even after she'd questioned him about all the scratches he'd gotten from the rose bushes. Seemed like a pattern, him trying to be her knight in shining armor and never quite making the grade. This time there wasn't anywhere to hide and no way to lie about his mistakes. Facing the music wouldn't be so painful if he didn't know the Whitfields had been waiting for him to fall short all these years.

He was surprised when Tori answered the door in a fancy jogging suit and reading glasses. She pulled them off and let them hang at her chest by a jeweled chain. "Jason? Were we expecting you?"

"No, Tori. I'm sorry for interrupting." More sorry than she would ever know.

She let him in the foyer and, after shutting the door, turned to face him. "You're not interrupting."

"Is Colin around?"

She glanced over his shoulder just as Jason heard Colin's loafers on the polished marble floor. "Jason." Colin heartily slapped his shoulder. "This is a surprise."

He had no idea. Jason returned his handshake. "If you've got a minute, Colin, I'd like to speak to you."

He eyed his wife inquisitively and winked at Jason like the politician he was. "Sure, sure, always have time for you." He led him into the study and, as if he knew Jason would like some privacy, shut the double pocket doors behind him. The study had always intimidated him, with Colin's law books lining the walls and the dark country club furniture. Jason felt like a caddy who'd been summoned for a scolding. Colin took a seat in one of the Chippendale chairs by the fireplace and looked up at Jason quizzically. "What can I do for you?"

He was sweating even though they kept the house cold, so cold Colin wore a sweater with his perfectly pressed slacks. Jason felt ridiculously casual in his jeans and ratty t-shirt. He ran both of his hands through his hair and blew a breath out of his mouth. Because he couldn't sit still—and hadn't been offered a seat—he began to pace back and forth in front of the fireplace where he could spill the ugly truth without having to look Colin in the eye.

"I hired a private detective to follow Pace while I was out-of-town last week. He took some pictures of you at the Ritz after you'd had lunch with Pace. Some…" Christ, how did he say this? "…damaging pictures. He asked me to pay him fifty thousand for them, but I could only come up with twenty-five. He said he could get more elsewhere. He called it the open market. I thought you needed to know."

Colin sat as still as a statue in the chair, his fingers laced together over his crossed legs, staring at Jason as if he'd just sung the national anthem slightly out of key. Colin said nothing, his expression gave nothing away. He finally stood up and walked over to the desk in the corner. He picked up the phone, dialed a number, and after a moment said into the receiver, "I need you here. Now. There's a situation." He paused, said, "Fine," and hung up the phone. He sighed and turned to look Jason in the eye.

Now Jason could see the rage on his face under the veil of his normally affable expression. There was a vein pulsing on his forehead and his fists were clenched at his sides. "What were you thinking having Pace followed? Do you really think my little girl deserves to be stalked around town like some kind of cheap whore?"

It was everything he expected to hear and yet it still stung. "Colin…"

"Do you have any idea what you've done? Do you have any idea what kind of effect this will have on my campaign?"

It took him a few seconds to realize he'd said campaign and not marriage. Silly, naive Jason, he thought Colin would have worried about his marriage.

"I'm sorry, Sir. I didn't want to have to tell you. I didn't want my mistake to turn into your problem."

"You." He pointed his manicured finger in Jason's face. "You've never understood your role in this family. You've never understood what you signed on for when you married Pace."

He was so sick of hearing about the responsibility of being a part of the Whitfield family. "With all due respect, Senator, I married Pace, not you and your wife."

"One and the same."

He snorted his disagreement and was about to argue his case when Trey burst through the doors and shut them before turning around to sneer at Jason. Just when he thought it couldn't get any worse.

"I should have known." Trey panted breathlessly and his normally perfect hair looked tussled.

"Do you live here now?" Jason asked.

Colin moved to stand between them and focused his attention on Trey. "Jason hired a private detective. He's got pictures of me and a woman."

Jason almost enjoyed the look of shock on Trey's face. Almost.

"What the hell were you thinking?"

"Look," Jason leaned over Colin's shoulder, "I'm not answering to you, you son of a bitch."

His pale cheeks turned red with anger. "You'll do whatever I want you to do."

Colin held his hands up between them. "Just calm down, both of you." He kept a hand to Jason's chest and looked at Trey. "What do we need to do?"

Trey flicked his hair from his eyes and looked at Jason like he'd just keyed his car. "Who's the detective?"

"Frank DeAngelo. He wants fifty grand for the pictures."

"Did you see the pictures or did he just tell you he had them?"

Jason cast a quick glance at Colin. He was afraid he'd never be able to forget. "I saw them."

"Fuck." Trey paced toward the window and turned back with a jerk. "Did you refuse to pay?"

"I didn't have enough and he said he could get twice as much on the open market."

Trey slapped his face with both hands. "You are such a fucking idiot, Kelly. Dammit!" He pounded his fist into the desk and reached for a notepad. "Give me all the information on DeAngelo. Phone numbers, email, everything."

Jason pulled out his blackberry, flipped through his contacts, and wrote down everything he knew. He pushed the pad toward Trey.

"What were you hoping to gain by having Colin followed?"

Colin sniffed at Jason before he answered, "He had Pace followed. I'm just a side benefit."

"Pace?" Trey laughed mockingly. "You had Pace followed?" He shook his head and smirked. "I always knew you were trouble. I always knew you'd bring her down, but this… Colin's got real competition for the first time in years. This could blow us out of the water and implode the whole campaign." He glided over to stand in front of Jason, hands on his hips. Jason would have known by the smell of him—the cut grass and sweat smell—that he'd been on the golf course even if he weren't wearing ridiculous madras pants and a bright green golf shirt. What in the hell had Pace ever seen in this asshole? "You'd better hope I can head this off, but know this much; you're going to pay for your stupidity, Kelly. I'll see to it you do."

Colin took a seat in the chair and steepled his fingers. "Keep me abreast of whatever you find out." He dismissed Trey with the flick of his eyes and Trey disappeared through the door.

"Colin, I never meant for this to happen. If I'd known…"

Colin silenced Jason with a steely look that betrayed his casual posture. "I've put up with your less than stellar attitude towards this family for the sake of my daughter's happiness. But now my little girl is unhappy and that alone is reason enough for me to be upset with you. When you throw in the detective…" He shook his head. "I'm taking off the kid gloves, Jason. Trey's not the only one with an ax to grind now. If I go down, you go down."

* * *

"What in the world was that all about?" Tori asked Colin when he finally reemerged from his study after hours on the phone.

"Nothing. Just some snafu with a press release."

"What does Jason have to do with a press release?"

Colin seemed startled, like he'd forgotten about Jason's visit and Trey's abrupt entry and exit. He made a beeline to the bar in the den.

"He needed a favor. Some zoning variance he's having trouble with." He waved his hand in front of his face and took a gulp of scotch. "I told him I'd make some calls."

Tori watched him refill his glass and take another sip. "It's a little early for cocktails."

"Not after the week I've had." Colin paced to the windows and turned around in a fury. "That damn Stan Michaels. He's never been more than a county commissioner and he's mounting a full fledged run for my seat. *My* seat. This country is at a turning point and the last thing we need in the Senate is a wet behind the ears upstart who wouldn't know a real crisis if it bit him in the ass."

Something more than a snafu had lit his flame. She hadn't seen him this upset in years. "Are you really that worried about losing your seat?"

"Hell yes, I'm worried." He slammed his drink on a side table and pumped his fist in the air. "People are tired of the status quo, no matter how hard I've fought for their interests. When is this country going to wake up and realize the problem isn't the politicians, but the whole system—the same system that allows a person with no experience, no background, and not a lick of sense to vote on important legislation that shapes their lives? The man doesn't even have a law degree! He couldn't decipher a bill with a year and twenty Harvard aids to help him."

"Colin…" She moved toward him and he waved her away.

"I'm alright, Tori." He ran his hands through his hair and let out an exasperated breath. "This whole damn election has me tied in knots. I haven't had competition in so long I guess I've forgotten how it weighs on me." He attempted a weak smile. "I'm too old for this."

"Old?" Tori laughed and tugged him over to the couch. "You look better now than you did during your first term." She reached out and ran her hand over the streaks of gray by his temple. "People will see through his rhetoric before the end of the year, you wait and see." She was ridiculously grateful to be able to comfort him, not to be the vulnerable one. She leaned over and kissed his lips. They tasted of scotch and fear.

He pulled her into a hard hug. "I love you, Tori. I need you."

It was everything she wanted to hear. "Then show me."

CHAPTER 20

Jason had been acting...weird ever since he'd dragged Pace to bed and then announced after a phone call he had to run to the office for some sort of emergency. He came back a few hours later looking like he'd been wrestling with demons. When she'd asked him about what had happened, he'd shrugged it off and said he'd taken care of it.

But something wasn't right with him.

He'd been going to work, coming home, and playing with the boys and he even agreed to go Christmas shopping with Pace—something he hated to do. At night when they'd slip into bed, he reached for her in a way that felt...different. She couldn't put her finger on it exactly, but there was a desperation to his love making that left her unsettled and unable to sleep afterward. She had started to think things were back to normal and now things just seemed strange.

During the last week the kids were in school before Christmas break, Pace managed to ferret some time for lunch with Amanda. She hadn't talked to her about anything personal since they'd started seeing Dr. Falcon. She'd talked with her on the phone several times about work, but Amanda knew she and Jason were back together.

"So everything's back to normal?" Amanda asked as they dove for a free table at the crowded deli around the corner from her office.

Pace knew what she was asking, but things seemed so far from normal these days that she hesitated before saying, "Yes, as normal as they can be."

"What does that mean?"

"I mean things are crazy right now. I told you Jason's planning to leave the firm. He's working around the clock and with the holidays…"

"Pace," she interrupted. "I mean your marriage. I've been seriously worried about you two."

She knew Amanda wanted to talk about her marriage and reconciliation, but for some reason, she didn't want to talk about it. At their last session with Dr. Falcon he'd said, "There's been a breach of trust in your relationship. You've faced it head on and are starting to heal. What I don't want is for you two to pretend it didn't happen, pretend that everything is fine, because you'll end up right back where you started if you don't acknowledge what you've been through and how far you've come. You've got to keep talking about it and how you feel when you hit a bump in the road."

As Amanda waited patiently for her to give details, his words echoed in her head. They were doing exactly what he'd told them not to do. It was like they'd wiped the slate clean and they didn't ever mention what had happened or what got them there. So talking to Amanda about something she and Jason avoided like the plague seemed…weird. "We're fine. Better than fine." Pace took a big bite and watched Amanda's eyes narrow as she chewed. "In fact," she rambled on, hoping she'd drop it, "we haven't been so close, physically, since college. We can't keep our hands off each other." That wasn't exactly true, nothing could compare to the crazy, lustful state of new love, but compared to how they'd been a few months ago, their sex life had definitely recharged. Besides, Pace felt like the marriage merchant of doom and she needed to throw Amanda some nugget of hope as she skipped toward the altar.

She didn't seem appeased. "So…you never mention it? It never creeps up on you?"

"What?"

"The fact that he thought you cheated? The fact that he didn't believe you? The fact that neither of you trusted each other for about a month?"

"Oh..." Pace felt like Dr. Falcon had sent her to check on them. She tried to shrug it off. "It doesn't come up."

"It doesn't come up?" Amanda nibbled at her turkey club before putting it down. "How can it not come up?"

She should have known Amanda couldn't be thwarted. "We're busy, the kids are thrilled we're getting along...we don't want to rock the boat." She popped a chip in her mouth and glanced around the restaurant. Couldn't someone drop a tray or choke on some food? She really needed a lifeline.

"Are you sure he's past it?" she asked. "I just don't buy that it never bothers him. What if you don't answer your cell phone or...or you go out with your girlfriends—he doesn't think, for just a second, that you may be with someone else?"

Her patience with Amanda's line of questioning quickly evaporated. "First of all, whose side are you on, anyway? And second of all, I sure don't have many girlfriends left."

Amanda backtracked before Pace had even finished her uncharacteristic show of annoyance, her hands lifted in the air above the table. "I'm on your side and you know it. It just seems...I don't know, unhealthy to act like you didn't go through something so big."

Amanda took another bite of her sandwich and studied her. Pace could almost see the wheels in her head grinding. She wiped her mouth and reached her hand across the table where Pace's hands lay limply beside her plate. Her appetite had vanished. "Pace, I'm not bashing you or Jason, I just don't see how this doesn't come back to bite you over and over again. I don't see how Jason can have his reputation and his manhood questioned like that and then just shrug it off. There isn't a guy on the face of this earth who wouldn't let stuff like that eat away at him."

She couldn't stand to hear her friend's logic. Maybe because it was Amanda, someone who wasn't even married yet, that made hearing it so upsetting. "So what are you saying? I should try to bring it up, initiate conversations about how he's feeling and if he's still worried I'm running off every free second to have sex with some other guy?"

"Don't get pissy with me. I'm just saying..."

"Yeah, well…after you've been married a few years, then we'll talk."

Amanda straightened in her seat and Pace knew she'd hurt her friend. She hadn't even asked about Paul and the wedding plans. She sure couldn't ask now. Amanda switched into work mode, bringing up the clients most likely to give Pace trouble, what projects needed more attention than others, her tone stilted. When the waiter came and took their plates away and Pace saw her rooting around in yet another designer bag for her lipstick, she knew she only had a few minutes to try and undo the mess she'd made earlier.

"Amanda?"

She glanced up, but continued pushing things aside in the huge purse.

"I'm sorry. I appreciate your concern and your honesty. I know you're right. I just don't know how to broach the subject."

Amanda sighed and pulled out a tube of red lipstick. "You're like watching a train wreck, Pace, and I'm about to get on the train." She uncapped the tube and expertly applied a fresh coat without a thought. She smacked her lips together and tossed the lipstick back into her purse. "It's a little bit scary."

"How are the wedding plans coming?"

She rolled her eyes, but behind the bluster Pace could sense her excitement. "Crazy. Even with me trying to keep it simple it seems to have taken on a life of its own."

"They have a way of doing that."

"You know, the worst part is the thought of meshing our families together. You know how simple my parents are? Well, Paul's family is Upper East Side New York. I just keep having nightmares of his mother speaking to mine like she's the help."

Pace laughed and thought of the look on her mother's face when she'd told her about the rehearsal dinner. Tori had gasped and clutched her chest. Pace thought she'd given her mother a heart attack. "You'll get through it, Amanda. We all do."

Pace left the restaurant feeling securely back in Amanda's good graces, with an armful of research, and the very distinct feeling she needed to talk to her husband.

The strangeness continued when Tori paid a surprise visit one afternoon, just a few hours before the boys got home.

"Mom?" Pace opened the door and found her standing on the porch wearing a bright purple overcoat, her hair and makeup picture perfect. She followed her mother's gaze as she silently critiqued her yoga pants and t-shirt. Her expression all but said, "You're a complete disappointment to me." Pace felt instantly irritated. No one could get under her skin the way her mother did without even saying a word. "What are you doing here?"

"Can I come in?" The wind blew a section of her hair over her eyes and she swiped it away.

Pace stepped back and closed the door behind her. Tori stood in the foyer and glanced around the den before taking off her coat. Underneath, she wore black tailored slacks, a white tunic, and a purple print cardigan sweater wrap. She could have come from a charity lunch or shopping at the mall. Either way, she managed to look more put together than if Pace had spent all day trying—which she rarely did. "I didn't know you were coming by. You're lucky I'm home."

She handed Pace her coat, which Pace tossed over the stair rail to her mother's utter dismay. Unfortunately, her coat closet was filled to overflowing with their coats and jackets. "I was in the neighborhood." Tori walked into the den and eyed the piles of magazines Pace had spread over the coffee table. Amanda had her doing some research and she'd just gotten started. "Doing a little reading?"

"No. What do you mean you were in the neighborhood?"

Pace lived about a half-hour north of the city, way outside the perimeter, the highway boundary that separated the haves from the have-nots. Tori never came up their way unless the boys had a game or she'd been invited by Pace, the only person Tori knew who lived in what her mother considered no man's land.

She shrugged and continued to scan the room with critical eyes. "You really need to get some window treatments in here, Pace. I told you before I'd send Marsha up."

"I don't want window treatments, Mom. I like the light and the clean lines of the wood shades."

Tori scrunched her nose. "It just looks so informal."

"We're informal people." Pace moved toward her and waited until she looked her in the eye. "You haven't answered my question."

"What question?"

Her mother was stalling and Pace felt frustrated with the games and the fact that she was intruding on her only time to work while the kids were at school. "Why are you here?"

Tori carefully lowered herself onto the sofa as if the middle class of their house could somehow rub off on her. She sighed down at her lap before looking up at Pace. "I...I take it things with you and Jason are better?"

She'd made a surprise appearance at Dillon's basketball game the prior weekend. She'd watched with curious eyes as Jason rubbed the sore shoulder muscle Pace had pulled while walking the puppy. Tori hadn't said a word then.

"Yes." Pace hesitated to go into the details with her mother. She couldn't tell if she was happy her marriage was back on track or upset that her list of possible son-in-laws would go to waste.

"Good. Your father and I have been very worried about you."

"You needn't be. I'm fine. I'm happy."

Tori looked around the room and Pace did too, trying to see it through her mother's judgmental eyes. The toys, the clutter, the dog hair, all the things that screamed home to Pace probably screamed disaster to her mother. Oh well. She'd never been able to please her.

"Your father's still worried, even after I told him you and Jason seemed to be getting along fine." Tori flicked one of Cooper's hairs from her sweater.

She thought back to her lunch with her father, his willingness for her to walk away from her marriage. "Daddy has nothing to worry about and neither do you."

"Good." Tori slapped her knees and stood to retrieve her coat.

"That's it? You drove all the way up here for that?"

Her mother sighed and pushed Pace's hair behind her ear like she'd done countless times since Pace was a child. "I wanted to make sure my only daughter was doing okay."

"You could have called and saved yourself the trip."

"You and I both know you don't always answer when I phone. I wanted to see for myself."

Busted. "I hope you'll pass on the good news to Daddy."

"Oh, I will." With a brief kiss on the cheek, she breezed out to her car.

Pace wrapped presents in the basement one morning while the kids were at school and Jason was at the office. He'd called not long after he'd left for work to ask Pace to check his desk for a file he thought he may have left at home. She went into his office and found the file, sitting right on the credenza where he stacked his things before shoving them into his case. She'd always been amazed at how clean he kept his work space, when he used the rest of the house as a dumping ground for his shoes and discarded clothes. Whenever she found a food wrapper on the floor or in the den, she was never sure if it had come from one of the kids or from her husband. He thanked her, told her to leave the file on his desk, and hung up the phone.

Pace stood up to get back to wrapping presents when she noticed his trash can was filled to overflowing. The boys had obviously skipped Jason's office on their weekly trash run. She lifted the heaving can in her arms and took it upstairs to dump in the big can outside. She didn't see Cooper sprawled on the hallway rug and tripped over his slumbering body. With all the grace of an NFL lineman, she fell face first onto the floor and lay stunned while trash drifted around her prone body like confetti after a Super Bowl win. Cooper lifted his head and started to lick Pace's face as if she'd just decided to join him in the hallway for a nap. She got up, rubbed her sore elbow which had taken the brunt of the fall, and gave Cooper a smacking kiss before shoving him out the back door. She didn't need his "help" to clean up the mess.

Pace was on her hands and knees, stuffing food wrappers, discarded drawings, and work correspondence back in the receptacle when she spotted a crumpled note card. She opened it up and read the unfamiliar looped handwriting.

> *Jason,*
> *Mr. Bisbain asked me to send you this picture of a building in Salt Lake City. He saw it in a magazine and wanted your thoughts on whether you can incorporate this type of look into your drawings. I would have emailed it, but our scanner is on the blink. I hope to see you before the holidays so I can wish you a very Merry Christmas in person.*
> *Yours,*
> *Deborah.*

Pace slumped against the wall and reread the note over and over again. There wasn't anything in the words that should make her stomach roll the way it decided to do just then, as if the cereal she'd eaten might come back up at any moment. Bisbain was his client from New York. New York was where she had heard a woman call his name from the restaurant the night he'd called, the call that had put her hackles up and had left her suspicious for days. She'd forgotten the phone call until just then as she stared at what may or may not have been evidence against him. *Please, no. Jason, please, please, please no.*

She thought back to the day he'd started acting weird. He'd blamed a work emergency and was gone for hours. No matter how many different times or ways she tried to ask him about it, he gave nothing away. Without even thinking about what she was doing, Pace went back downstairs to Jason's home office and logged onto his computer. She felt guilty for looking through his personal stuff, but not guilty enough to stop. He'd discovered the doctor's email by snooping on her computer.

He was as meticulous with his work on the computer as he was with his office. Every email was filed under the client's name. It only took a moment for her to find Bisbain Mellon and start wading through the forty or so emails. A third of a way down the list she spotted an email from Deborah. She'd put a smiley face next to her name and the tone of the email seemed more friendly than professional. Pace's stomach tightened as she scrolled down and read the rest of the emails from Deborah. There was a snippet of business in each email, but they all contained a personal aside: she'd complimented his attire, the lack of grey in his hair, and his mood on more than one occasion. With each email, her language got more and more personal, so personal, in fact, that if she were standing in front of Pace right then, she probably would have been tempted to slap her. Pace had never struck another person in her life.

Who communicated with clients that way? She switched over to Jason's sent items and read all the items directed to anyone at Bisbain. There were only two to Deborah, both brief and businesslike, but she couldn't help but feel suspicious. As she stared at the emails on Jason's computer screen and tapped her fingers on the surface of his desk, Pace had to wonder if Jason was having an affair in retaliation for her botched pregnancy results. And if he was having an affair, did their abrupt reconciliation and his unusual behavior since have everything to do with guilt?

CHAPTER 21

Pace didn't say anything to Jason about the note or the emails. For days she obsessed about Deborah, wondering what she looked like, how old she was, and what she'd done with her husband. She watched him when she could, took note of when they kissed, if it felt different, if he held her differently, if he orchestrated some new move when they were together. But strangely enough, he'd been more attentive to Pace than ever and she couldn't help but think it was guilt at having been with Deborah that was responsible for the change in his behavior.

Pace checked his emails daily, sometimes twice a day. Once he almost caught her. She'd gone downstairs before bed to put some presents in the closet where they hid gifts and couldn't help but check if there were any new emails. Jason had done about thirty minutes of work earlier in the evening and she wanted with every fiber of her being to know if he'd contacted Deborah or if she'd contacted him. Pace had just logged on when she heard his footsteps on the stairs. She quickly closed out of the screen and made up some lie as she lunged for the hall, telling him she'd smelled something weird and wanted to make sure he hadn't put some food item in the trash. He didn't seem to notice she was lying, perhaps because she suggested he take her to bed and have his way with her. Nothing like a little sex to distract a man.

Later in the week Deborah sent another email—the same stuff, clarification about some email and the ever present "Hope to see you soon." Pace was still sneering at the screen when she scrolled down and saw Deborah's last name attached to her signature before the company name and address. Deborah

Thigley. She logged off, shot up the stairs to her computer, and had executed a Google search within minutes. There was only one Deborah Thigley listed in the small New York town. Pace found an article in the local paper from a few years ago with a picture. She'd been Miss Constilligna County and sat atop the flower decorated float, her double D's on full display even though the image was grainy. Deborah was gorgeous and could have easily hopped on a plane to Orlando and filled in for Belle from Beauty and the Beast at the Disney character breakfast. Crap.

* * *

Jason was walking on egg shells, except he was so damn angry at Colin and Trey he may as well have been stomping. Something, sometime soon was going to break. He felt like he and Pace were circling each other. He kept watching her to be sure Trey hadn't decided she needed to know what he'd done and she watched him because he was acting so...intense. He was freaking her out, Jason could tell, but he couldn't seem to help it. The only way to act natural would be for him to let his guard down and if he did that, he was convinced she'd find out he'd had her followed. Damn it, he'd never consider hiring house painters without soliciting three bids and recommendations from neighbors and he eenie-meenie-minie-moed his choice for a private dick from the internet? What the hell had he been thinking? But who could he have called and asked for a reference?

The more he thought about it and, to be honest, he thought about it all the time, what could Trey do about the pictures other than offer to buy them from DeAngelo? And if he'd done that, and he must have because Jason hadn't heard or seen a thing about any of it in the news or on the web, why hadn't Colin or Trey called and gloated about their success and let him know the danger had passed? Was he supposed to crawl back to Colin and make sure Trey had covered his ass? That would be the day. But the longer he worried about it, the more he let it eat away at the lining of his stomach, the more convinced he became that the other shoe was about to drop.

He was working on the environmental impact study for his client in New York and fielding miscellaneous phone calls when Tarks came into his office and shut the door. He was decked out in his typical taupe suit and Jason's favorite—loafers. He plopped down in a chair uninvited and picked at his nails until Jason got off the phone.

"Kelly." He started talking before the receiver even hit the cradle. "How are things going in New York?"

Tarks had left him pretty much alone on the project and Jason wasn't sure if he thought the scope of the deal was beneath his interference or if he'd given him a wide berth considering his well-known personal problems. Nothing like a little office gossip to keep the boss off your ass. No matter the reason, he was thrilled to be flying under his radar and could feel his stomach muscles clench when Tarks mentioned the project he'd already dubbed solely his.

"Fine." Jason scribbled some notes and closed the file on his computer so Tarks couldn't wander behind his desk as he sometimes did to peek at what he worked on. "What can I do for you?" Tarks just sat there, lounging in Jason's chair as if he had nowhere to go and nothing to do. He must have gotten bored with lording over his employees and checking his image in the mirror.

"Just checking in." He leaned forward, bracing his hands on his knees. Jason could smell his spicy cologne settle over the room. "We've got our big meeting in January to strategize and plan for the coming year. I thought you might be interested to know I've recommended you for partner."

Smile, Jason told himself, act happy. "Well...that's a surprise."

"It shouldn't be. You've been with us long enough and you've certainly proved your worth." Tarks stood up and walked to the door. He turned around before opening it. "Of course, this isn't public knowledge, so I wouldn't discuss it with anyone just yet."

"Of course." Tarks winked and closed the door behind him. Jesus. If he'd known his status as a ladies man would earn him a partnership, he'd have faked a mistress years ago.

Shit. Had Tarks somehow figured out he was planning to leave? But how would he? Jason hadn't said anything to anyone except a former classmate from Indianapolis whose brain he'd picked and he'd specifically asked him to keep it to himself. Damn it. The idea of making partner in this firm was about as appealing as setting his skin on fire, but he'd hoped to have more time before making anything official. They usually announced partners right after the meeting in mid-January, so now he had a deadline to worry about.

He opened up the design for New York. It was too good a project to walk away from. He was going to have to talk to the guys at Bisbain Mellon about his leaving the firm and try to get a commitment from them to follow, which meant another trip to New York. And leaving Pace and the kids for any amount of time was the last thing he wanted to do, considering he didn't trust Colin or Trey to strike while he was away.

Jason's fears were unwarranted, he realized, when he came home that night and found Pace waiting for him when he opened the door. "Hey." She stood in the middle of the kitchen glaring at him with her chin in the air and her nostrils flaring. His mouth went dry and he felt like he'd stepped into an ambush.

"I thought you trusted me!" Her voice sounded thick with righteous anger.

He lowered his case to the ground and shut the door. "What are you talking about?"

She pulled something from behind her back, a manila envelope, and shoved it into his chest. "You had me followed!"

She stormed out of the kitchen and he took a step to go after her, but stopped. He opened the envelope and peeked inside. Black and white 8x10's of Pace shopping, Pace meeting with Amanda and that guy from work, Pace and her father having lunch… A white piece of paper with one printed line slipped out. *Who wants to know what you do when he's away?* Fuck. Jason flipped the envelope over and saw it was mailed locally with no return address.

He should have known.

CHAPTER 22

If Tori had to eat another chicken dinner, she was going to toss her plate against the wall. In the last two weeks she'd had lemon chicken, almond chicken, rosemary chicken, crab stuffed chicken, glazed chicken, chicken, chicken, chicken… Didn't anyone eat red meat anymore?

She glanced around at the people milling about the ballroom of the Intercontinental Hotel. The five-hundred-dollar a plate charity event was packed and she'd made the rounds to just about everyone with whom she'd hoped to get some face time. She felt physically exhausted, but more mentally challenged than she had in years. Politics was a game, a game she'd always been very good at, and a game she'd avoided playing for the last fifteen years. But now, with Colin fighting so hard to hold onto his place in history, she felt as though every conversation she had, every contact she made, every false compliment to the wife of a supporter, was done with a greater good in mind. She and Colin were a team, even on nights like tonight when he couldn't get away and she worked the room alone.

She was about to leave, standing in a short line at the coat check closet, when she was approached by a well known reporter from one of the city's largest television stations. Tori hadn't seen her in the ballroom and was thrilled to have a chance to plug Colin's success with a bill the reporter had once referred to as impassable.

"Deidre, you're looking lovely." As would anyone with a professional make-up artist and a plastic surgeon on retainer. "I simply adore your brooch."

She smiled and in her eyes Tori saw the hint of trouble. Deidre was known to pry where her smarter peers had learned to look away. "I didn't see your husband tonight, Tori. Is he burning the midnight oil again?"

There was something in her question, in the tilt of her head, the lilt of her voice that told Tori she was on a fishing expedition. "There's a lot to be done for the state. You've covered politics long enough to know there's no such thing as a break."

"Oh, I don't know." She grinned and passed the attendant her ticket as Tori's mink arrived. "Seems like Senator Whitfield knows how to recharge his batteries, if you know what I mean."

Tori did know what she meant and so did the attendant, the couple behind them in line, and the security guard smirking only a few feet from where she stood bolted to the ground. *It was only a fling*, she wanted to shout at Deidre after she'd slapped the superior look right off her face. *It's not going on anymore*, Tori screamed inside her head. But as she took leave of the reporter with a scornful glance and slowly, methodically made her way to the valet station, she knew the only one stupid enough to believe it was her.

* * *

How could Pace have thought Jason had simply had a sudden change of heart? That one night of fabulous sex would make him realize she'd never give herself to another man? She couldn't believe it. After hours of looking at the photos that had arrived in the mail, after hours of piecing together what he'd done, she still couldn't believe he'd done it. And the look on his face! The minute she'd said it, the minute she'd shoved the envelope into his chest, he'd known he'd been caught.

She swirled around the den, too keyed up to sit, too upset to do anything but wait for him to come out of the kitchen and explain himself. Ha. There couldn't be an explanation for having her followed. How could he have done that to her, to them?

"Pace...." He'd removed his jacket and loosened his tie. He looked guilty; the shifty eyes, the grim expression, guilt was written all over his face.

"Don't you dare tell me you didn't have me followed. There was a note, just in case I didn't understand."

"I can explain."

Pace lunged for him, her hand outstretched, her finger poking into his chest. "Explain? What a joke!" She'd backed him into the wall, a ridiculous sight for any onlooker considering he was almost a foot taller. "There couldn't be an explanation good enough for this!"

"Pace, please. Just hear me out."

His voice was pleading. The scene was going to get ugly and she felt so thankful the boys had gone to the movies with Sherry. To think she'd been looking forward to an evening alone with her husband. "Just admit it. For once just be honest with me." He ducked his head and ran his hands through his hair. When he looked up and met her eyes, Pace nearly fell to the ground. How did they get so far down this dirty road?

"I had you followed."

She yowled, something between a cry and a scream, and she couldn't stop. Jason seemed alarmed, she could tell by the way he just stood there watching her, his eyes wide. He didn't move, didn't speak. She wanted to hit him so hard he felt like she did, like someone had tilted his world upside down with nothing to hold onto. She wanted to duck her head and ram him in the chest like an angry bull. She wanted to slap him across the face so hard her hand print would be permanently affixed to his cheek. But the surge of unthinkable violence, so unlike anything she'd ever experienced before, left her too confused to move or think or breathe.

Jason finally stepped toward her and she waved him off and took a deep breath.

"Honey, you need to sit down. You need to calm down so we can talk about this."

"Calm down? Calm down?" She laughed and circled the coffee table. She felt tempted to flick the family photo of them across the room. She sat on the couch, crossed her legs, and knitted her hands together over her knee, the picture of demure innocence. "Please, Jason. Join me on the couch and tell me all about the reasons you had me followed and photographed like some kind of low life insurance frauder, like some kind of…cheating scum." She patted the cushion next to her for emphasis and was glad to see from his posture that her sarcasm had lit his short fuse. "Hope you didn't pay a lot of money to catch me dastardly trying to earn some extra money, shopping for those nefarious groceries, or plotting your death with my father." Pace wanted him mad. She wanted them to scream at each other until all of the hurt and fury had escaped her system and she could breathe again.

He stood in front of her, his hands on his hips, and sneered. "You think this is funny?"

"No, Jason, I don't think this is the least bit funny. But I deserve to know why you had me followed."

He breathed hard, twisting his lips together, and Pace knew she was about to get her wish. "When I walked in your parent's house on Thanksgiving Day and found Trey Conway with his hands all over you…" he threw his arms in the air, "…I lost it."

Pace shot up from the couch. "Trey? Trey and his harmless flirtation? Uhhhh. Are we back to this again? What do I have to do to convince you I don't want him, Jason? Take a blood oath?"

"There's nothing harmless about Trey!" he shouted. "And what the hell is a blood oath?"

Pace shook her head and growled in frustration. Now was not the time to explain the bizarre antics of young couples in love as explained by late night cable television.

"You don't have any idea what it's like to have to deal with him," he continued. "How would you feel if every time you turned around you came face-to-face with someone I used to care about? Someone I'd had a serious relationship with? Someone who still wanted to have a relationship with me even though I'm married?"

"Jason…" Pace never thought she'd have to defend herself after what he'd done. She knew he and Trey didn't like each other, but this fury… And what could she say? She'd never even been to his hometown, never met anyone he'd dated before. "I don't care about Trey at all. The last time we were together I was seventeen-years-old. I can't believe you're jealous of a high school romance."

"Do you know how many times I've heard him talk about when the two of you were together? Have you ever noticed how he looks at you? And he's always touching you, Pace, and you never do anything about it!"

"That's not true. I don't encourage him, that's just how he is. It means nothing."

"Well, I hate it!"

"If you hate it so much, then why haven't you ever said anything? Why haven't you talked to me about it or…or… asked him to stop?"

He gave a half laugh and shook his head. "You know I hate it, Pace, just like you know I hate him. And if I asked him to stop, I'd do it with my fists and considering your parents think he walks on water, they'd only hate me even more."

Pace was about to scream back at him that her parents didn't hate him, but she stopped just as the words were on the tip of her tongue. Her mother's feelings had never been a secret and after lunch with her father, she couldn't deny the truth. Her parents may not hate him, but they certainly didn't like him very much. Wasn't that what had led her to seduce him back to bed? "Jason, I don't have any feelings for Trey whatsoever. If you want to punch him in the face, go right ahead."

He snorted sarcastically. "Please, Pace. You'd probably be the first one to coo over his injuries."

"I don't know what to say to you to convince you I don't care about him. I love *you*, Jason. I married *you*."

"He would have you back in a heartbeat. Who do you think sent those pictures?"

Pace fell back on the couch and just stared at him. She knew him inside and out—or she thought she did, before she opened that envelope and her world shattered in her hands. She knew every imperfection on his impossibly handsome face; the tiny chip in his left eye tooth from a fall he took as a child, the mole over his right ear that she teasingly called his beauty mark, the dent in his skull from when his head hit the corner of a locker in his only middle school fight. How could she know all of those things and not know he had it in him to question her love again?

"I don't care who sent the pictures, Jason. I only care that you had them taken in the first place."

He ran his fingers through his hair, let out a big breath, and let his hands fall to his sides. "I shouldn't have done it. I shouldn't have had you followed, no question. I'm sorry."

"You're sorry you did it or sorry I found out?"

"Both."

Pace, who had always thought of herself as above petty one-upmanship, the one everyone described as the nicest person in the world, couldn't accept a simple apology. She couldn't chalk it up to a natural reaction to jealousy. She wished she were a big enough person to let it go, but she couldn't. If Jason could get it all off his chest, then so could Pace. "How would you feel if I had you followed when you were out-of-town? If I had some sleazy private detective watch your every move? What would I see then, Jason? Would I have actual proof that you flirt with your client's receptionists or just the emails I've already read?"

Jason's eyes narrowed as he looked at her; he opened his mouth to say something and then shut it again. He shifted his weight and put his hands on his hips—typical stressed out avoidance move—and then tried again. "What the hell are you talking about?"

"Oh, please. You know exactly what I'm talking about!" When he lifted his hands in the air she said, "Deborah? Don't tell me you've forgotten her name? Or do you just say, 'Ooohh, Baby, don't stop?"

"Pace, really…"

"What? It's okay for you to think I sleep with my high school boyfriend and not okay for me to assume you'd do something with a former beauty queen who practically throws herself at you every time you see her?"

"I've never touched her, Pace. I wouldn't." His even tempered response after her outburst made her feel foolish. Jason stared at her and shook his head. "How the hell did you even know about her emails?"

"You think you're the only one who can snoop?" When she realized she'd compared her snooping on his computer to hiring a private detective, she tried to explain. "I thought you'd worked it out and were ready to move on the night we made love. I thought you'd realized on your own that I'd never look at another man, much less sleep with one. And then you turn all weird and blame it on work. I found a crumpled note from her in your trash can and got suspicious. So I went through your emails."

"That's a little like the pot calling the kettle black, don't you think?"

"I wasn't looking for evidence against you, Jason. I was looking for a way to clear you." Pace had no pride left at this point and rushed ahead with what had been nagging at her for weeks. "I heard a woman's voice say your name the night you called from a restaurant when you were in New York. Was it her? Was it Deborah? Have you...?"

He looked confused, his brows knitted together, and then his expression turned smug. "That was Amelia."

"Amelia?" For a moment she couldn't place the name.

"Your niece."

She felt like an idiot. "You got in touch with Adam?"

"We had dinner with the kids."

Pace felt like the couch had swallowed her up. "You didn't tell me."

He shrugged, lifted his hand to scratch the back of his neck. "You didn't ask."

They stared at each other for a long moment. She didn't know what else to say, what else she expected him to say. At this point, even if he threw himself on her feet and begged for her forgiveness, she wouldn't have been moved. And he sure as heck wasn't tripping over himself apologizing.

"Christ, Pace. Don't you see what you're doing? You're accusing me of the exact same thing I accused you of—cheating on you because of a misunderstanding." He skirted the coffee table and stood above her. "Are we even now?"

She stood up and felt smaller than she'd ever felt before. "I wouldn't need a private detective and some photos to believe you didn't cheat on me, Jason. All I'd need is your word."

"You've got it. I wouldn't lie to you."

She snorted and fell back onto the couch. By the look on his face she could tell he recognized the absurdity of his statement. "I wouldn't lie to you about that."

CHAPTER 23

"I swear to God Trey is going to pay for this." It was all Jason could think to say as Pace looked at him like he was a stranger. That pretty-boy, madras pants wearing fucker was going to pay.

"How in the world would Trey even know about these photographs? How can you blame him for something you did? My God, Jason, didn't the detective exonerate me and Trey?"

He stared at her, so hurt, so accusing. He knew what he did was wrong and he also knew there was no way to explain how Trey was behind the pictures without telling her everything. And telling her everything was going to crush her worse than the photos. But she wouldn't get past this, they wouldn't make it past this if he couldn't be honest. She wanted the truth; she was going to get it. "He knows and so does your father."

She shot to her feet. "My father?"

Jason hated telling her, shattering her illusions about her perfect father. No matter how he spun this, she'd blame him. The messenger would lose again.

"The private detective I hired got some pictures of your father. Trey obviously took care of it so it didn't leak to the press."

Her eyes narrowed and her face looked pinched. "What kind of pictures?"

He swallowed hard and stared into her eyes, willing her to understand without him having to say the words out loud. "Incriminating pictures."

Her breath came out in small gasps, like she couldn't stand what he'd said, like she knew what he was about to confess. He could tell by the look in her eyes that her mind was working a thousand miles a minute trying to figure out how her dad was blameless. "Incriminating how?"

He couldn't say it to her. He just couldn't. "How do you think?"

She shook her head, her eyes wide. "Don't play games with me, Jason."

"Pictures of your dad with a woman."

She gripped the sides of her head with her hands, pressing against her ears. "No," she said over and over again. "You're lying."

"Pace." He moved to touch her, to try and calm her down. She reminded him of the horse that used to live on his grandfather's farm, wild and a little bit crazy. "Why would I lie about this?"

She dropped her hands and her voice sounded low and angry. "I don't believe you."

"Honey, I saw the pictures." They were ingrained in his memory like a brand. "It's true."

Her fists were bunched at her sides and she stared at Jason like she couldn't quite figure out who he was. Was he the man she married, the man who'd promised to love, honor, and cherish her, or was he a stranger hell bent on destroying her life? At this point Jason wasn't even sure. She abruptly turned and walked out of the room.

He followed her into the kitchen. "Where are you going?"

"I need to get out of here." She began searching through the junk drawer for her keys. When she found them, she went straight to the garage door.

"Pace."

She turned to look at him, an irritated line between her brows. "What?"

"Where are the kids?"

"They're at the movies." Her eyes flicked to the clock on the oven. "Sherry will drop them off later." She turned to leave again and Jason lunged forward and grabbed the door.

"Wait just a minute. It's dark out and you don't even have your coat." He looked down at her empty hands. "Or your purse."

"Oh." She reached behind him and scooped up her purse from the counter. When he just stood there and didn't let her move she said, "I'll be back later. Go ahead and feed the kids. There are some leftovers in the fridge or you can make sandwiches." She stared at him as he just stood there blocking the door. He could stop her and they both knew it, but he'd never be physically rough with her, no matter how much he didn't want her to walk out.

"Please don't walk out on me, Pace. We need to talk about this."

"I can't even think right now, Jason." She tugged the straps to her purse over her shoulder and straightened her back. She looked like she was about to break and he wanted to scoop her into his arms and hold her until she was okay, until he felt sure they'd both be okay. But the look in her eyes kept him from even laying a finger on her. He lowered his arm and let her pass. From the entrance of the garage, he watched as she drove down the street and out of his line of sight.

* * *

Pace wondered what her father would say when she asked him point blank if he'd cheated on her mother. She wondered if he'd deny it or if he'd circle back around to Jason and what he'd done. She wondered if she was doing the right thing, confronting him, accusing him, or if she'd be better off, if they'd all be better off, if she just went home and tried to deal with her marriage.

After driving around for hours, Pace found her car in the garage of his office. She heard the click of her shoes on the hard concrete, listened to the familiar ding of the elevator, and felt the ascent in her empty stomach. She hadn't eaten since breakfast, since before her world fell apart, and she felt like she'd been put through the wash and dry cycles of the laundry and was sure she looked about the same. He'd probably gone home, she told herself as she stepped onto his floor and walked toward the glass doors of his suite, but the lights were on and she heard voices down the hall when she entered the eerily quiet headquarters.

His office sat empty and dark except for the spotlight he'd left on the American flag in the corner, but she saw light coming from Trey's office. When Pace approached his door, she saw him behind his desk. He'd loosened his tie, his feet were crossed at the ankles on the desk's surface, and he laughed into the receiver. She wouldn't have been surprised if he was talking to a woman from the flirtatious tone of his voice and the cocky set of his shoulders.

She leaned against the door jam and watched him for a minute, thinking back to all the hundreds of phone conversations they'd had when they were kids. The things he'd talked her into—sneaking out to go to a concert downtown, sneaking in to have fumbling sex under her parents' noses. Trey had dazzled her from the moment he'd waltzed into the country club wearing Doc Martens, khaki shorts, and his trademark monogrammed argyle sweater. Every girl had wanted to be on his arm and under his spell. For awhile, in their little bubble where life meant no more than fancy cars and expensive clothes, they'd been inseparable.

When Pace had broken up with him for good, she'd been dating Jason for about a month and had come home for Thanksgiving. Trey was there with his parents and, as usual, he'd expected the two of them to pick up where they'd left off. They'd dated other people at college, but somehow when they were home they'd slip back into the comfortable existence of boyfriend and girlfriend. She hadn't told her parents she and Jason were dating and had no intention of telling them for awhile, but she had to say something to Trey, especially since slipping back into their roles meant slipping back into bed. They'd left the house one night to go meet up with a group of friends when Pace had asked him if they could skip it because she had to talk to him about something important. He'd parked along a side street near Chastain Park and she'd told him as quickly and painlessly as possible that she'd met someone.

"That's great, Pace," he'd said and wrapped his fingers around the ends of her very long hair. "Anyone I know?"

She remembered feeling stunned at how well he'd taken the news, how she'd thought she'd completely overreacted in having been so nervous about telling him. "Just someone I met at school. He's not from around here."

"Well…" He'd scooted a little closer. She remembered distinctly the smell of his Drakkar Noir as it mixed with the new leather of his convertible BMW. "That doesn't mean we can't have a little fun while he's not around."

His mouth had started to working on her neck before she'd realized he hadn't understood a word she'd said. "Trey." She'd pushed him away and watched his wounded eyes focus on her face after he'd flicked his hair back into place. "We can't do this anymore."

"Sure we can." He'd swooped back in for more.

"Trey, stop it." When she'd turned to open the door and make her escape into the night, he'd caught her arm and held her in place.

"Pace, I get it. You met someone, you really like him, and you feel guilty for being with me like this, right? But listen, we both knew we'd…experiment while we were apart. There's nothing wrong with that and I applaud your instincts to want to be faithful to this guy. You obviously care about him. But nothing can come between us, Pace. Not your guy back at school, not the girls I date at Yale, no one."

That's when she'd had to remind herself who she was dealing with. No one told Trey he couldn't do something or have something he wanted. No one. Not his parents, not any authority figure, and certainly not Pace. "I'm in love with him, Trey. I love him," she'd repeated so he could understand exactly what she was saying and what it meant to the two of them as a couple.

He'd laughed. Not at first, of course. There was a moment when he'd had to consider if what she was saying could be true. But then he'd laughed it off because he couldn't fathom she'd actually meant what she'd said. They'd never used words like love with each other. Pace simply belonged to him like his shoes and his car and the whole world. "Okay, okay, have some fun with someone new for awhile. I'll be here when you're done."

Had he been waiting all these years for her to be done with Jason? Could he have sent the pictures, not because he wanted so desperately for them to be together—she'd seen him happily bounce from one beautiful girl to the next—but because she'd dared to tell him no all those years ago?

Trey saw her, or rather her reflection in the window, and plopped his feet on the floor and straightened in his seat. "Pace? What's wrong?"

She stared at him and lifted her brows. She wanted him to hang up the phone so she could grill him without an audience.

"Ahhh, I've got to go," he said into the receiver. "I'll call you tomorrow." He stood up and came toward her, all smiles and charm. "To what do I owe this pleasure?"

Could he have done it—sent the photos in an attempt to destroy her marriage? Was she too inclined to see the harmlessness in him to notice? "Did you do it?"

He cocked his head to the side and a boyish lock of blond hair fell over his brows. "Do what?"

He struck the picture of innocence, but if he did send the photos and cover up for her father, he was capable of anything. "Did you send me those pictures?"

"Pictures?"

"Darn it, Trey. I want a straight answer."

"It would be easier to answer if I knew what you were talking about." He led her inside and closed the door. "You're freezing. Where's your coat?"

Before Pace knew it, he'd started massaging her shoulders after he'd eased her into a chair. "Stop it." She shooed his hands away. He frowned down at her after leaning back against the desk.

"What's going on? You're obviously upset about something."

It was clear he wasn't going to confess under pressure, but maybe he'd give something away without meaning to. "Is my father having an affair?"

He bolted upright, laughing at what still sounded to her like a preposterous question. "What? Why would you ask me that?"

She stood up and wandered around his office. There was a small flag on his desk, two large artificial plants flanking the window and a floor to ceiling bookcase. He had pictures on the shelves of him with important people—other senators, some semi-celebrities at a golf outing, a formal one of his parents, and one of him and her father. Pace walked over and picked it up. They were in the rotunda of the capital building, clasping hands and smiling for the camera. There was visible affection on their faces, apparent respect and admiration for each other. Her father loved Trey like a son, had said so on numerous occasions, probably within earshot of Jason. Darn it, she didn't want to believe what Jason had told her.

"Jason had me followed."

Trey contorted his face into a Popeye smirk. "Like by a detective followed?" When she nodded he said, "I'm sorry?" Pace read lots of things in his expression—sympathy, an 'I told you so' glimmer in his eyes—but no surprise.

"You don't seem surprised."

"I'm not. Your husband is a jealous man. Always has been."

He was so sure of himself and so unabashed in his hatred of Jason. "And you enjoy fanning the flames, don't you, Trey?"

He flashed a quick grin. "Guilty." He walked to where Pace leaned against the bookcase and took the picture from her hand, placed it back on the shelf. He gripped her empty hands in his. "He's not good enough for you, Pace. He never has been. I'm glad you finally see that now."

"Now that I've seen the pictures, you mean?"

"What pictures?" He grabbed her shoulders and gave her a little shake. "Pace, you're talking in circles."

He was right about that, but he was the one laying the tracks. She began to think Jason was right about Trey sending the pictures. She felt all but convinced of it after her unannounced visit. "You didn't answer my question."

"I don't know anything about pictures. Why don't you come and sit down and I'll make you a drink?"

Pace wiggled out of his grasp. "Is my father having an affair? That's the question you didn't answer."

He sighed at her like she was a spoiled three-year-old. "How does Jason having you followed lead you to believing your father is having an affair? Connect the dots for me, please?"

"Yes or no, Trey? How I got there is not your concern." She folded her arms over her chest and waited. Just as she knew Trey was lying about the pictures, with every second he didn't respond, with every sigh of breath he took, she knew she'd gotten her answer.

"No, not as far as I know he isn't."

She grabbed her purse from the chair and turned to leave.

"Pace? Where are you going?" he called as she sprinted for the elevator.

If only she knew.

CHAPTER 24

Tori fell asleep before Colin got home. It could have been the two glasses of wine she'd had when she got back from the dinner or maybe the sleeping pill. Had she taken the pill? She remembered pulling it out of the tiny jar and holding it in her palm, watching the white oval dip and sway over the lines of her hand. Her old woman's hand. She honestly couldn't remember if she'd put it back or swallowed it down with the alcohol. She felt pretty sure she would have more than just a nagging headache today if she'd taken it, but who really cared?

He'd left a note on her vanity, scrawled in his familiar block writing. *Unlike sleeping beauty, you didn't rouse at my kiss. We'll try again later...* Perhaps that was because he wasn't a knight in shining armor and she wasn't a princess. Or maybe she was a princess, an air-headed bubble brain who blindly stood by and waited for her prince to sweep her away and make everything clean. But all she felt was dirty. Dirty and ashamed of herself for believing he loved her enough to end his affair. She stuck the note in the drawer where she kept them, a pile of pithy phrases that meant...nothing.

She stepped into the steaming hot shower and let the water ease the knots from her shoulders. Her father's affairs and her mother's unbendable pride had driven her parents to divorce and her mother into a lifelong affair with alcohol. So Tori had sucked it up when Colin first slipped, tried to avoid her own free-fall into depression, and shielded Pace from the humiliation of divorce and a divided family. She'd never been close with her own father, not with his second and third wives and the multitude of half-siblings left in his wake. She knew she'd done the right thing, keeping their family together, but why did it eat at her so? And why now, of all times, when they should have been enjoying their life together, traveling, spending time relaxing, did his betrayal feel so heartrending? She'd deluded herself all these years into thinking it didn't matter, that he loved her more than he needed the other women. She was running out of fight and yet she felt too old to move on. Tori looked down at her body. Her skin was never firm, despite her strict diet and exercise routine. There wouldn't be any exercise on this day, she thought as she leaned over and felt her head sway.

The housemaid had made the bed while she'd showered and had left coffee and the newspaper on the ottoman's tray. She took a tentative sip and flipped through the paper. When she saw herself, smiling and confident, looking out at her from the lifestyle section, she pulled it from the rest and eased into the chair. Would anyone know how broken she was inside from the carefree look on her face? She pushed the paper away and stared outside at the gray day.

She wondered what she was more afraid of—what she thought of leaving Colin or what other people would think of her. Either way it would kill his campaign and the thought of it gave Tori a tingle in her belly. He'd probably make something up, blame her for leaving, avoid all mention of his adultery. She had evidence on her side, lots of it, but was she strong enough to use it? She'd never considered herself vicious or retaliatory, but she had to admit it would feel good to destroy something he wanted so badly. But would leaving him destroy her as well?

* * *

Pace was gone for hours. Jason spent most of the night pacing the floor of their den after finally getting the kids to bed. He'd put together peanut butter and jelly sandwiches for them and pieced together a story about why Mommy wasn't around for dinner and bedtime. When they wouldn't drop it after he'd said she had to go out and she'd be back later, he flat out lied and told them she went to the movies with a girlfriend. With everything their family had been through in the last month, and considering he'd been an absolute mess since she'd walked out of the house, he didn't think they believed him. He sure as hell couldn't blame them.

Jason didn't know how to feel. Should he be mad at her for walking out without an explanation? Should he be worried she'd gone to Trey or her father? He felt a little of both. But more than anything, he was pissed off at Trey. As soon as Pace got back and the sun came up, he planned to pound his fist into whatever body part of Trey's he could reach. Just as he imagined Trey's head snapping back under the weight of his knuckles, Jason heard the garage door open and saw the flash of Pace's headlights in the front windows. His stomach plunged to his knees.

She dropped her purse on the counter after coming inside, threw her keys in the drawer, and looked up at him with tired, red-rimmed eyes.

"I'm surprised you're still up," she said.

He followed her to the base of the stairs and watched her begin to climb. "Where are you going?"

She didn't stop. "To bed. I'm tired."

Jason scrambled up after her and stayed two steps behind as she poked her head into each of the boys' rooms. "They've been out since eight-thirty. I told them you went to the movies."

She closed Mitchell's door and went into their room, straight into the closet and began to unbutton her blouse. He waited for her to say something, tell him something about where she'd been, what she'd decided to do about everything she'd discovered that day, but she seemed content to undress and get ready for bed like it was a normal night. When she scooted past him into the bathroom he said, "Pace, we need to talk about this."

Her answer was to stick her toothbrush in her mouth and stare at him in the mirror. She spit into the sink, wiped her mouth, and gargled with mouthwash before responding. "Not now we don't." She slipped into bed and turned out her bedside lamp.

"Pace." He was pissed off at her for going to bed when he'd been waiting for hours to hash this out.

She sighed, but didn't sit up. "Jason, I can't do this right now. I need to go to sleep; I need to have some time to let things sit for awhile." She sounded as defeated as he'd ever heard her. "I know that's not what you want to hear, but it's the best I can give you right now." She rolled to her side as if the discussion were over.

Damn it. How in the hell was he supposed to sleep? How was he supposed to just go to bed with all the questions bouncing around his head? He watched her until her breathing sounded deep and slow. He undressed and slipped into bed beside her, wrapping his body around her if only to reassure himself she was there and to let her know he wasn't going away. He tried to feel grateful she was home, but he hated not knowing what to expect in the morning.

He didn't rush off to work the next day, but waited for Pace to come back from the bus stop. She'd slept like a baby while he'd tossed and turned all night. Surely she could talk to him after such a restful night's sleep.

"Jason?" She came in the door and saw him sitting at the kitchen table. "I thought you'd be gone by now."

"We need to talk about this, Pace. I need to know what you're thinking, what you're planning to do."

She draped her coat over the kitchen chair, walked to the coffee pot, filled her cup, and brought it over to the table where he sat. She slowly pulled out a chair and joined him at the table, tapping her fingers on the side of the mug. If he didn't know her better, he'd think he was keeping her from something. When they'd first started dating and they'd try to study together, she'd unconsciously tap her pencil against her book until he couldn't take it any longer and he'd reach over and pull the pencil from her hand. He was afraid of what she'd do now if he tried to reach over and still her fingers.

"I think we need to go back to Dr. Falcon."

"What?" Jason pushed away the newspaper he wasn't reading and glared at her. "I'm not really sure how he helped the last time."

"You didn't exactly try very hard last time." She waited for him to rise to her bait, but he didn't. Yelling at her wasn't going to get them anywhere. "Things are different now, Jason. There are things we need to work out. We've both made mistakes this time."

"Pace, I've explained about the private detective, I've apologized."

She took a deep breath, stared into her coffee before lifting her eyes to his. "I'm not sure I can forgive you without some help. If you agree to see Dr. Falcon with me, it would be…like a vow, a commitment to making this work."

"That sounds like a threat. See Dr. Falcon or we get divorced. Is that what you want?"

"It's not an ultimatum, Jason, it's a request. Frankly, it's the least you can do."

The idea of hashing it out with Dr. Falcon again made him want to scream. Why did it always come back to counseling? "I'll tell you what I can do. I can remind you that I don't need a damn shrink to mediate what we need to say to each other." Her expression hardened and he realized he was going about patching up their relationship the wrong way. He couldn't yell at her and get her to see his side of things. He was still in the dog house and probably would be for some time. He softened his voice and reached out to touch her arm. "I love you, Pace. I'm sorry I had you followed, I'm sorry it brought up all this stuff about your father, but I don't need Dr. Falcon to tell me what I want. I want you. I want our family. I thought that's what you wanted too."

Her face crumbled and a tear streaked down her cheek. "I don't even know who I am anymore."

Christ, he had no defense against her crying. He never had. But he wouldn't agree to see Falcon just because she was vulnerable. "If you need to see Dr. Falcon, that's fine with me. But I won't go through all that again. I don't need it. I already know what I want."

She used one of the kids' napkins to blow her nose and pulled herself back together. "I don't want you throwing the expense of it in my face every time I turn around. If I have to, I can pay for it with my own earnings in January."

"I just said I don't care if you see him." Jason reached out and put her cold hand in his. She looked across the table at him with tear filled eyes. "If he can help you get past everything that's happened..." *maybe convince you it never happened* "...it'll be money well spent."

Trey wasn't at his office when Jason arrived around nine. He'd driven through the parking garage three times and still hadn't seen his sporty red Porsche with his stupid vanity plates. He finally secured a spot near the entrance of the lot and waited for him to come in. He was answering an email on his Blackberry when he heard the purr of an engine and glanced up to see Trey's cocky blonde head behind the wheel before he did a quick hair pin turn around the corner. Jason started his engine and followed.

He'd just blocked Trey's car in his space and gotten out of his sedan as Trey folded himself out of the matchbox car. He seemed prepared to yell at a stranger when he recognized Jason and his face turned to stone.

"Kelly. What the hell are you doing?"

Before Trey could react or think or dodge, Jason punched him in the nose and watched with immense satisfaction as a trickle of blood dripped onto the collar of his shirt. Trey swiped his nose with the back of his hand, his eyes wide with shock.

Jason grabbed the lapel of his suit and tossed him back against the Porsche. "You sent those pictures to my wife, you son of a bitch."

"I could have you arrested for assault!" His lip was swelling and he acted like a scared little boy without the senator as backup. He knew Trey had never started a fight without a wingman.

"I haven't even gotten started." Jason shoved him back and waited for him to retaliate, but Trey just touched his lip with his tongue and straightened his suit.

"You're a fucking idiot. You have Pace followed, you put Colin's future on the line, and you think punching me is going to get you anywhere but put in jail?"

"She knows you sent the pictures. She knows about her father."

He laughed and shook his head. "She knows nothing except for the fact that you had her followed. I told her last night I don't know anything about pictures and she believed me."

Jason felt momentarily stunned. He told her last night? She went to him? "I know you did it. You're the only one who had reason to."

He righted his tie and cocked a brow. "Prove it." He dabbed his nose with a handkerchief he'd pulled from his suit pocket. "Your days are numbered, Kelly. Colin wants you out of the family. Pace sure as hell isn't some delicate wallflower who'll stand by you after you had her tracked like a dog. If I were you, I'd get myself a real good lawyer because by the time I'm done with you, you'll be asking my permission to speak to Pace." He tucked the hanky back in his pocket. "And if you're lucky, I might occasionally let you see your kids."

Trey's stupid, pathetic words were all talk and just as effective, more really, than a strong right hook. Jason lunged for him, but this time he'd set his feet and squared off. They both landed a punch. Jason delivered a direct hit to Trey's gut and had him doubling over; Trey caught Jason's jaw in what felt like a mosquito bite. *"Pussy fights like a girl,"* he thought. Just as he reached for Trey to lift him up for another punch, a security guard rounded the corner and they both paused as his brakes screeched on the concrete. Jason dropped his hands and Trey pushed himself up by the knees. Breathing heavily, they watched the security guard approach.

"Everything okay here, Mr. Conway?" Trey looked at Jason and seemed to weigh his options. The senator's campaign manager would have a hell of a time explaining a fist fight with his boss's son-in-law.

"Yeah, Steve. Everything's fine."

The guard examined Jason warily. "You're going to have to move your car, Sir. Can't have you blocking other vehicles."

"No problem." Jason stared at Trey. Blood smeared his face and collar and his shirt was untucked. He couldn't tell in the dim light, but he hoped like hell he'd broken Trey's nose. One thing was for sure, his pretty little face wasn't so pretty anymore. "I'm done here, anyway."

As Jason drove to work, his jaw beginning to throb, he thanked God for the security guard's interference. He would have killed Trey, he was all but sure of it. He couldn't believe Pace had gone to Trey last night. Damn it, the whole situation got worse by the second.

CHAPTER 25

Pace managed to shower and dress and she even applied some makeup. What did it say about her that she was trying to put on a good front for her therapist?

After she'd brought him up to speed with the goings on of her roller coaster marriage and Jason's accusations about her father, he asked how she felt. "I feel like an explorer who just found out the world is round. It just changes your perception of everything. I can't quite seem to wrap my mind around any of it."

"Pace." Dr. Falcon sat up in his chair and pushed his glasses back up his nose. He never seemed surprised when he saw her again or when she told him about Jason. She assumed he'd heard worse, but just then she couldn't imagine. "Are you depressed?"

"Depressed?" She let the word sink into her brain, absorb into her blood and flow through her veins. Could one word adequately describe the state she was in, the free-falling without a net to catch her state? "Probably."

"I can prescribe something to help you."

"No. I don't want anything to dull my senses." She rubbed her eyes and then remembered she had on mascara. Great. "I need to work through this."

He jotted something on his pad and stared thoughtfully over her shoulder before he asked, "So now Jason wants to move past this and you can't?"

"I want things back the way they were before, when we were a team, when we trusted each other implicitly. It won't ever be like that again and I don't know if I want to live with anything less."

Dr. Falcon stared at her without blinking. He did this, she now knew, when he tried to figure out what to say, how to proceed. It always made her feel uncomfortable.

"Are you thinking of leaving him?"

"No. I don't know. I don't think so."

"You have to be willing to work at this, Pace. He can't do it all."

She pushed away from the couch because she couldn't stand the condescension in his voice. "I just found out he had me followed by a private investigator and that my father is probably cheating on my mother. Jason won't even consider more therapy. Aren't I allowed some time to wallow?" She walked to his bookshelf and picked up a glass figurine in the shape of an angel or maybe a bird. It felt cool to the touch and heavier than it looked. If she threw it at him, she wondered if it would knock him out or just irritate him. "I don't know how to work at it." She put it back on the shelf when the thought of chucking it through the window held an almost unstoppable appeal. She sat back down again, deflated, weary.

"Maybe you and Jason should try to get away together, just the two of you. You're letting the days pass, letting life get in the way of dealing with your emotions. It can't go on forever before one or both of you breaks."

She started shaking her head even before he'd finished his point. "Can't. Jason's too busy with work." Hopefully all he was busy with was work. "I'm in no position to take off right now."

Dr. Falcon leaned forward with his ankle resting on his knee. She saw the argyle socks he wore under his corduroy pants. "Do you still want to be married to Jason? Do you still want to spend the rest of your life with him?"

Being without Jason would be like cutting off her air supply or severing a limb on purpose. How could this man who'd lost his wife ask her such a question? "I want to be married to Jason, I *am* married to him and I don't want to stop. I love him, Dr. Falcon. I just don't like him a whole lot right now.

"What about your father?"

"What about him? He did it. I don't necessarily trust Jason all that much right now, but I know he wouldn't have lied to me about that. And Trey all but confirmed it."

"What are you going to do about it?"

She picked at the dog hair on her pants. "I think I have to tell my mother."

"Pace…" He put both feet on the floor and leaned toward her. "You need to give it a little time and think about whether or not that's the best thing to do."

"You think I should just pretend like I don't know? I don't think I can do that."

"This is your mother's life you're talking about. It's not about what you can or can't do. It's about what's best for her."

"You think it's best if she doesn't know?"

He sat back in his seat and tapped his pen against the yellow pad. "What if she already knows?"

A bubble of laughter spewed out of her mouth. She slapped her hand over her lips. "Oh, God, I didn't think I could laugh about any of this." She took a deep breath and tried to answer him seriously. "I'm sorry, Dr. Falcon, but that's the most ridiculous thing you've ever said. My mother is the strongest, most fearsome woman in the world. If she knew my father was having an affair, she'd have cut his balls off—*if* she let him live."

* * *

Tori was on the phone arguing with the caterer about her Holiday Tea when Pace unexpectedly walked in her study. Tori usually looked forward to hosting the annual event, but this year she couldn't seem to muster much enthusiasm. She raised her hand at Pace, silently asking her to wait while she instructed the baker to make all the petit fours look like presents. Last year they'd done a mixture—trees, reindeer, and such, but the presents went first so she wanted them all alike. She expected her highest turnout this year and the kids loved the petit fours.

"This is a nice surprise." Tori stood up to greet Pace after she'd gotten off the phone. "I wasn't expecting you."

"I know." Pace stopped and stared at her blankly. Tori had just started not worrying about her daughter, but she looked awful. Her mascara was smeared and she had bags under her eyes. "I—"

Colin walked into the room and stopped Pace cold. Tori had never seen her look at her father like she did then, her eyes narrowed, her glare accusing. She glanced at her husband to see what could have caused such a reaction. He wore an affable grin, his usual suit and tie, and he carried an overnight bag. She struggled not to cringe at the sight of it. He'd mentioned his trip to Washington in passing. She hoped he had real business to do because it didn't matter whether he met his mistress at home or in D.C.

"Pace, darling." He kissed her cheek and she visibly flinched. What in the world? "Did you come to see me off?"

"See you off?" She scooted around the couch and out of his reach.

"I'm heading to Washington for a few days. Seems my challenger is stumping for support inside the beltway." He was oblivious to her reaction, tugging the cuffs out from his coat and playing with his tie. "There's always something."

"Anyone going with you?" Pace asked.

Colin seemed taken aback. She never asked about his job. "Noooo." He shook his head and chuckled at her as if she were a child.

The words, *She's older than your lover,* were on the tip of Tori's tongue, but she held them back as he approached. When he leaned in to kiss her, she stiffened her spine and offered him her cheek. She'd avoided all physical contact since her run-in with Deidre. He hadn't noticed her cold shoulder either. "I'll call you when we land."

Tori stole a glance at Pace, who stood watching them raptly. As soon as Colin had gone, Pace wandered out from behind the couch. "He seems awfully chipper to be heading out-of-town right before Christmas and to be dealing with opposition."

Tori jotted a note in her appointment book and closed it forcefully. Too forcefully, she could tell when she looked up and realized Pace studied her suspiciously. She forced a smile and tried to distract her. "He thrives on competition and I'm sure he's grateful to be out of the house while I work on the details for the tea." Tori sat on the sofa and was pleased when Pace followed. "So, why the visit? Were you in the neighborhood?"

Pace stared at lap and said, "I was worried about you."

If her earlier behavior hadn't already peaked Tori's interest, Pace's statement would have put her on alert. She'd always been the least of Pace's worries. "Worried about me? Why?"

When Pace only shrugged, Tori wondered if what she said next would be the truth or something to throw her off. The whole situation felt like a trap.

"I was just wondering how you're doing," Pace said. "You've been so busy with stuff, all the luncheons and dinners. I can't remember you throwing yourself into a campaign like this before, especially so early in the game, and I just wanted to check on you."

Tori felt ridiculously close to tears. It was the most care Pace had shown her...ever.

"I mean, when you came by the house the other day, it seemed like you wanted to talk about something. Something important."

Tori's breath hitched in her throat. It felt like Pace was trying to lead her somewhere, but she didn't know where or if she wanted to go. Pace sat on the edge of the cushion, her hands clasped tightly together, her eyes intent. "I was worried about *you*," Tori explained. "I wondered how *you* were doing. There was no nefarious intent, I assure you."

Pace blinked her eyes quickly, tapped her fingers on her legs. She was nervous. How very interesting. "You know you can talk to me, Mom, about anything that's bothering you." Pace reached over and grabbed her hand. Tori felt a spurt of anger toward Jason for the calluses on her palm. "I'll listen if you just need to talk."

What in the hell was going on here? Did she know about her father's affair? "The way you open up with me?" Her reply was born of panicked fear instead of compassion for her daughter's kindness. She pulled her hand from Pace's and flicked the hair from her face. Tori wondered what was wrong with her? Why did she take her anger out on Pace? "I'm sorry. I didn't mean to sound so disingenuous." She had to get away from Pace's stare, the concern on her face, the seeking glare in her eyes. She walked to the window, tried to get a grip on her emotions. She took a deep breath and, when she thought she could disguise her feelings, turned to face her daughter. "What's gotten into you lately? Why so serious?"

Pace looked so sad sitting there on the big leather couch. It seemed like just yesterday when her feet barely touched the ground.

"No reason." She shrugged and kept tapping away on her pants. "It's just that we're both adults, both married women with children. I'd like us to be closer than we are."

Tori's mind was reeling. Where the hell was this coming from?

"I'd like us to be friends."

Her mouth was dry as cotton. "Friends?"

"Why not?" She popped up and approached Tori's spot by the window. She was afraid if her daughter came any closer, she'd smell her fear. "We're both married to very demanding men, men who travel a lot, men who expect us to handle the details of life while they're gone."

"That's certainly true." Tori felt like they were dancing to music only one of them could hear.

They stared at each other for a long time and in Pace's expression, it seemed as if she was wrestling with something. "We have to trust our husbands to be faithful when they're gone, when they're free to act on certain desires."

It hit Tori all at once that it wasn't Colin she was talking about, but Jason. "What's going on, Pace?" Tori gripped her shoulders, felt the taut muscle beneath. "Has Jason…"

"No, no, I don't think so." Pace wrapped her arms tightly around her chest and closed her eyes as if to gather strength. When she opened them, Tori knew she was about to tell her the truth. "He's been getting some emails from a client. Some suggestive emails. He says they're harmless, that he'd never do anything, but…it bothers me."

Tori was shocked that Pace would come to her with a crisis and tried to guide her as best she could. Lord knew she'd had some experience with this kind of thing. It was one thing for Tori to put up with infidelity, but she wouldn't stand by and watch her baby be treated that way. "You asked him about the emails?"

"Yes. I tried to sit on them, pretend they didn't mean what I thought they did, but I just couldn't do it. I needed to hear him tell me there wasn't anything going on."

Tori was so proud of Pace for being stronger than she was at her age. When she'd first suspected. "And you believe him?"

"Yes, I believe him." Tori didn't say anything for minute, tried to get her thoughts in order. She didn't want Pace following blindly down the path she'd forged. Pace waited expectantly for a response, her eyes wide with alarm. "You don't think I should believe him?"

"I think you should be careful. I think you should protect yourself."

Her brow furrowed. "Protect myself how?"

How did Tori warn her about the danger to her soul if she didn't put her needs before his and take nothing for granted? "Don't let up about what's going on. Let him know if he cheats on you, it's over. I mean it, Pace. Don't stand by and let him walk all over you. You deserve better than that."

She looked like a scared teenager; not quite a child, not quite a woman. Those had been the hardest years between them. "Okay, okay, I'll make sure he knows how I feel."

"Do it, Pace." Tori gripped Pace's arms tight and had to stop herself from shaking her senseless. "Because once you let your guard down, once you let him get away with something, there isn't any turning back."

* * *

Pace stared at her mother, panting and lightheaded like she was going to pass out. She felt as though she might actually pass out. Or throw up. Or both. Did her mother just admit her father had had an affair? "Mom, you're making it sound like you've been through this before."

Tori dropped her arms and swirled away. Pace was frantic to see her face, read what she could from her mother's expression, but her back stayed turned and all she could hear was the slight tremble of her mother's voice when she said, "Don't be ridiculous."

She still wouldn't turn around, but stood facing the window. The shifting clouds made strange shadows drift across the room. "Mom?"

Pace placed her hand on Tori's arm and turned her just as the sun slipped out from behind a cloud and shot a glare into her eyes. All she could see was her mother's silhouette. "Your father is a politician, honey. Politicians are notorious for having affairs and the rumors run rampant even when they're not true. Of course I've suffered with doubt and insecurity. Every woman has."

Oh, it sounded nice, her very politically correct answer. Her very vague, admit-nothing answer. Pace could hear Dr. Falcon's warning in her head, but forged ahead anyway. She may never get this chance again. "I'm not talking about every woman, Mom. I'm talking about you. You and Daddy."

"Pace." Tori led her to the couch and they both sat. She could see her mother clearly now and the look she gave her was the same as when Pace was a teenager about to get a lecture. "Your father and I have been married a very long time. He's handsome, successful, and in a powerful position. Women are drawn to him and I've learned to deal with their admiring glances and…sometimes more. If you make it clear to your husband that you won't stand by while he uses you as a doormat, he won't."

Pace nodded her head and hoped she would go on, expound a little on her theories like she always had in the past, but her mother slapped her hands on her knees and stood up.

"I've got a thousand things to do for this tea. Is there anything else you needed?"

Pace rose onto unsteady legs. *A straight answer*, she wanted to shout as her mother flipped open her appointment book and lifted the phone from its cradle. But as Tori began to dial and sat behind her desk, Pace knew she'd been dismissed and that she wasn't going to get one.

CHAPTER 26

By the time Jason got home, his jaw was swollen, a little pink, and, as much as he hated to admit it, hurt like hell. He wondered if Pace would notice, if she'd even care, or if she already knew he'd attacked her old boyfriend. He should regret it, punching him without any thought to the consequences from his father-in-law and his wife, but he couldn't. He'd had nearly two decades' worth of anger building and finally letting it out felt too damn good to regret.

They sat through a painfully normal dinner, the kids scarfing down their food and talking about some kid getting in trouble on the bus for cussing. Normally Jason would've been concerned, but he couldn't seem to work up much enthusiasm. The kid cussed, he got in trouble, drama over. Pace watched him while they ate, her brown eyes suspicious as he tenderly spooned food into his mouth and tried to chew without biting his swollen cheek.

After dinner, he whipped the kids at video games while she did the dishes. The boys didn't seem to know something was going on with them because he and Pace were working double time to act like things were normal. Their problems had taken an enormous toll on the boys last time and he knew if they sensed a crack between them, they'd crumble. When they'd gotten them bathed and put to bed, Jason followed Pace into the den and prepared to interrogate her about Trey.

"What happened to your face?" She stood in the middle of the room, her arms crossed, her expression grim.

Jason reached for the remote and turned off an annoyingly loud sitcom that had come on while they'd been upstairs. It seemed like just a few years ago they would race to get the kids in bed so they could sit in front of their favorite shows. "You don't know?"

"What do you mean?"

"I went to see Trey."

She dropped her arms and her whole body seemed to deflate. "You got into a fight with Trey?"

"He sent those pictures. He dared me to prove it." He didn't know what he expected her to do, how he expected her to react, but the non-reaction seemed strange and only added fuel to his fire. "Damn it, Pace. The man's obsessed with you."

"You're the one obsessed." She rubbed her temples with her hands. "I already told you I don't care about Trey."

"He's trying to break up our marriage. Don't you care about that?"

"Trey can't break up our marriage, Jason. Only we can do that."

She couldn't have delivered a better knock-out punch in her quiet, measured tone. Right between the eyes. "Is that what you want?" Jason asked.

"No, that's not what I want." She walked over to where he stood, placed a hand on his puffy cheek. "Does it hurt?"

Jason nodded, staring into her eyes. It felt more like a bee sting, but he'd milk it for all it was worth if it made Pace feel sorry for him—feel anything for him. She was everything he'd ever wanted. Just as he leaned down to kiss her, to tell her he needed her, she turned and walked toward the kitchen. "Where are you going?"

She didn't answer, but he heard her rustling around in the freezer. She was back a moment later with an ice bag. "Frozen peas would work better, but this is the best I can do."

"Pace." He grabbed her hand before she could pull away. "I love you. I've always loved you and I'll never stop loving you. I want us to get back to the way things were."

She sat on the couch and stared up at him. "You used to trust me."

"I still trust you. It's Trey I don't trust."

"That's not true, Jason." She leaned back against the couch and sighed. She looked exhausted and way too thin. "When the nurse called with those test results, you didn't think twice about me cheating on you. You knew I wouldn't do it. And I understand how you must have felt after your test and the doctor's email, but instead of thinking about us and me and figuring out I would never cheat on you, you went out and hired a private detective—"

"I said I was sorry, Pace. Please, if I could undo what I did, I would. If it hadn't been for Trey, the whole thing would have blown over, but when he had his hands on you I saw red."

"I know that. I believe that. But you still did it." She sat up and braced her hands on her knees. She wore jeans and a sweater and they were gaping where they used to cling. How had he not noticed how much weight she'd lost? "It's more than the detective. The emails, Jason. I just can't get the emails out of my head."

He was on his knees in front of her, threw the ice pack on the coffee table, and took her hands in his. "I told you there's nothing going on. She's an infatuated young girl. I haven't done anything to encourage her." Shit. He needed to tell her about his trip. He leaned back on his heels. "I have to go back to New York. I leave the day after tomorrow."

"What?" She pulled her hands out of his grasp. "Why now? It's almost Christmas."

"Tarks says he's nominating me for partner."

She eyed Jason skeptically. "Why do you sound so upset and what does this have to do with you going to New York?"

"If Tarks caught wind of my plans to leave, this could be a tactical maneuver to keep me."

"From everything you've said, making partner is too big a deal for him to use it to keep you. He's probably worried because you're too good to keep without making partner. It seems flattering to me and about time. What's the problem?"

He couldn't help but smile at her die-hard support, even in the face of their issues. "If I make partner and turn it down, I'm going to have to leave...I mean, I'm leaving anyway, but now I have to leave before they announce who made partner or else I risk them taking my projects from me—which they may do anyway."

"So you can't wait until spring like you'd planned?"

"No, I've got a month, tops." The stress of it, on top of everything else, felt like a boulder on his spine. He had to find an office to lease, get incorporated, hire a support staff, figure out insurance… "I think I can convince my New York account to come with me. I need them to, Pace. This is too big a deal to let slip away."

She fell back against the cushions and looked up at the ceiling. "Then I guess you have to go."

Her face looked pale and completely blank. He knew he had to do this, for him, for their family, but leaving her when she seemed so fragile felt like a betrayal. "You can trust me, Pace." He reached out and cupped her cheek in his palm. "I love you. I don't want to leave you now. I admit it was flattering to have someone interested in me, especially when everything here was such a mess, but I never did anything to provoke it."

She leveled him with her honest brown eyes. "You didn't do anything to stop it, either."

"Honestly, I didn't know how. I thought ignoring it would be best. It seemed too risky to make a big deal of it before I had a commitment from them."

Her mouth quirked in annoyance. "So you'd rather risk losing me than risk losing them as a client?"

"No, that's not what I meant." He rubbed his eyes with the heels of his hands and tried to start over. It wouldn't do any good to get pissed. "I won't go if you tell me not to."

She snorted sarcastically. "I won't tell you not to go. Don't put that on me."

"I mean it, Pace. If you don't want me to go to New York, I won't."

"Where does that get me? If I tell you to stay, you'll resent me and if I tell you to go, it's like I'm giving you permission."

"If you tell me to go, it's like you trust me. You're going to have to trust me, Pace, just like I'm going to have to trust you."

He studied her then, the hollows under her eyes, the way her shoulder blades poked out sharply. Jesus, how did he not notice how worn out she was? "When was the last time you ate a decent meal?"

She seemed surprised at his question. "We just had dinner."

"No, you didn't put more than three bites in your mouth." He grabbed her shoulders and could feel her bones against his palms. "You're fading away, Pace."

She closed her eyes slowly. "It certainly feels that way."

Jason had a million things to do before his trip the following day, but the first thing he did in the morning was phone Dr. Falcon and insist on seeing him. He couldn't seem to hold his anger at Trey and he'd found a new target.

Falcon squeezed him in at four and as he opened the door, Jason bounded past him before he could say hello.

"Jason," he said in that damn calm manner of his. "Have a seat, won't you?"

He whipped around to face their counselor. "I don't want to sit down. Have you looked at her?" he asked. "Have you seen how depressed she is?"

Dr. Falcon stood by the closed door, slipped his hands into the pockets of his khaki pants. "Have you?"

Jason stepped up to his face and through sheer will power didn't poke him in the chest.

"Jason," he said with a warning in his tone. "Sit down and tell me what happened."

Jason let out a big breath and sat in the chair. Dr. Falcon took the seat across from him and waited with his brows lifted. "She's…slipping away."

"How?"

"She's not eating enough, her clothes are falling off of her, she's tired, she doesn't seem to care about anything anymore."

"Classic signs of depression and not that surprising considering your situation."

"What do you mean?"

"She's grieving, Jason. She's grieving for your marriage as if someone or something has died." He shifted in his seat and reached for his pad. "What happened?"

"I'm sure she told you I had her followed." Jason glanced up and felt shameful. He knew Falcon already knew the details, but admitting it was like swallowing a bitter pill. This must have been what it felt like to get in trouble by parents who actually gave a damn. "And about the emails from my client's receptionist. Plus this stuff with her father. I know that's enough to put anyone over the edge, but...she's pale and thinner than I've ever seen her."

"Physical side effects of an internal conflict are normal. If you're concerned, you should try to get her to see a doctor."

Jason gripped the arms of the chair. If a genie had popped out of a magic bottle and offered him one wish, he'd ask to start all over again. "That's what got us into this mess."

"What do you mean?" Falcon asked.

He thought back to her complaining of her lack of energy, the leg cramps and headaches, tingly hands and feet. He'd insisted she see a doctor.

"She wasn't feeling normal. She was having headaches and was tired all the time." He rubbed his eyes. God, that seemed like a lifetime ago. "That's why she went to the doctor, who ran the blood test, who told her she was pregnant."

Dr. Falcon stared at him over the top of his glasses before pulling them off. "Jason, if there was an error at the lab as she continues to insist there was, she could be suffering from some undiagnosed condition." The thought of Pace having an illness had him sitting up in his seat. "Or it could be from the stress of what she's gone through. Either way, I'd encourage her to get a complete physical."

"Are you sure there's nothing you're not telling me? You'd have to tell me if you thought she was sick, wouldn't you?"

"I'm not obligated to reveal anything."

"But you said she's depressed and grieving."

"Yes."

"And I'm to blame."

Falcon sighed and put his glasses back on. "Casting blame isn't going to help."

Jason looked at the doctor they both thought could save them. "I can't lose her, Dr. Falcon. I won't."

* * *

Jason left in the morning wearing his best suit and the tie Pace had given him for Christmas last year. He'd kissed the boys as they ate breakfast and pulled her into the garage for a pep talk of sorts. "I'll be back as soon as I can. You can trust me, Pace. I love you." He'd kissed her, long and deep, the kind of kiss that promised to forgive things lost and promised things to come. Pace had had a lump in her throat as his car backed out of their driveway and by the time he'd rounded the corner at the end of the street, she was crying. And the thing of it was, she wasn't sure why.

She hadn't cried about him leaving town since his first business trip after Dillon was born. She'd quit her job to stay home with him and her days were spent with the sleep deprived tedium that defined the first few months of a newborn's life and a new mom's existence. She'd been at times weepy, at times so tired she didn't know up from down, and at times so confused about her role in life—in Dillon's life, in Jason's, and her own—that she'd wondered if she should have been so hasty in quitting her job and giving up every shred of what had for so long been her identity.

Jason had been nervously excited about the prospect he'd planned to see, a construction company that later became one of the firm's biggest clients, and Pace had dreaded the three days he planned to be gone as if when he left, her life would cease to exist until he'd returned. And it did, in some ways. Seven o'clock came and went and no one was there to scoop Dillon from her arms and give her a moment's rest until he woke screaming again three hours later just to nurse and the endless cycle continued. Jason hadn't been there to put Dillon in the crib after she'd fall asleep in the glider and usher her back to bed for a few minutes sleep before he had to leave for work. She'd simultaneously envied and yearned for him with equal fervor. When Jason did come back, flushed with success and giddy with his burgeoning career, he'd seemed a little frightened at what he'd come back to—Pace's just shy of losing it behavior and the somewhat alarming appearance of both the house and the woman he'd married. Showers and housekeeping had been very low on her priority list.

There were more trips, of course, and each one filled her with less terror than the last. Each time she'd miss her husband less and less until, at some point, she came to look a little bit forward to the freedom his being gone afforded her and the fact that there was one less person to look after, at least for a few days. By the time Mitchell came along and Jason's travel picked back up again, Pace found it easier to cope when he was away and harder to remember what had filled her with such anxiety the first time he'd left.

And now she stood crying in her garage as he left them for the millionth time. Was she sad to see him go? Yes, but it wasn't the same terror that used to fill her. Was she mad at him for leaving so close to Christmas and that he headed back to see the girl who kept emailing him? Yes, but she understood he had to go. He'd always wanted to work for himself and having a client on board could mean the difference between success and failure. Did she trust him to be faithful while he was gone? Yes, Pace knew his guilt and nerves at having to talk to his client would be enough to keep him from doing anything stupid.

He'd said it was flattering—Deborah's flirting. No matter how subtle it had appeared, she'd flirted with her husband. Was that why Pace had let Trey call her gorgeous and make suggestive comments? Did she crave the kind of flattery she and Jason were too busy to give one another after 12 years of marriage? Was this whole thing more about the two of them, about the way they didn't really even see each other anymore, than about some silly receptionist and her old boyfriend?

Of course it was.

And of course she realized the truth now that he'd gone and she couldn't talk to him about it.

She took a deep breath, wiped her eyes, and went back in the house to get the boys on the bus for their last day of school before Christmas break. She tried to busy herself with things she couldn't do easily once they were home. She wrapped the last of their presents, ran to the grocery store, checked her emails. She logged onto the computer and, after deleting most of the spam and responding to what needed addressing, she flipped over to her homepage to scan the news.

It didn't register at first, what she was seeing; at least Pace didn't process it as anything other than a tabloid style headline concerning a United States Senator. When she looked at the picture of her father, a head shot where he was smiling like the statesman she'd always known him to be, her head began to spin and there was a ringing in her ears that sounded like an alarm bell. A teaser promised exclusive photos and intimate details of Senator Whitfield's tryst if she just clicked on the article, but Pace couldn't seem to make her fingers move to click the picture or the more damaging headline. She swiveled away from the computer and put her head between her knees when it felt like she was going to throw up or lose consciousness.

As she took slow, deep breaths in and out and tried to concentrate on what was real and true—she was in her home, her tennis shoes had white laces and were neatly double knotted, the hardwood floors needed a good scrubbing—Pace realized she'd been fooling herself with some sort of fantasy that Jason hadn't really seen pictures of her father with another woman, that in his anxiety over being caught having her followed he'd made that little detail up to make his betrayal seem less important. She sat up slowly, inch by inch, and let the blood settle back in her stomach, let the room come back into focus. With a combination of dread and defeat, she turned back to the computer and read the headlines. Two were from local news organizations and one, the big one, was from the Associated Press.

That meant the news had spread.

That meant her mother knew.

Her father was dead man.

CHAPTER 27

Tori lifted the shutter with shaking hands and watched the scene unfold outside her bedroom window. There were television vans around the block. Reporters milled around the base of the drive, either turned away per her instructions to the staff or showing an unprecedented shred of respect for her and what she was going through.

She was about to avert her gaze when she recognized Pace's SUV as it eased around the crowd and up the drive. Pace. Not for the first time, she wondered if she'd done the right thing. Moments later she heard her footsteps in the hallway followed by a plea from the maid for Pace not to disturb Mrs. Whitfield. Pace knocked on the closed bedroom door and peeked her head inside.

"Mom?"

She looked scared and a little shocked to see her mother dry-eyed and alert. She probably expected to find her in a puddle of tears on the bed. Tori needed to be strong for both of them now.

"I should have expected you, Pace. I probably should have called."

"Mom, I'm..." She swallowed and leaned her head against the door. "Can I come in?"

She waved her inside. "I take it you've heard."

Pace entered the darkened room and closed the door behind her. "Mom, are you okay?"

"I'm..." Tori brushed the hair away from her face and tried to compose herself. "I don't really know how I am, other than mortally embarrassed." She dropped her arms and frowned. "I should have thought of you, of what this would do to you."

Muted light speared through the window. The temperature was close to forty degrees outside and the sky appeared ominous with low hanging clouds. She'd purposely left the room dark in keeping with her mood, but now that Pace had arrived, she turned on the light by her bed. When Pace stared at her, her face pinched with worry, Tori knew just how she looked. She'd been staring at herself in the mirror all day, wincing at her shell-shocked expression and the shadows under her eyes.

"This is all my fault." Pace burst into tears and lunged like a child into Tori's arms, giant racking sobs escaped that left her breathless and choking. Tori rocked her daughter and ran her hands over her bony back. Her little girl. She shouldn't have done this to her. How in the world could Pace blame herself? When Pace stopped hiccupping, she pulled back, her face blotchy face framing her eyes swollen.

"What on earth are you talking about?"

"Jason had me followed by a private detective." Her voice sounded little more than a whisper. "He—the detective—took the pictures of Daddy." She averted her gaze and her pale face flushed with color. "Jason told me Trey took care of it."

"Trey." Tori hadn't thought of all the people who knew, all the people who'd helped Colin cover his tracks. Of course Trey would know and take care of the little details for Colin. How humiliating. "Yes, he is the loyal one, isn't he?" So this was why Pace had come to see her the other day, this was why she'd looked at her father so accusingly. She already knew.

She led Pace to the settee and handed her a box of tissues from the nightstand. She waited until she'd composed herself before sitting down beside her. "How long have you known?"

Pace shrugged. "A few days."

Tori felt ashamed of herself for not doing something sooner. Maybe if she had, Pace would never have found out. "Why on earth did Jason have you followed by a private detective?"

"It's a long story, but he thought I'd cheated on him. No," she held up her hand when Tori opened her mouth, "I didn't, but he had good reason to believe I did. We've been through a lot—which sounds ridiculous considering what you're going through." She was babbling and looked like she was about to start crying again. She stopped abruptly and grabbed Tori's hand. "Why aren't you falling apart? At the very least I thought you'd have him in front of a firing squad or I'd find you waiting for him with a set of brass knuckles."

"Pace," Tori laughed. "Jason should be very afraid of you."

She blushed and waved her comment away. "I've been watching a lot of late night TV. I'm serious, Mom, I don't get your reaction."

It was time to be honest. "The news is painful, dreadful really, but only a surprise to one of us."

Pace gripped the cushion of the settee. She stared at Tori intently, waiting for her to explain something she clearly didn't understand. "What do you mean?"

This was what she'd been dreading. This was why she never made demands on Colin, she now realized, as Pace stared at her with wide-eyed horror. The truth was shattering her daughter; it would have shattered her at any age. "Oh, Pace, you know how charismatic your father is. People get caught up in his whirlwind. I know I did."

She couldn't look at Pace while she destroyed her illusions of her father and their marriage. She rose and walked toward the window, lifted the slat of the blind and stared out into the gray day. "I was so young when we got married, so blinded by my faith in your father, in what he wanted to do, how he wanted to change things. Being around him was like being on a carnival ride." She let go of the blind and it snapped into place. The sound brought Tori back from the past and into the present where her daughter was all that mattered. She turned around to face her. "Real life eventually caught up with us. I guess I got off the roller coaster first and he's kept on going. I couldn't keep up, especially after you were born. And now he keeps people around him who provide a certain level of...adulation. Trey, the young zealots, women. He craves what they give him, what I can't give him anymore."

Pace's mouth tried to form the words she couldn't make her heart believe. "You mean this isn't the first time? He's done this before? Since I was born?"

"I shouldn't have let it go on for so long."

Tori could see in her expression that she was adjusting her whole perception of her mother and father and their marriage. "You make it sound like he's blameless, like you've let him do this awful thing to you."

Tori shrugged and sat down, pulled at a loose thread in the throw absently draped over the back. "He chooses to accept what others give freely. By not asking for more, by not demanding he stop, I've let him, Pace. All these years I've known."

Her despair turned to anger in a flash. "Why do you let him?" she asked. "My God, Mom, you of all people."

Pace asked the question Tori had been unable to answer for over thirty years. She gave her the truth and the only answer that made any sense. "I love your father."

"I don't understand how you can love someone who treats you this way."

"No, I don't suppose you would." Pace was shaking; her knee bouncing up and down. The air around her seemed to snap with an electric charge. Tori reached over and stilled her leg. "You're such a confident woman. I've tried so hard to raise you with a strong sense of self. I know my interference has annoyed you, but I worry."

"I hate what he's done to you." She hopped up and began to pace. "I hate the way I've treated you all these years. I thought...all this time, I thought you led him around by the nose. I thought he innocently followed because he didn't want to be bullied." To see her skulk around the room like a caged animal, to have the blinders pulled away, was more painful than Tori could ever have imagined. "I wish I'd known."

Tori let out a mirthless laugh. The sound of it startled them both. "Oh, Pace. What good would that have done?" Her smile drifted away and she sighed. "I've known about your father's affairs for a very long time now. When he first...slipped, I was devastated. When I confronted him, he cried and begged me to forgive him, promised he wouldn't do it again. Because I loved him and believed his sincerity, I forgave him and we moved on. When it happened again..." She shrugged and leaned back into the settee. She tried not to dwell on those days, when she'd been so young and naïve. When discovering the truth had felt like a knife to her heart. His infidelity had shaped her life in so many ways. "Something inside of me died. I guess it was hope, or faith, but things were different then. We had you and he'd just been elected lieutenant governor. Leaving him had many consequences I wasn't willing to face. I had nowhere to go, no way to support you and his career would have been ruined. I couldn't bring myself to kill so many things in order to save face, so I let it go."

She'd always believed if she acted like things were normal and healthy, things would be normal and healthy. Especially for Pace. But witnessing her daughter's fragility after hearing the truth felt shaming. With much more that needed to be said, she cleared her throat and finished.

"He knows that I know and he tries hard to be discreet...or at least he did. It's something I've come to accept about him, the same way women learn to live with their husband's drinking or snoring. It doesn't lessen what we have together or the people we are on our own."

"Mom..."

"I don't expect you to understand, Pace."

"I don't understand. What makes you think you don't deserve a genuine love that doesn't involve infidelity? I know it's your choice..." She threw her hands on her hips and paused. "I'm sorry, Mom, but I can't stand by and let him publically humiliate you like this. I won't."

"I know our marriage isn't ideal," Tori explained. "I know you think I should expect better and many times I have. But, every time I thought about leaving him, I realized I didn't really want to. I do love him and, in his own way, he loves me, too. He's never asked for a divorce, he's always treated me with respect and kindness, and we want to be together for you." But even as she said those things, even as she defended her husband, she wondered if they were true. Would she have done what she did if she wanted to stay with Colin? Or did she just want him to suffer?

"I'm thirty-five, Mom. If you want to leave him, you don't have to consider me any longer."

Tori attempted a weak smile. "If I were going to leave him, I'd have done it already." That, she knew, was the most truthful thing she'd admitted.

"But…"

"Everything you're dying to ask me I've already asked myself a thousand times over."

"How do you know what I'm going to say?"

She ambled to where Pace stood ramrod straight and defiant and ran the back of her hand along Pace's cheek. "You wear it all on your face, my dear child. You always have. I'm still here. I'm not at all happy about what we're facing because of this, but we'll face it."

"You shouldn't have to face this alone. Where is he?"

"Washington." Tori thought back to their stilted conversation before dawn, his quiet admission and promise to come home as soon as possible. "He's making arrangements to come home."

"How can you stay with him? How can you face the throngs of people with your head held high? God, Mother, this must be killing you."

It was killing her, but if she admitted it to Pace, she'd crumble. She had to be strong for her. This had been her choice. If that was all she had, for now, it had to be enough. "It's not pleasant, but we'll deal with it. We have to present a united front if he has any chance of keeping his seat."

"His seat?" Pace swiped at the tears on her face. "This is your life, your marriage we're talking about, not his job. Please, Mother, for once, can't you put your life and your needs ahead of his?"

She knew her decision to stay would incite Pace's anger, cause her to lose sight of the bigger picture. Tori had reconciled her role in Colin's affair as it played out in the media and had decided to let things unfold as they must. "In many ways, his job is our life. Everything he's done, everything we've been able to accomplish, is because of his position. He's a good man. He has flaws, like everyone. I'm not in this blind, Pace. I had a choice and I made it." She tried to convince Pace she'd made up her mind, but she still wasn't sure. "I don't want this to change the way you feel about your father. He's a good man and has been an excellent father to you."

"I don't think I can forgive him for this. I don't think I want to."

Tori gripped her shoulders and squeezed gently. "It's not your place to forgive him. He's your father. He didn't do this to you."

Pace shook her head in disbelief. "He's done it to all of us."

* * *

Jason was so nervous he felt nauseous as he stared at his reflection in the airplane bathroom. He looked like shit, with a decidedly green pallor that could have been him or just the lighting. Considering all he'd eaten that day was a pack of crackers and a Coke, it was no wonder he seemed a little unsteady on his feet. Why did he want to go out on his own again? He tried to focus on having the freedom to design as he pleased as the plane jerked to a stop in the snowy weather. As he maneuvered his carry on around a man in a wheelchair along the crowded terminal walkway, he tried to think about taking on projects that interested him—this project for starters—instead of manufacturing cookie cutter buildings with no character.

There were people everywhere, most appeared to be heading out of town on vacation, skiing or to some warm Caribbean island, or maybe home to be with Grandma for the holidays. Everyone looked happy except for the business travelers like him, traipsing from state to state while the rest of the country settled in for Santa's arrival.

He was going to have to do this anyway, approach Bisbain about coming with him, trusting him with their business. Trust. Hadn't he spent the night before and the morning trying to convince his wife that he was trustworthy? Was her doubt rubbing off and making his meeting harder to face than it normally should've been? *Stop thinking the worst.* There was nothing he could do to change what went on at home, but there sure as hell was something he could do to make sure his family was taken care of in the future. Pace believed in him, in his work, in what he could do. She understood why he was there, she knew he'd be back. She knew he loved her. He hoped it was enough.

He'd stopped at a newsstand and waited in line to pay for a pack of gum when he glanced at the television mounted along the back wall. The news was on, CNN or some other twenty-four-hour cable channel. The girl on the screen was talking about the weather. It had been an unusually cold fall and winter along the east coast and yet another storm was brewing over the great lakes that seemed determined to hinder his flight home. Perfect, Jason thought as the man in front of him collected his change and walked away. He didn't need to get stuck in New York City over Christmas. He stepped forward and put the gum on the counter. He thought he heard the name Colin Whitfield come from the news announcer's mouth. He passed over a five dollar bill and had his hand outstretched for his change when he looked back up at the TV and saw a picture of his father-in-law.

"Sir?" The girl at the counter asked as he ignored her question and pushed through two women looking at magazines to get closer to the television. "Sir, do you want your change?"

Jason stood under the television, as close as he could possibly get, and tried desperately to hear what was being said over the counter girl's shouting and the noise from the tiny store. Before he was able to figure out what had happened, if it was anything other than some bill Colin had proposed or some stance he'd taken on something, the announcer moved to a story about the presidential dog. Damn it. Every time Colin's name was mentioned, Jason freaked out and assumed the pictures had leaked.

He stepped out into the terminal and glanced around. He knew he should find a bar or go back to the gate and find a television—they were everywhere back there, but if he was going to make his meeting on time, he had to move on toward baggage claim and find his driver. Just as he stepped off the escalator and reached for his phone to call Pace, he saw a driver waiting with his name on a cheap piece of copy paper.

"Mr. Kelly?" A beefy black man in a loose fitted suit smiled widely when Jason nodded. Jason followed the driver out into the wet snow.

He slid into the back of a Ford crown car and was whisked away toward Manhattan. He'd made arrangements to meet Mark and his partner, Steve, for a late lunch and drinks at a restaurant in the city. Mark had mentioned it was one of their favorites and Jason thought the gesture might help sway their decision to stay with his new firm. He'd have done just about anything short of breaking the law to make a favorable impression. He'd drawn up a business prospectus and had the latest designs in a proposal package. Whatever their decision, they wouldn't walk away because he hadn't been thorough. In fact, Jason planned to use the individual attention their project would receive as a big selling point.

He'd have been lying if he didn't admit part of the reason he wanted to meet in the city was to avoid seeing Deborah. After everything he and Pace had discussed, he wasn't so sure he'd be able to be cordial to her without letting on about the problems she'd caused in his marriage. Her stupidly inappropriate, yet completely harmless comments had snowballed into yet another notch in his undoing.

Jason pulled his Blackberry out of his case. He thought he should be able to track Pace down before he got to the restaurant, but hesitated before connecting and looked out the window. If something had happened with her father, did he really need that hanging over his head while he tried to convince a very important potential client to follow him as he opened his own firm? He was already a bundle of nerves. Did he really want guilt at what may or may not have been going on at home to join him at the table like an unwanted guest? Even the guilt he felt for not calling to see what was going on made him feel guilty. He couldn't handle any more guilt!

He was about to tuck the phone back into his case and watch the sea of concrete buildings outside the dirty window when he realized what a stupid move that would be. If the shit had hit the fan, Pace would need him. He dialed her number and, of course, she didn't answer. It would have been easier to dismantle a ticking bomb than to locate her phone in the cavern she called her purse. He hung up without leaving a message and figured she'd call if something had happened.

He looked out the window as a distraction and tried to get his bearings on the way into town, but found it impossible. He could have been close to his brother's office in the financial district or miles away. He wondered if Adam had had any success winning Lydia back and what he'd have to say about everything Jason had done in the past month. He'd probably shake his head and say "I told you so." As the car pulled up to the restaurant and Jason stepped out with his case in a death grip by his side, he felt ready to plead his case to Bisbain Mellon. Because going home with another failure on his back was out of the question.

CHAPTER 28

Leaving her mother's house took twice as long as it had taken to get in because there were even more news trucks around the property. In this day and age, Pace didn't think a cheating senator would garner so much attention. Perhaps it was his position as chairman of the Ethics Committee or his image as a true southern gentleman. Either way, she realized she'd been wrong on all counts as far as her father was concerned. "Right is right, Pace," she remembered him saying when she was a teenager and she'd begged him to get her tickets to the sold out REM concert. "If I used my influence to get you tickets, I wouldn't be setting a very good example, now would I?" What a joke.

As Pace inched around a news van and punched on the gas, she couldn't get her mom's last words out of her head. "Your father needs your support now, Pace. Don't turn your back on him when he needs you the most."

How in the world could her mother shove her own personal hell to the background and put his needs before hers after everything he'd put her through? He'd cheated on her for years—decades! Her parents were not the people she'd thought they were. Pace had wanted to stay and argue, try to talk some sense into her stubborn mother, but she had to go home and collect the boys. What was she going to say to them? How was she going to explain what had happened to them or would she be able to shield them from their grandfather's mistake?

As the anger began to recede and Pace was left with a numb acceptance of what her father had done, she wanted to talk to Jason more than anything. She fished her cell phone out of her bag and realized he'd called her hours ago. He must have heard, but he didn't leave a message. Pace needed to talk to him without trying to dodge the boys and, with no school for the next three weeks, their bedtimes were a very long way off. So she dialed and hoped she could catch him while she was in the car and he wasn't in the middle of his meeting. Her call went straight to voicemail. She drove the rest of the way home clutching the phone like a crack addict with an empty pipe. She knew his meeting was important—hell, it was vital to his future, to their future, but she needed him now more than ever.

* * *

Tori heard a tentative knock on the door and then Mylia—the new staff member whose name she finally remembered—began speaking to her, telling her there was a call from Caroline. She'd been in Denver with Bethany and baby Chloe and Tori hadn't spoken to her in over a week. When she picked up the phone, Caroline sounded exhausted.

"Tori? You're harder to get in touch with than God. Wait," she sighed. "Let me start over. I just turned on the news. How are you?"

"Well..." She wasn't sure how to answer because she really didn't know how she felt. She thought she could handle Colin's public ruination. She'd told Pace they had to stand firm behind Colin, but now that Pace had left, she realized how ridiculous that sounded considering everything. "I've been better."

"What in the hell happened? How did the pictures leak?"

"They're reporting an anonymous source close to the campaign. Which means we'll never know." Thank God.

"How are you holding up? Is the press swarming?"

"Of course they are. You should see them, Caro. They're around the block as far as the eye can see."

"Where's Colin?"

Tori could hear the sound of a newborn in the background and some gentle shushing. "Oh, Caro. How is Chloe?"

"Beautiful." Even through the phone line she could tell Caroline beamed. "I'll email you some pictures. You forget how tiny they are."

"And Bethany?"

"She's a trouper. I tell you, Tori, they kick you out of the hospital as soon as they get you cleaned up, it seems. Nothing like when we had our babies. She's exhausted, hell, we all are, but she's doing great. Third time for her, so I guess she's used to the chaos."

"Give her my best."

"I will, but I didn't call to talk about the baby. I want to know where Colin is and what you're going to do."

"He's in Washington." Tori thought again of their conversation that morning, after she'd spotted the first report. It had taken him twenty-three minutes to call. He'd sounded…embarrassed and ashamed, but more under the gun than anything. "He'll be home as soon as he can."

"Did he admit it?" Caroline asked. "Offer an explanation?"

"He didn't have time. As bad as it is here with the press, I think they've ambushed him. He sounded a little stressed out."

"When he comes back in the house, it better be on his hands and knees."

Tori smiled at the image of him crawling, begging her forgiveness. "We both know him better than that. He thinks I don't know about the others—the ones in between. To him, this is a slip after years of fidelity."

"Did you tell him you knew?"

"We haven't talked since this morning. We'll get into all that when he gets home."

"I wish I was there for you. You know I'd be there if I could."

It was probably best that Caroline wasn't around. Tori had started this mess on her own and she needed to finish it on her own. "Of course I know. You give that baby a big kiss from me and enjoy your grandchildren. I'll call you if I need you."

She hung up and glanced out the window. The press looked like they weren't going anywhere anytime soon. She needed to plan her next move.

* * *

The sun had gone down in New York and it had begun to snow. Jason was pleased with the meeting so far. Mark Bisbain and

Steve Mellon sat across the four top table laughing at a story Jason had just told. They'd seen the prospectus, done a lot of head bobbing between the array of questions and scenarios they'd thrown at him since they'd sat down almost—Jason peeked at his watch—two hours ago, and he thought things were going about as well as he could have expected. Better than he'd dreamed, as a matter of fact. They'd just sent the waitress back to the bar for another round of drinks when Jason felt his cell phone vibrate inside his case when he leaned his leg against it. He reached down and noticed that he'd missed three calls from Pace.

"Excuse me, guys…" Jason threw his napkin to the table and stood up. "I've got to return a quick call. I'll be right back."

They waved him away and he weaved through the happy-hour crowd, out the front door, and into the cold night. He'd dialed Pace even before he reached the door.

"Jason?" Her voice sounded weird and very hard to hear on the busy New York street.

"I'm sorry I didn't call sooner, honey, I've been with the Bisbain guys since I landed. What's going on?"

"Somebody leaked the pictures, Jason. My dad's all over the news."

And just like that, his little balloon of optimism popped. "The pictures are out? Where?"

She let out a biting laugh. "Everywhere. I can't believe you haven't heard."

"Jesus." Jason rubbed his forehead and waited for the sound of a siren to pass. "How's your mom?"

"She knew. Jason, she's known for years."

As he stood on the street, people passing quickly with their heads ducked against the bitter wind and falling snow, Jason realized Pace was quietly crying because her whole world had fallen apart.

"I'm coming home, baby. I'll catch the next flight out."

"No." Her voice sounded stronger than it had since she'd said hello. "I don't want you to leave your meeting. There's nothing to do here anyway."

"Pace…" He glanced back toward the restaurant and looked through the window where Mark and Steve seemed to be enjoying their newly delivered drinks and conversation. "Things here are going well. I don't think it would be a problem to bug out if I claim a family emergency." All his talk about putting her before anything would go up in smoke if he stayed in New York and wasn't there when she needed him.

"Take care of things there, Jason. We'll be all right until you get back."

He hung up with a promise to call her later and slumped back against the icy window. Damn. He didn't want to look like a flake in front of his clients, and he certainly didn't want to own up to his relation to the Whitfields, but he knew in his gut that no matter what Pace said on the phone, she wouldn't be all right. He had to hand it to DeAngelo; he'd timed the leak perfectly. Absolutely nothing was going on in Washington the few days before Christmas and the media was salivating for any kind of story. The fall of mighty Senator Colin Whitfield provided a very tasty morsel.

CHAPTER 29

"Mom?" Pace looked over Tori's shoulder to the street where a Mercedes sat gleaming by the curb. Pace, still in her pajamas, was waiting for the coffee to finish brewing when she'd heard the doorbell. The kids hadn't even gotten up yet. She had Cooper by the collar and it took all her strength to hold him back. "What's happened?"

"Is that any way to welcome me?" She pushed past her as Pace wrestled the dog inside. Tori unsheathed her coat to reveal perfectly pressed slacks and a black turtleneck. She tossed her coat onto the staircase newel and marched into the den. When she turned around, Pace could tell her mother hadn't gotten any sleep.

"Let me get him outside." She shut the front door and dragged Cooper to the backyard where he thankfully took off after a bird. When she returned to face her mother, she just stared. Tori stood still as a statue in the middle of the den, hugging her arms around her waist. After their conversations the day before, Pace had a terrible feeling in the pit of her stomach about the reason for her visit. "Why are you here at the crack of dawn? What's going on?"

"Your father is coming home today and the house is already a zoo. I had to get out of there before I could be spotted."

Pace ushered her mother into the kitchen and poured them both a steaming cup of coffee. "Whose car are you driving?"

"Caroline Prenzy's. The news trucks blocked the driveway and she's out of town. Bethany had her third. A girl this time."

Pace thought back to the last time she'd seen Bethany Prenzy-Collier. She'd flown in from Denver for her parent's anniversary last summer, the same pixie blonde she'd always been sporting an adorable baby bump. Pace remembered the envy she'd felt looking at her in her trendy maternity wear. Bethany was one of those evil women who made pregnancy look like a snap.

"If she's out-of-town, how'd you get the car?" Pace tried to envision her mother hoofing it through the backyard in her designer boots, around the hedge of cypress trees, and over the small creek to get to the Prenzy's house.

"Mylia gave me a ride in her car. I had to lie down in the back seat so the press wouldn't see." Pace laughed despite the reason for her tactics and then immediately regretted it when her mother's face contorted in pain. "I'm glad you find this funny."

"I'm sorry." She quickly took a seat and wrapped her hands around the warm mug. "So you've talked to Dad?" She spit out his name, hoping her mother would understand how mad she was at him. Tori either ignored her tone or didn't notice.

"Yes. His flight lands at one and he's scheduled a press conference for three."

"A press conference?" Pace's imported coffee, one of her few indulgences, turned to vinegar in her mouth. "Does he plan to dispute the pictures?"

"No, he plans to apologize."

"Has he apologized to you?"

She looked as if Pace had hit her, or rather she'd hit on a very sore subject. "This isn't about me."

"This is absolutely about you and, from your non-answer, I take it he hasn't apologized." She shot up from the table and went into the pantry to look for something to serve her mother. Why couldn't she have had coffee cake fresh from the oven or had made muffins earlier in the week? Why did she have to be a complete failure as a hostess at a time when her mother might actually have been soothed by some sort of baked good? She didn't think her mom would appreciate or accept a Pop Tart, of which they had plenty. "Can I make you some breakfast?"

"No." She sighed and, for the first time, seemed ready to let down her stoic wall. "I couldn't eat right now. Coffee is fine."

"Mom." Pace flung herself into a chair and reached for her hand. "What did he say?"

"He's mad, of course, that the pictures were taken in the first place. I'm afraid your husband is the current target of his wrath. And apparently Trey is on the warpath."

"Mom." Pace squeezed her cold fingers. "What has he said to you? Has he even asked how you're doing?"

"Of course he has, darling. I've told him about the circus at the house, how the phones are ringing off the hook, how I've even had a few emails from reporters seeking an exclusive on my side of the woman-scorned story." She shrugged her shoulders. "I'm dealing with it. I almost wish for some sort of natural disaster or…terrorist plot so the vultures will move on."

"Mother, do you hear yourself? You're not dealing with anything but the logistics."

"That's what we need to focus on right now." She sat up and pulled her hand from Pace's grasp. "Your father wants you and the boys at the press conference."

She almost choked on her sip of coffee. "Is he delusional?"

"Now is not the time for theatrics," Tori scolded.

"Then let me be clear. I'm not going. Please tell me you're not going either."

"How can I not?" Tori stood up and stepped to the sink, grabbed the edge of the counter, and turned around dramatically. "He's having it on the front lawn. He asked me to be by his side. It was an apology of sorts," she said when Pace just shook her head. She couldn't believe her father's nerve. "It's the most he can offer right now. The campaign…"

Pace stood up and approached her mother, made sure she had her attention. "The campaign is a job, an elected position that will go on whether or not he's the one to fill it."

"His job means everything to him."

Pace studied her beautiful mother. She was so strong and worthy of love. She was hurting right now. She'd been hurting for years. "I feel sorry for him then, because that's very sad."

"I can't deal with my emotions about this until the press stops staking out the house and sticking microphones in my face every time I turn around. Your father swears once the press conference is over, our lives will return to normal and then we'll deal with it."

"Nothing is going to return to normal! Nothing *is* normal!"

"Pace..." She masked her pain with dignity. "This is normal for me. The only thing different is that everyone knows."

"You're going to have to deal with it, Mom. Dad is going to have to face what he's done to you." Pace reached out and gripped her shoulders. "Please, tell me you're not going to stand by him as if he got caught running a red light."

Her mother looked as raw and defeated as Pace had ever seen her. "I don't know what else to do."

Pace didn't relent, she couldn't. No matter how she felt about her father's behavior—angry, disgusted, hurt, and humiliated—she wouldn't agree to parade herself and the boys around some trumped up press conference. The nerve of him, asking Pace to come and put her sons on display as if they condoned his behavior, asking his wife to act as if he hadn't done anything wrong, as he apologized to his constituents for his affair. How about apologizing to his wife? His daughter? His grandchildren? She'd always thought they meant more to him than his career, but now she could see she'd been blinded in all matters concerning her father.

Her mother drank a few sips of coffee and tried in vain to convince Pace to join her and the throngs of so-called journalists for his televised confession. When she realized her attempt fell on deaf ears, she put her arms in her coat as if the effort took every ounce of her energy. Pace opened the door and strolled arm in arm with her outside where the rising sun blinded them as it bounced off the frosted tips of their lawn. They were just pulling apart from a hug when Pace glanced up to see Jason's car pull into the drive.

She felt like the cavalry had arrived when the driver door opened and he stepped out looking ready to drop. The suit he'd left in the day before was wrinkled and his tie was so loose he could have slipped it right over his head. He stopped when their eyes met. Without a second thought, Pace barreled toward him, her bare feet slipping on the wet grass. He dropped his case as she lunged for him and he grabbed her in a bone crushing embrace. Here was the balm she needed, Pace thought as she inhaled the familiar scent of his skin, the elixir to all that ailed her.

"Jason," she muttered into his neck. She didn't realize she'd started crying until he put her down and she felt the pads of his thumbs wiping away tears on her cheeks. "I can't believe you're here."

"I would have been here sooner, but I had to go standby and the airport was a zoo because of the snowstorm. I couldn't let you deal with this alone."

The click-clock of heels on concrete reminded her that her mother stood behind them. Tori was the one left to deal with the ordeal alone and, now that Jason had arrived, Pace's heart broke for her all over again.

"I'm glad you're home where you should be," Tori said to Jason with very little conviction in her voice. "Watching my daughter's face bloom when she saw you..." she shrugged and tapped him on the arm. "You're a good man."

"I'm sorry, Tori." He reached out a hand and laid it on her shoulder. He'd embrace her, Pace felt sure, if she could bring herself to let him go. She didn't know if she could stand alone now that he'd come back to support her; her relief at having him home was more than she could express. "I'm sorry for everything."

"It's a mess. An absolute mess." She slid her Chanel glasses onto her nose and tried to smile. "Think about what I said."

Pace nodded and watched as her mother approached the sleek German car. No one would ever have known she was embroiled in a crisis judging by her long, confident strides and the quick flick of her hair as she sank behind the wheel. They both watched her pull away from the curb and round the corner. Pace nestled into Jason again.

"How is she?"

"I don't know. She won't deal with anything but how this affects his career. It's not healthy."

"How are you? Other than freezing." He scooped Pace off her feet.

"I can walk." She giggled and patted his chest. It felt so good to be in his arms.

"Not when I'm carrying you, you can't. You should know better than to come outside without shoes."

He carried her inside, pushed the door closed with his foot, and continued on to their bedroom. They fell onto the bed with a thud.

"I could sleep for a week." He rolled over onto his back and rubbed his eyes before sitting up and staring down at Pace. "You didn't answer me. How are you?"

She sighed and tried to think of what to say. "Numb. I didn't really believe it until I saw the pictures. A part of me still can't."

"This is my fault, Pace. All of it. I'm so sorry."

She sat up to face him. "It's his fault, Jason. My dad did this, not you."

"No one would know if I hadn't hired that private detective."

"Would that be better?" She ran her hands through her knotted hair and pulled in frustration. "Really, Jason, would it be better not to know?"

"Better for your mom."

She fell back against the pillows and groaned. "Nothing is what I thought it was. I feel like someone has pulled the rug out from under me. And it's a thousand times worse for my mother and she won't admit it."

"If she'd told you she was dying inside, that she's humiliated beyond belief, would that have helped?"

"At least it would be honest." Pace stared at him, the tired eyes, the tousled hair, the shadow of a beard on his chin. He was there with her, when he should have been asleep in his hotel room preparing for another round of meetings. "He's called a press conference for this afternoon. She wants us to go."

"You don't want to."

"Not for him, no. But I don't know that I can stay away and leave her there to deal with it alone. She's alone in this, Jason. He's done this to her for years, since I was a baby."

"Then we'll go, for Tori."

Pace shook her head no even though she knew what he said was the right thing to do. "She said my dad blames you. I don't want a confrontation."

Jason leaned down and pulled her chin toward his face. "I've owned up to my part in this. I went to him first. I'll apologize again, but beyond that, there's nothing more to do. And I won't stay away when you need me." He kissed the tip of her nose like he sometimes did with the kids. "We'll both be there for your mom."

"I love you, Jason. I can't tell you how much it means to me that you're here."

He bent forward and rubbed his lips against hers. The whiskers of his beard tickled her skin. "I wouldn't be anywhere else."

* * *

Trey must have picked Colin up from the airport because Tori could hear them both downstairs preparing for the press conference, ordering the staff around as if directing a stage play. She waited patiently in the bedroom.

For the first time since the pictures had hit the newswire, she realized the magnitude of what had happened. It wasn't the relentlessness of the news crews that made her face the truth, the endless phone calls, or hibernating in the house. It was the look on Colin's face when he came upstairs, his skin pallid, his eyes haunted and sagging. Tori had wanted him to pay, yes, she'd wanted him to suffer for his weakness, but facing the suffering, seeing what it had done to him, made her feel sick inside.

"Tori?" He called her name because she just stared at him, a familiar stranger, a shadow of the man she'd married.

"Come in." She sat on the settee, dressed and ready for the press conference in the same outfit she'd worn to a funeral. It seemed appropriate.

He joined her and lifted her hand from her lap. "I really messed things up with you."

Was he expecting her to say he was wrong? To tell him she was okay with him having sex with a twenty-year-old? Even if he weren't her husband, even if she didn't know the girl and her family, she'd think it was wrong. "I'm not going to disagree with you, Colin."

"I need you, Tori. The press..." He glanced out the window where she knew the press had hounded him upon his arrival and had begun preparing for his statement. "They're having a field day with this."

"You've given them a lot to work with."

He looked at her and in his eyes she could see shame and just a hint of anger. "Jason..." His fury at Jason seemed so misplaced. He bounded up and went into the closet. Tori could hear him shuffling through his suits. "I should make him stand up there and explain his part in all of this. Christ, to think we've treated him like a member of this family all these years."

Tori moved to the closet door and leaned against the jam. "He is a member of this family. From the pictures I've seen, he was nowhere around when you were fucking your little whore."

He stopped moving, his arms fell to his sides, and he dropped his head to his chest. He let out a big sigh before lifting his gaze to hers. For a moment she thought he might defend his lover. "I screwed up, Tor. I shouldn't have done it."

"No, Colin, you shouldn't have."

He took a step toward her and she pulled herself up straight. The movement, her show of confidence and the don't-touch-me glare, stopped him in his tracks. He shoved his hands into his pants pockets. "I'll spend every second of every day making this up to you. Please, don't let my stupid mistake ruin everything we have together."

He sounded remorseful and certainly appeared exhausted. Was it enough, she wondered for the millionth time, to have him repent so they could move forward? She simply lifted her brows and turned around. He prevented her escape by laying a hand on her arm.

"I was weak. I got caught up in the excitement of the campaign. She doesn't mean anything to me, I swear." When Tori glared at him and the hand that held her arm, he moved his hands to her shoulders and began to rub. "I need you at the conference, Tori. I need you to stand by me today so that I can move forward and start making things right by you. Please, I know I don't even have the right to ask, but I'm begging you."

She eyed her husband. She'd spent nearly forty years standing by his side, smiling for the cameras, playing the roll she'd come to both love and loath. He looked so much like he had at their wedding, nervous and expectant in front of all the people, the people he would come to charm and whose attention he would eventually covet. Had she ever had a choice?

"I'll stand by you, Colin, but don't expect me to defend your actions."

"Oh, Tor." He grabbed her in a powerful hug. "I knew you'd come through. Thank you." He leaned in to kiss her and changed his mind when he saw her expression. He patted his wife's shoulder and went back into the closet to change.

"Colin?" He'd removed his tie and was unbuttoning his shirt. "Is it over?"

He turned to face her, his smile bright and a little too forced. "Yes." He crumpled his shirt and tossed it into the laundry bin. "It was only once, I swear it."

CHAPTER 30

Jason and Pace couldn't get within five hundred yards of the Whitfield's house and were forced to park in a private school lot. Jason felt pretty sure the car was going to get towed, but short of going home and then taking a cab, there didn't seem to be an alternative. Pace had been a jumble of nerves beside him in the car on the ride into town. She'd twisted her hands, checked herself in the mirror at least ten times, and tapped out what sounded like the national anthem on her legs twice.

Jason reached over and grabbed her hand as they walked along the sidewalk. She was trying hard to remember the shortcut she used to take through two neighborhoods twenty years ago while Jason still tried to figure out what he'd seen on the internet before they'd left. "Do you know where we're going?"

"What?" She was a million miles away. "Oh, um…" She looked around with her brow furrowed and pointed to a side street. "I think we turn there and then look for a white brick house with black shutters and a red front door."

"Let's hope they haven't painted," he mumbled and followed behind.

"I'll probably recognize it anyway."

"Pace?" He yanked on her arm to make her stop. "Honey, are you okay?"

"Yes." She pulled free and rubbed her gloved hands over her puffy white parka. "No. I just want this over with."

"It will be soon."

She lifted up her sleeve and pushed her glove down to see her watch. "Let's get going. I want to make sure Mom knows we're at the house before she faces the cameras."

They found the white brick house, amazingly just as Pace had described it, trudged over a creek and squeezed between towering cypress trees that separated the Whitfield's yard from another family. As they approached the pool house and the back door, they could hear the bustle of people scurrying around the front of the house setting up cameras and microphones for the big event. Jason would have sworn Colin planned an outdoor press conference in December to show his love to the media. On second thought, he'd bet it had been Trey.

Pace pressed her face against the windows of the French doors. "They're all huddled around my father." She glanced over at Jason with the weight of the world in her weary eyes. "Are you ready?"

"Ready when you are."

She knocked on the glass pane and the door opened within seconds. Tori answered, unable to hide the surprise on her face. "I thought you weren't coming." She dragged her inside and Jason followed.

"We're here for you, Mom," Pace whispered into her mother's ear as she hugged her tight. "Only for you." She pulled off her gloves and unzipped her jacket. Jason saw her mother's critical gaze at Pace's jeans and sweater, but, to her credit, she didn't say anything.

"What the hell is he doing here?" Trey lorded over the scene from the middle of the den with a clipboard and an angry scowl. Colin sat in a chair while a woman hovered around him patting his face with powder.

Jason had expected a hostile reception and came prepared to defend himself. What he hadn't expected was for Pace to shove a hand in her old boyfriend's chest and get in Trey's face before Jason had the chance to respond.

"Back off, Trey. He's here with me and we're both here for my mother."

Trey glared over her shoulder at Jason and snarled. "Get out of here, Kelly, before I throw you out."

Jason stepped forward and watched in astonishment as Pace shoved Trey back with both hands. He swayed backwards, his eyes wide with shock, but didn't budge. The fact that he remained on his feet didn't make his wife's actions any less remarkable. "I've had it with the way you speak to him. He's my husband and he's here because I want him here. If anyone is going to get thrown out, it's you."

"Pace." Colin stood up and adjusted his tie. From the look on her face, Jason could tell she was about to crumble. He stepped next to her and squeezed her hand. She gripped his fingers tight. "Your husband is the cause of this fiasco. I don't suppose he's mentioned the private detective he hired to tail you."

"I know all about the private detective." Her voice revealed a confidence Jason knew she didn't feel. "And the only cause of this fiasco is you."

He'd never seen Colin look at Pace the way he did now, as if she was worthless and practically see-through. It was the same way he looked at Tori. "I'm sorry you feel that way." He held his hand out to Tori. "Ready, darling?"

Tori stared at his hand like he'd presented her with a stick of dynamite. She glanced at Pace who reached out to grip her mother's arm. "Whatever you decide, Mom, we're here."

Tori shook her hair back from her face and stole a quick breath. "I won't be standing with you during the press conference, Colin, and don't touch me. I won't play act for you in front of reporters."

Colin dropped his hand and appeared as stunned as Jason at her words, as well as the disdainful tone she'd used to deliver them. "I thought we agreed you'd be with me. I thought you understood how important it is for us to present a united front."

"You haven't thought about anyone but yourself in a very long time." She jutted her chin in the air and looked down her nose at her husband. "You're on your own with this one, *darling*."

The room was so quiet it was like everyone was afraid to breathe. Colin stood gaping at Tori, completely dumbfounded. He never considered she might stand up to him.

Trey cleared his throat. "Senator, we really need to go."

Colin nodded and turned to leave. At the threshold, he stopped abruptly and whipped around to face his family. "Jason, you'd better be gone when I get back."

Tori gently coughed and stepped forward. "Jason's not the one who leaked the pictures. I did."

Jason finally understood. Colin slumped against the wall, too amazed to believe the truth, as was everyone else in the room. Everyone but Jason. "I…how?"

"You've gotten careless," Tori said. "And a little too brash. Two detectives, Ed Prenzy, and some boys from the club. Do you think you're invisible? Or just invincible?"

"Why, Tori? Why would you do this to me? Why would you ruin everything? Revenge?"

She shrugged her shoulders and pursed her lips contemptuously. She showed her strength in withstanding the heat of his fury, the look of hatred in his eye. Jason would think her heart impervious if he couldn't see the tremble in the hands she'd tightly clasped behind her back. "I didn't do this to you, Colin. You did this to yourself."

When she glared at him, challenged him to rebuke her, he took a quick look around the room. His minions, the staff who'd followed him blindly, wouldn't meet his eye. "Well, then. We'll discuss this later." He turned and strode toward the anxious press.

Everyone ambled into the foyer behind him and Pace and Jason stayed behind, alone in the room except for the makeup artist, who quickly packed her stuff in a large case, and Tori, who hadn't moved.

Pace rushed to her mother's side and searched her face. "Mom? Are you alright?"

Jason let the makeup artist out through the back door.

"Mom, please," Pace pleaded. "Talk to me. Tell me you're okay."

"I did this." Tori's voice was void of inflection. "If he loses the election, it's because of me."

"If he loses the election, it's because of him. Stop blaming yourself for his mistakes."

Tori stumbled toward the foyer and, for a second, Jason thought she might have changed her mind about joining Colin at the press conference. But she listened for a moment and then spun around to face them. "I'm sorry you had to see that, Pace."

Tori gave Jason a quick shrug and a pitiful look of appeal. "I let you be the fall guy, Jason. I'm sorry about that."

He felt staggered, not only by her admission, but that she'd apologized. "I wondered. Not right away, of course. I assumed it was the private detective I hired. But then when I saw the pictures, I knew it couldn't have been because of me."

Pace threw her arms in the air. "Will one of you please tell me what's going on?"

Tori wandered back into the room and ushered Pace to a chair by the fire. She slumped into the chair across from her. "I suspected your father of having an affair. I had him followed."

"You had Dad followed? When?"

"A month or so ago."

Pace shook her head, like she couldn't quite absorb everything her mother admitted. "You two should have gone in together, maybe gotten a two-for-one discount. Sorry," she said with a quick glimpse at Jason. "So you've known about this girl for awhile?"

Tori nodded and exhaled loudly. "I was furious, Pace. She's twenty and the daughter of a friend. I was humiliated and felt betrayed, the same way I always feel when he does this. But this time it was worse. I don't know if it was her age or the way he'd skip around the house like a love struck teenager, but I just couldn't bury my feelings and wait for him to end it. I felt threatened for the first time in a very long time."

"Oh, Mom."

"But then...he seemed to need me again with the campaign, in a way he hasn't for years. I buried it, I guess, tried to forget. I thought he'd realize how stupid it was to run around with a girl more than half his age while his seat was under attack. I thought he'd ended it. I was wrong."

"Why did you press me to stand by him? Why did you insist on taking his side when you were the one who'd outed him? I don't understand."

"I couldn't go through with it—standing up for myself, demanding he change. I thought I could, but when I talked to him, when I saw how destroyed he looked, I folded. He did need me then and I so desperately wanted him to." She seemed close to tears and her chin began to quiver. "But he lied to me only moments after begging my forgiveness. And then when I saw you here today, for me, I couldn't go through with it. I owe it to you to be strong."

Pace started crying and she slid out of the chair to her knees. She grabbed her mother's hands and put her head in her lap. "You don't owe me anything, Mom. I'm so very proud of you."

Tori stroked her hair and Jason tried to back out of the room. He not only felt uncomfortable overhearing Tori's private business, but the poignant moment seemed only for them.

"Jason?"

The sound of Tori's clipped tone halted his progress. He peeked around and saw her straining to look at him. "Thank you for taking responsibility for the pictures, even though they weren't yours."

Jason couldn't help but smile. "No need, Tori. I didn't really care if he thought it was me. It just as easily could have been."

Jason tried again to slip out when she stopped him. "Jason, stay." She patted Pace on the back and they both got to their feet.

"Mom, are you going to be okay?"

"I'm fine. I'm going upstairs to change my clothes and pack a bag."

Pace gripped her arms before she could go. "What? Where are you going?"

Tori flashed a cunning smile. "I'm not going anywhere. Your father needs to face more than just the reporters alone."

She winked at Pace and disappeared into the hallway and up the stairs.

Pace looked to Jason with wide-eyed wonder. "You knew?"

"I checked online while you were in the shower. The pictures were from a different location and..." *Should he tell her?* "...it wasn't the same woman. I knew they weren't mine."

Pace fell back into a chair. "Are you sure?"

"The woman in my pictures was blonde and she sure as hell didn't look twenty."

"Holy shit."

"Pace?" Jason had never heard her cuss. "God, I shouldn't have told you."

"No, no, of course you should have. No more lies, remember."

He pulled her to her feet. "No more lies."

"You let everyone think you were responsible. You were willing to take the blame."

"Your father hates me, Pace. He always has. No matter where the pictures came from, it doesn't change the way he feels."

"I always thought he liked you." She lowered her forehead to his chest. "I'm such a fool."

He lifted her head until she met his eyes. "You're nobody's fool, Pace Kelly. Your father is the fool for throwing all of you away so carelessly." And a very busy man. Damn.

She glanced toward the doorway where her mother had escaped. "Do you think she'll be okay? Do you think she'll really leave him?" She gripped his jacket tight. "Do you think I should tell her about the other woman?"

Jason shrugged and pulled her into a hug. She looked like she could use a big one. "I definitely don't think you should tell her about the other woman. I don't know if she'll leave him, but I'm glad to see her stand up to him."

She buried her head in his chest and groaned. "I hate this for her. I hate him for doing this to her. Two women?"

"I hate to bring this up, but he's still your father."

She wiped her face with the end of his scarf. When she leaned back and caught him smiling she said, "What?"

"You. I enjoyed watching you yell at Trey more than I enjoyed hitting him myself."

She snorted and yanked on the scarf. "Trey's an ass."

Jason threw his hands in the air. "I've said that all along!"

"You were right." She reached up and cupped his face, hauled him down for a kiss. "Thank you again for being here."

"Oh, baby." He reached back and wrapped his fingers around her ponytail. She could have passed for a teenager. "I love you." He gave her hair a tug. "For better or worse, remember."

When she smiled up at him, Jason knew they could get through anything. "I remember."

EPILOGUE

The ice cream shop was packed, three deep at the counter and a crowd milled around waiting for their names to be called so they could retrieve their orders. It was stifling outside with temperatures hovering near ninety degrees. Jason and Pace waited along with the rest of the lucky few inside the air conditioned shop. Tori had the boys outside and Pace could see her through the window trying to fan her face with a napkin. They ran circles around the table she held for them. It was only May, but promised to be the hottest summer on record.

"Your mom looks happy." Jason shuffled to let another patron through the door.

"Yeah, she does." Pace glanced back outside the window and watched her grab Mitchell after he almost ran over a toddler with bouncy blonde curls and a dripping waffle cone. "I'm so proud of her for moving on with her life."

"It only took thirty-eight years and a national scandal."

"She told me he called and asked her for a date. She said no."

Jason lifted his brows in surprise. "How long do you think she'll hold him off?"

If this ordeal had taught Pace anything, it was that her mother was not predictable. "He's sent her flowers every day since. It doesn't seem to be having an effect on her." She stole a glimpse behind the counter to see if anyone was making any sundaes or shakes. The line was getting longer by the minute and the teenage workers seemed like they were goofing off.

"How do you feel about that?"

She stared up at her husband. "Marriage takes work and trust." She nudged him with her shoulder. They'd learned a thing or two about trust. "They're my parents and, as much as I hate what he did and especially the way he treated her, a very small and selfish part of me would like to see them together if he could be faithful. But I'm not sure he can and it's not about what I want." She snuck a glance out the window and watched Tori throw her head back and laugh at Dillon's antics. "I don't think she can ever trust him again. I think she likes the person she is now. I know I do."

Jason followed her gaze and nodded. "I do, too. She's a lot easier to take without the attitude. Your dad on the other hand…"

In the months since the scandal had hit, Colin's attitude toward them had vacillated between indignation and remorse. He still blamed Jason for having to retire his seat. Until he was ready to take full responsibility for the destruction of their family, his marriage, and his career, Pace didn't have much to say to him. Their relationship, what little was left, was strained and kept her up some nights. "I hope he owns up to his mistakes, but until then…"

She squeaked the last word out as she got knocked in the back. She turned around to see the flushed face of a very pregnant woman. "Sorry." She rubbed her hand over her belly. "I forget to allow for this extra load sometimes."

"No problem." She scooched closer to Jason to give the pregnant woman more room. God knew she remembered what it felt like to be pregnant in the heat of the summer. "When are you due?"

A teenager called "McCalister" over the din of the crowd and a man with three small children rushed forward. "The end of June," she said as she blew her bangs out of her eyes.

Pace remembered her pregnancy scare. She'd calculated her due date to be the end of June. She watched the girl, sweating, bloated, and ready to pop. God, that could've been her. How different would their life have been now if she'd really been pregnant?

A pimply faced boy came forward with another tray of ice cream. "Pace?" he announced to the crowd. Jason tried to muscle his way forward at the same time the pregnant woman next to Pace patted her belly and said, "That's us."

Pace watched them both arrive at the counter. "Um, I think you have my order." She smiled at Jason as he picked up the tray and turned back toward Pace.

"Uh, no." He looked down at the two kid sundaes they'd ordered for Dillon and Mitchell, the shake he and Pace would split, and the smoothie her mother had requested. "This is ours."

Her brow furrowed and she twisted back to the teenager who watched raptly, as if he didn't have three thousand other orders to fill. "Didn't you say Pace?"

"Yessss…"

She looked back at Jason. "That's my wife's name," he explained.

Pace moved to his side. "Is there a problem?"

The woman laughed. "I'm sorry," she said. "Pace is my last name. I should have said Kelly…I never know which one to give."

They all laughed it off and Jason and Pace made for the door. Just as the humid air slapped Pace in the face, she was slapped with an outrageous thought. She spun around, squeezed back through the crowd, and tapped the woman on the shoulder. "Your name is Kelly Pace?"

As she nodded her head and smiled quizzically, Pace wondered if the woman could explain everything.

"Who's your doctor?"

Her brows disappeared under her bangs. "Excuse me?"

"I'm sorry," Pace stammered. "Your obstetrician. Did you happen to see Dr. Hidel?"

She snorted and wrapped her hands around her belly in what resembled a protective gesture. "Well, I did at first, but he told me I was anemic when I just knew I was pregnant." She patted her swell. "I was right."

Anemic. Pace learned all about anemia after being diagnosed when Jason and her mother insisted she go for a physical. The doctor said she'd had it for awhile. She looked up at Jason. He stared at her with a strange look on his face as the tray he carried tipped dangerously to one side.

She reached out and righted the tray just before the shake tipped over and glanced back at Kelly Pace. "Congratulations on your baby."

As they walked out into the hot sun and passed out ice cream to the kids and her mom, Pace thought about all they'd been through in the last six months. Her parents had separated, her father floundered through retirement without her mom. Tori had been on a few dates—dates!—and she seemed happier, more carefree than Pace had ever seen her. Jason had started his new firm and worked insane hours—hours she would've most definitely resented him for if they hadn't almost lost everything. They made time for each other, had regularly scheduled date nights and organized family outings. Pace knew who her friends were, she knew how strong her marriage was, and she knew not to take anything for granted.

If she could go back and change what had happened, if she'd pressed the doctor to check into the blood test some more or had thought to have them check the appointment book, of course she would have, absolutely she would have headed off the near destruction of her marriage. But from where she sat now, knowing that they all came out of it a little bit smarter, a little bit more grateful for what they'd built, she honestly didn't know if she would. As Jason slurped the last of the shake they had planned to share and her mother smiled at her over the lip of her smoothie, Pace felt pretty sure she wouldn't change a thing. Not one little thing.

The End

ABOUT THE AUTHOR

Christy Hayes writes romance and romantic women's fiction. She lives outside Atlanta, Georgia, with her husband, two children, and two dogs.

Please visit her website at www.christyhayes.com for more information.